Praise for

MURDER ON
SEX ISLAND

"I'm so sad *Sex Island* isn't a real TV show, because I'd make a fantastic host."

—Stephen Colbert

"Once again the incomparable (and unhinged) Jo Firestone proves that she is damn funny."

—Ziwe, author of *Black Friend*

"The perfect combination of three incredibly addictive ingredients: murder, reality television, and Jo Firestone's brilliant comedic mind. *Murder on Sex Island* is a fun, fast-paced mystery that's also jam-packed with hard jokes. I laughed out loud so many times reading it. Jo Firestone is a genius and my hero—there is truly nothing she cannot do."

—Taylor Tomlinson

"A deliciously clever murder mystery drenched in scandal, satire, and sheer fun. *Murder on Sex Island* is an absolute riot from start to finish. I loved it!"

—Joanna Wallace, author of *You'd Look Better as a Ghost*

"Bless Jo Firestone's quiet, mad genius. . . . Hilarious and completely brilliant, [a] bloodstained love-letter to reality-dating television."

—*Vulture*

"A hilarious cozy . . . Firestone scores major points with her outrageous premise, laugh-out-loud one-liners, and fast-paced plot. It's a tropical blast of sun, sex, and sleuthing."

—*Publishers Weekly*

"Firestone writes comedy for TV [and] it's hilariously obvious here. Wear protection while reading (sunscreen, I mean)."

—*The Minnesota Star Tribune*

"A humorous whodunit."

—*US Weekly*

"Hilariously absurd and over the top, showcasing *Sex Island* as a nightmare fantasy world . . . Luella is a fantastic and funny narrator whose can-do attitude frequently places her in bizarre and dangerous situations. With a long list of suntanned suspects, the true identity of the killer remains a mystery right up until Luella puts the pieces together. This silly and surreal cozy mystery is truly unlike anything else."

—*Kirkus Reviews,* starred review

"A clever, broadly funny mystery . . . Fast-paced fun that will appeal to fans of Elle Cosimano's Finlay Donovan and Jesse Q. Sutanto's Meddelin Chan."

—*Library Journal,* starred review

"A delicious debut mystery . . . Both as sharp social satire on the illusions of so-called 'reality TV' and as a wickedly funny bit of entertainment on its own, Firestone's novel is quick, smart, and silly and a great, if temporary, escape from actual reality."

—The Boston Globe

SEX ON MURDER ISLAND

SEX ON MURDER ISLAND

A LUELLA VAN HORN MYSTERY

JO FIRESTONE

BANTAM

New York

Bantam Books
An imprint of Random House
A division of Penguin Random House LLC
1745 Broadway, New York, NY 10019
randomhousebooks.com
penguinrandomhouse.com

A Bantam Books Trade Paperback Original

ISBN 979-8-217-09147-8
Ebook ISBN 979-8-217-09148-5

Printed in the United States of America on acid-free paper

1st Printing

Book Team: Production editor: Cassie Gitkin • Managing editor: Saige Francis • Production manager: Linnea Knollmueller • Copy editor: Faren Bachelis • Proofreaders: Julie Ehlers, Andrea Gordon, Russell Powers, Nicole Ramirez

The authorized representative in the EU for product safety and compliance is Penguin Random House Ireland, Morrison Chambers, 32 Nassau Street, Dublin D02 YH68, Ireland. https://eu-contact.penguin.ie

For Mike.

CAST OF CHARACTERS

LUELLA VAN HORN: The private detective alter ego of mousy ex–social worker Marie Jones. Also your narrator.

LESLIE JONES: Marie Jones's ex-husband. Not the woman who was on *SNL*.

JOAN CLYBORNE: A fifty-five-year-old librarian with a sense of adventure.

BETSY CLENCH: The first mate on the Murder Island ferry, which arrives once a day.

CAITLIN MCCARTHY: A wealthy property owner on Murder Island who is married to Mark Fontaine.

MARK FONTAINE: Caitlin's husband, who suspects her of cheating.

YANNI TOUMIS: The McCarthys' hunky handyman.

FRANK FISHER: The McCarthys' longtime dutiful house manager.

JOSH AND CARLA JORKAVIC: Neighbors of the McCarthys on Murder Island. Josh is a doctor.

BRADFORD AND DEBRA TYLER: Neighbors of the McCarthys on Murder Island. Debra is a doctor. They have a loyal butler who takes care of more than he should.

BRYANT AND LINDSAY PETERSON: Neighbors of the McCarthys on Murder Island. The only renters.

EDMUND AND SIERRA HUNT: Neighbors of the McCarthys on Murder Island. They own the Peterson property, as well.

LENORE FISHER: An actress visiting Murder Island.

SYBIL WILLIAMS: The Hunts' longtime house manager.

PAUL ANIONE: A very attractive waiter. He works at Morgan's, Murder Island's only bistro.

If we command our wealth, we shall be rich and free. If our wealth commands us, we are poor indeed.

—Edmund Burke

I want a divorce. Fuck you!

—Tamra Judge, *Real Housewives of Orange County*

SEX ON MURDER ISLAND

1

Midtown Manhattan is a terrible place to hit rock bottom. Surrounded by hundreds of bowl restaurants . . . you know you actually can't get food served on a plate here? They legally have to give it to you in a cardboard bowl that costs fifteen dollars. When they ask if you want bread with it, you can say yes, but know it's a trap.

And yet there I was: broke, alone, and in Midtown during an August heat wave. To top it all off, I was in the middle of moving. I'd gotten up early to beat the sun, but the temperature was already ninety degrees outside. Humidity like soup. Of course the window AC unit was the first thing I'd been able to sell on Craigslist. I was so angry at myself for only charging fifty dollars. That thing was worth its weight in gold. I should've held out for the highest bidder, but with a checking account balance of seventeen bucks, I found it hard to be economically strategic.

If you asked me three months ago if I would be in this situation, I would've laughed. Three months ago I was doing great. I—well, my sexy alter ego Private Detective Luella van Horn— had recently solved a big case, one that paid me two months' rent, and I was even starting to date again. Well, I was swiping, but that takes bravery! How were so many men in New York City able to catch and pose with giant fish? Where were they getting these fish, the Hudson River? Seemed like red flags.

I'd been a social worker before I'd gone into the seedy world of private investigating. I'd been married, a homeowner even. But I threw it all away for an exciting life of tracking down bad guys and insisting they give back the dogs they stole from little old ladies. That's most PI work, it turns out.

But the PI jobs just sort of stopped coming in. I figured maybe the criminal world had slowed down. But I read the papers, and I knew that wasn't true. Crime was higher than ever. So why wasn't I getting called? Blame it on a couple of bad reviews, or no word of mouth, or lack of TikTok. Hell, maybe someone at the bowl restaurants ratted me out for saying yes to bread. Whatever it was, I was running out of money fast.

My lease wasn't up until November, but it was August, and I couldn't afford this or next month's rent. I made a deal with my landlord—I'd give up my deposit if he let me out of my lease early. I was missing that deposit money right about now, but knowing my landlord, he would've kept it regardless.

So I sat there, sweat-soaked, packing up my belongings into limp cardboard boxes. I'd just sealed the box labeled KITCHEN 2 when the panic came back. My plan was to put my stuff in storage for a while and sleep on some friends' couches until I could make enough money to get another place. But the sticky part was, well, I didn't really have any friends. There was my neighbor Sophie, but she lived in a studio. There was no room for me, even if she wanted me there, which she made clear she did not. The only other people I knew were back on Staten Island, and I wasn't on the best terms with any of them. I had reconnected with my old friend Lauren on Luella's last case, but a cold call asking for indefinite lodging for me and my two cats? I didn't foresee that going well.

I truly had nowhere to go.

But I would figure this out. It was Thursday, and I had a week and a half until I had to be *out* out. The first step was to get everything packed and into storage. I stood up and rubbed the knotty muscles around my jaw. My body was covered in sweat and dust. It was time to box up the office.

Office was a generous term. It's a metal desk with two locking drawers and a corkboard I used for mapping clues from time to time. Plus a big, shaggy scrapbook where I kept all my press clippings. I flipped through the book absentmindedly, maybe to lightly torture myself. There were a lot of lost dogs and cheating spouses, sure, but there were also bigger cases. I'd done good work for a couple of high-profile businesses, plus there were the *Sex Island* and Taylor Bell cases.

Look at all these jobs you used to have. What happened to you?

I paused on a page with a single business card in the plastic casing. In bold capital letters was the name ENDEAVORS.

That case had been a strange one from the start. I'd kept seeing those business cards everywhere I went. All they said was ENDEAVORS, with a phone number underneath, and they were up everywhere. Posted in my laundromat and my coffeeshop, taped to the lampposts I regularly walked by. I thought it odd: these cards never said what the business did, but they were ubiquitous. When I looked into the company online, nothing came up.

Then one day I came home and found an Endeavors business card had been slipped under my door. I was starting to think someone from the company wanted to get in touch. Sometimes I'm bright like that.

I'd called the number, and to my surprise, a young woman picked up, though she refused to give her name.

"It seems like someone from Endeavors is trying to reach me. What do you guys want?"

"Hold one moment," the woman said. A minute later I was on the phone with a man with a high, raspy voice. Joe Pesci–esque.

The man had told me his name was F, "as in F off." Real friendly type. F said he had a problem with his business partner, wanted to know if he was cheating him out of his fair share of the money. Eventually I tracked the partner down and confirmed what F had suspected. The business partner was having a grand old time, embezzling money from the company to such a degree I tipped off the NYPD. But something seemed odd about the whole thing—it was almost too easy. I couldn't help feeling like a pawn.

Looking at the card now brought it all back. Endeavors had to be some sort of front, though I never figured out what for. I never actually met F. In the end, I was told to pick up my check from an empty office on the fourteenth floor (which was technically the thirteenth floor) of an art deco building in Times Square. When I got off the elevator, I remember there were three hallways and I got lost on my way to the office. I tried calling the Endeavors number, but it'd already been disconnected.

When I finally found the office, the door was propped open but the lights were off. The word ENDEAVORS and maybe a drawing of an animal were engraved in the marbled glass. My check was right where F said it'd be—lying on the front desk. The whole situation gave me the heebie-jeebies. I grabbed my money and got the hell out of there. At least the check cleared.

But it always plagued me—why did F target me specifically, and in such a bizarre way? The crooked businessman I'd reported had to serve time. In the paper, F wasn't listed as a business partner. And what's really bizarre: The check was signed by the crooked business partner, Dave McCarthy. Why would the man pay me to send himself to jail?

My hands were sticking to the laminated pages of the scrapbook. It was too hot to go down memory lane. I needed to cool down, so I grabbed a bag of frozen peas from the freezer and rubbed it all over my body. This was a trick I'd learned on summer stakeouts, sitting in a hot car, slathering myself with a thawing bag of frozen vegetables. It's actually a life hack, and if you think it's weird, then congratulations on working in a climate-controlled environment. You've made it.

Dripping everywhere, I checked my phone. One missed call from my ex-husband, Leslie. I was married to him before I started moonlighting as Private Detective Luella van Horn, back when I was Marie Jones, a social worker on Staten Island. If you're doing the math, yes his name is Leslie Jones, like the woman who was on *Saturday Night Live*. He lived to tell people his full name then watch them get excited, like they were meeting her, not some random engineer from New York's trash heap. This was the person I willingly married. At one point, I think we were even in love.

I'd called Leslie in a moment of desperation a couple of nights ago, thinking if anyone would take my sorry ass in, it'd be him. But he didn't pick up, and I didn't blame him. It'd been a few days, so I figured we both planned to forget that I'd called.

Seeing his name on my phone screen, I felt shame stinging my throat. I wiped the bag of peas around my neck and took a deep breath. Unfortunately, I was still in that moment of desperation—indeed, it was an ongoing moment. Maybe he was feeling generous. Maybe things would work out. I called him back.

It rang four times, and I was about to hang up when Leslie answered.

"Hello, Marie! So nice to hear from you! I was just in the city. Can you believe that?"

"Wow, we were both in New York City, where there are eight million people on any given day. What a crazy coincidence," I said. I reminded myself to cool it on the sarcasm. I needed him more than he needed me.

"Did you mean to call me a few nights ago?" he asked.

"Yeah . . . I— Um, Leslie, I'm in a bad spot."

"What do you mean?"

"Well, I need somewhere to stay for a couple weeks . . . or more," I mumbled.

"Oh man, Marie, I'm so sorry to hear that! I wish I'd heard from you earlier!"

"Listen, Leslie, if you're going to be passive-aggressive about it . . ." I said.

"No, really! See, I'm not living in our house anymore. I put it on Airbnb, and I just got someone to take it for the next couple months."

"Huh, that's too bad," I said, the panic slowly rising in my voice.

"See, I'm actually living in the city! Marie, I'm going to become an actor!"

Okay, I was wrong before. Broke, alone, moving in August, and your ex-husband has discovered acting. This was actually rock bottom.

2

"Leslie, what do you mean you're going to become an actor?"

"Well, I'll start by taking classes, and auditioning whenever I can, and in my downtime, I'll work on my physique." He sounded chipper. I felt nauseated.

"When did you decide this?" I asked, trying desperately to stay neutral.

"Oh, it's always been at the back of my mind. When we were together, I felt all this pressure to be the breadwinner. But now you're off pursuing your dream, and I felt I should be able to also! You know what they say . . ."

"They say don't become an actor."

"No, Marie. They say it's never too late."

I pressed my fingers to the bridge of my nose. What had I done to deserve this?

"Well, where are you staying in the city? Can I join you? Even if it's a closet, I could make it work." This was pathetic, even for me.

"I'm going to be staying on my friend Davis's couch, and there's no room for you or your pets. I'm sorry."

"Who the hell is Davis?" I asked.

"He's a good friend, and the fact that you don't know him speaks volumes for how far apart we've grown. Take care of yourself, Marie." And with that Leslie hung up.

Meatball, the smaller of my two cats, brushed his head against my hand. I knew this meant it was time for me to feed him, but I took it as a much-needed sign of affection. I had nowhere to go. I looked around my studio apartment. Half-packed boxes everywhere. Nothing finished, except KITCHEN 2. I hadn't even started packing KITCHEN 1.

I needed a break.

I lowered the shades and set out a cooling station for the cats—ice water in their bowls and four bags of frozen corn set out fortress-style around their scratching pole. Then I headed out. I needed to take a walk, get a ten-dollar iced coffee with my last seventeen dollars, and, if I was lucky, possibly get dripped on by other people's air conditioners.

The streets of Midtown were filled with people looking their best. I couldn't believe it: crisp linens, designer shoes, full blowouts. Was I the only person in this city without any money? It was starting to feel that way. I stopped in to my local bodega for a Coke. At least I could still afford a Coke.

Moments later I was back on the sidewalk holding the most expensive Coke I'd ever bought in my life. Three dollars and fifty cents for a can? It wasn't even that cold! What was happening? I felt like I was living in another dimension. I was filthy and sweaty and drinking lukewarm cola . . . Had I ever been the sexy, glamorous private detective Luella van Horn? I had to get out of this heat. Somewhere with AC and preferably free.

I walked down the street in a huff, chugging my soda so hard it brought tears to my eyes. I burped, wiped my mouth with the back of my hand, and aimed the empty can at a nearby recycling bin. I missed, of course. But when I bent down to pick it up, I got that prickly feeling someone was watching me. I tossed it into the recycling bin and looked around. Then I spotted him. My body broke out in goosebumps. What the hell was he doing here?

Taylor Bell stood merely ten feet away, watching me. The murderer who'd been my social work client back when I was Marie Jones. At the time, he seemed so upset by his wife's disappearance I felt like I had to do something about it. So every night I'd put on a blond wig and go out looking for her as Private Detective Luella van Horn. I'd eventually found her severed fingers buried in Taylor's backyard. He'd played me.

I blinked to make sure I wasn't hallucinating and it wasn't the heat. My knees buckled and my throat felt tight—that's how I really knew it was him. And he knew I knew. A split second later, he ran. In my experience, Taylor always got away. When I learned he'd killed his wife, when the cops went to convict him. My first big case, a total flop. NYPD said I'd compromised the evidence. He was acquitted, justice never served. Maybe that's what started my downward spiral.

I thought about running after him, but part of me feared getting involved, and part of me was too hot for this bullshit. Damn, this day just kept getting better and better.

And that's how I ended up in the New York Public Library— the main branch on Forty-Second Street and Fifth Avenue with the columns and the lions and all that crap. I didn't even have a card, and I hadn't read a book in six years. But they had soft chairs and an air conditioner that made me shiver, and for ten minutes I could pretend this day was turning around. I wept with relief taking a seat near the back of the Rose Room. A bald man sitting across the table eyed me over his copy of *The New York Times*. I glared back. *Read your paper, bro.*

Before long, a librarian approached me. She was in her fifties, and her hair was done in a long gray braid. Her glasses hung on a turquoise beaded strap around her neck. It should be noted that I've never seen a nonlibrarian wear this kind of apparatus. It must be bestowed on them like a diploma upon getting their degree in library science. The woman had kind eyes and wore a wedding ring and a small brown leather wristwatch. I glanced at the time. It was 11:30 A.M.

"Hi, dear, are you Marie Jones?" she asked. I sat up straight and felt my cheeks flush.

"Did I do something wrong? Do I need to get a library card to be here? I've read books before, and I can start reading again anytime . . ." I stammered.

"No, dear, you're fine to stay here as long as you want," she said, smiling. "But there's a phone call for you."

A phone call? I fished my cellphone out of my sweat-drenched pocket and saw it was dead. But who would be trying to reach me, and at the library of all places? I'd never even been here before.

My stomach churned. This couldn't be Taylor Bell, right?

The librarian introduced herself as Joan Clyborne, and I followed her to the front desk where a landline phone sat blinking red. She pressed a button on the phone and held the receiver.

"Hello? Are you still there?" she asked. Someone on the phone must've confirmed, because she nodded. "Here she is, one second." Joan handed the receiver to me.

"Hello?" I croaked. "This is Marie."

"Marie Jones," a man with a gravelly voice replied. "It's been difficult getting ahold of you."

"Who is this?" I asked. The man didn't sound anything like Taylor Bell, thank god. My mind ran through the possibilities—an ambitious bill collector or maybe my bank telling me to go to hell?

"Don't be afraid. I'm only calling with a job for your little friend Luella van Horn." A job . . . that meant money! At the time, I was so shocked, it didn't occur to me to question how the caller knew both my real name and my alter ego's. Most days, I tried to keep my Marie and Luella lives separate.

"It's a job," I whispered to Joan, who was still standing nearby watching me closely. She nodded supportively.

"That's good, dear!" she whispered.

"What's the job?" I asked the man on the phone.

"I can't say much now," he replied. "But have you heard of a place called Murder Island?"

3

Murder Island was a small island off the coast of New York City, much like Governors or Roosevelt islands. In the eighteenth century, Dutch settlers had used the land as a prison colony for their most heinous criminals, calling it Moordenaar's Eiland. Over the years, it was shortened and anglicized into what it's called today: Murder Island. Why did I know all this? In the sixth grade, I did a school project on the smaller islands of New York City, and for some reason this stuck. But ask me to do long division? Impossible.

Its years as a penal colony were long gone, and it hadn't been open to the public for decades. Now it served as a private enclave for the über rich. It was the Hamptons of the Hamptons. Murder Island was so elite even Page Six couldn't get the scoop. Obviously I didn't know anyone who'd actually been there. The place had a quiet air of mystery about it.

There was a single ferry that came and went once a day, transporting comestibles and residents' employees in and out of the city. Most residents preferred to travel by helicopter or private plane. The gravelly voice instructed me to get myself on the next day's ferry, leaving at exactly 9 A.M. from the Twenty-Fourth Street Pier on the East River, then he hung up. I set the phone down and tried to process what had just been said.

"So you've got a job, dear?" Joan looked at me with friendly curiosity.

"I guess so," I responded. "Hey, do you have any books on Murder Island?"

"Let's see." Joan escorted me to a section on New York City history. "I believe we may have one book. It was written by a man named Stanford. First name Waldo, or was it Walter? Have you heard of him?"

I told her I hadn't.

"Brilliant man, but he never wrote another book after that."

"Really?" I said as Joan moved her finger along the spines.

"That's funny," she said, stopping at a gap in the books. "It didn't say it was checked out. I'm sorry, dear. Come back in a couple of weeks, I'm sure it'll turn up."

Joan somehow convinced me to sign up for a library card before I left. This day was filled with twists and turns.

As I walked the ten blocks home, the relief at finally getting a job was transitioning to pure anxiety. Why wouldn't the man tell me what the job entailed? What kind of people would I be dealing with? And how did he know I was at the library? Had someone followed me?

Was I being followed now? I suddenly turned. Everyone on the street seemed to be going about their business, rushing somewhere, looking at their phones, listening to music. A group of pigeons fought over an old chicken wing. One woman got shoved by another woman, and the shoved woman apologized. A dog pissed on a trash bag. Life in New York. Still, it didn't quash the feeling I was being surveilled. There was no sign of Taylor Bell, so I took that as a win and ran the rest of the way home.

Sweating and panting, I was thrilled to see both cats taking advantage of my cooling station. Meatball was draped over the frozen corn, while Meatloaf batted around an ice cube he'd found in his water bowl. At least these guys were having a fun summer. I hoped Sophie would agree to watch them for a few days.

I knocked on Sophie's door. To my surprise, she answered topless, and I did my best to avoid looking below her neck. Whatever was down there was knocking back and forth like a Newton's cradle.

"Do you want to put on a shirt?" I asked.

"No. Why?"

I decided it was safest to look up at the peeling ceiling paint. "I was wondering . . ."

"You cannot stay here!" she yelled.

"I know, I know. But I got a job, and I was wondering if my cats could stay with you for a bit?" I asked. "They adore you," I lied.

"They do adore me." Sophie groaned. "Oh, all right, but if this is some scam to off-load your pets on the elderly, I'll track you down and kill you." Imagine how desperate you'd have to be to ask this woman for favors.

With the cats taken care of, I began looking for my Luella gear. I knew I'd packed some of it in a box somewhere in this sweltering apartment. Eventually I excavated the blond wigs from a box labeled Cat Stuff and shoved some heels and dresses into an old suitcase.

Once I was all packed, I opened my computer and tried researching Murder Island to understand what I was getting myself into here. All that turned up was a map showing the islands of the East River, a very sparse Wikipedia page, and a link to that book by Walter Stanford. There was no book preview, and it seemed to be no longer in print.

I shut the computer and plopped down on my unmade bed, trying to wrap my head around it all. I had nowhere to live, Taylor Bell was roaming the streets, and New York City was the temperature of a testicle. A job on an island just outside of Manhattan might be the answer to all my prayers.

By 9 A.M. the next morning, I was standing at the Twenty-Fourth Street Pier in my blond wig, a pink leopard-print dress, and heels. A small yacht was anchored there, and a tall, buxom woman soon emerged from the cabin. She wore khaki shorts and a white button-down shirt, and her muscles bulged at the seams of both. She wore a white sailor hat over her short brown hair. This woman looked like she was made for the sea. She introduced herself as Betsy Clench, the ferry's first mate.

"You must be Lola van Horny," she said, firmly shaking my hand. I felt my knuckles crunch in her grip. "Welcome aboard! It'll just be a few minutes before we're out on that beautiful river.

We're waiting on a crate of caviar and three residents' employees. Make yourself comfortable!"

I walked onto the ship. The deck gleamed in the sun, and it looked like it'd been freshly polished. I moved toward the bow, passing a couple of crates labeled Emu Meat: Keep Cool. A flag I didn't recognize waved from the mast. There was a crest on it with a bear, a bat, and even a rooster. Maybe the boat belonged to some zoological nonprofit? I'd never seen a flag like that before.

By 9:02 a.m. the staff and caviar were all aboard, and we were sailing the East River toward Murder Island. Betsy Clench made a round of introductions. There was an older man, Frank Fisher, and a younger chiseled guy, Yanni Toumis. They worked as house manager and general handyman, respectively, for the McCarthy family. Sybil Williams, a blond woman in her late thirties, was a house manager for the Hunts' residence. Frank shook my hand.

"I would imagine it's your first time on Murder Island," he said.

I nodded. "How many years have you been going there?" I asked.

"I've been working for the McCarthys for close to forty summers."

"Does that family have any relation to Dave McCarthy?" I asked, thinking about that Endeavors guy I'd put in jail.

"I'm not sure," Frank said. Yanni looked to Frank, and Frank smiled passively.

Something about Frank reminded me of someone.

"Have we met before?" I asked him.

He shook his head quickly. "I don't think so. What brings you to the island?"

Before I had a chance to answer, Sybil spoke up. "I know why they're bringing you here." A smirk spread across her face. She whispered something to Yanni, who eyed me up and down.

"Why?" I asked.

Just then Betsy Clench pulled me aside. "Best to have discretion around here, hon. Everyone talks on Murder Island. It's mighty small."

I nodded as Betsy continued. "A lot goes on on that tiny island." There was a far-off look in her eyes. "A whole lot."

"What do you mean?" I asked.

She eyed Frank, Yanni, and Sybil, who all sat quietly, now gazing into their respective smartphones.

Betsy leaned in close and whispered, "The proclivities of the richest of the rich are none of my business, of course. But I wouldn't mind attending some of those parties I've heard about. Sex, drugs, and debauchery like you've never imagined. Bet you don't think I'm a bad girl, Louise, but I can be."

"It's Luella," I reminded her.

"Really?" Betsy asked. "Because you could be a Louise. I mean that in the best way. Three of my favorite people, I swear, all of them are named Louise." It was impossible not to be completely enamored with Betsy Clench. Even if she did think my name was Louise van Horny.

The East River made for a bumpy ride, but at least the wind was strong and cool. If my geographical knowledge of New York could be trusted, we passed Rikers Island, City Island, and Rat Island. As we sailed past the big cemetery on Hart Island, I couldn't help but wonder what this Murder Island case was all about. Had there been bloodshed? Would there be? Either way, I finally had a job. And maybe this could lead to others! Betsy said the island was small—maybe other rich people on Murder Island would start calling me for their private investigation needs, too. This could be a huge business opportunity. This could change my life. I looked out at the choppy gray water and breathed in deeply.

Man, this city smelled like shit.

4

I could've sworn the boat turned around at some point. When I'd googled "Murder Island," it wasn't anywhere near Long Island, which was where I thought we roughly were. I knew some people had the power to blur their homes from Google Street View, and maybe this was a situation like that. I wouldn't put it past the super rich to hide their private island. It'd only discourage nosy riffraff like me.

Our boat started approaching a land mass at 11 A.M. The heaving body of water—was it still even the East River?—had made us all a little green, and even Betsy looked peaked as she threw out the anchors and moored the boat.

Yanni sidled up next to me as we docked. He was so ripped he reminded me of the *Sex Island* contestants I'd met on my last case. That's when I first learned that six-pack abs were a sign of the devil.

"It's your first time," he said. I nodded. "You can't be too careful."

"What does that mean?" I asked as people started to unload the crates of food and liquor. A shockingly handsome man picked up a crate of caviar, tucked it under his arm, and winked at me. You know when someone is so attractive you want to take a picture of them to show your future grandkids? You'll hand them a yellowed photo and say, *Honey, this was the hottest person Grandma ever saw.* That was Caviar Guy.

"Where are you going with that?" Frank yelled, chasing after the hot man. Frank's voice was high-pitched but also raspy, like he'd smoked a pack a day since he was ten. I could've sworn I'd heard that voice before.

Yanni still hadn't explained what he meant, so I decided to pivot. "Have you worked with Frank a long time?"

"Sure, why?"

"He looks so familiar to me. Do you know if he's ever worked in the city?"

"Trust me, if you don't have a billion dollars, you're not running into old Frank Fisher. He's just got one of those faces. Anyway, grab your stuff. It's time to get back on dry land."

The dock was made of wide blond slabs of interlocking teakwood. A statue of a man I didn't recognize stood at the end of the dock, his bronze finger pointing toward the island, a bird perched on his shoulder. Then I looked closer—it wasn't a bird, it was a bat. What kind of man keeps a bat on his shoulder? I'm sure it wasn't the sculptor's intention, but the guy looked like plainclothes Dracula.

Sybil and Yanni walked briskly onto the dock as Frank yanked a wooden crate out of Caviar Guy's hands. Between the statue and Frank, I couldn't decide who was more off. Though I still couldn't place him, I knew I wasn't crazy. Where had I met Frank before?

As I stepped onto the immaculate dock, I immediately felt underdressed. My dress, which I swear was once stylish, now looked cheap and misshapen, and in the sunlight, I could see my patent leather heels were scuffed at the toes. I fluffed my wig, put on my sunglasses, and tried to stand up straight. I could, at the very least, have the posture of the upper crust.

The island looked like the kind of fictional small town that wealthy people craved. Neat sidewalks, tastefully rustic storefronts, manicured island flora. The downtown area could've been straight out of *Gilmore Girls*. But there was an eerie stillness to its streets.

I saw a bistro by the dock, though it looked empty, and next to the bistro, a designer swimsuit store that appeared to be closed. I watched a woman with a blond bob slowly drive by the dock in a white Range Rover. Murder Island seemed like one of those places that didn't see a whole lot of outside visitors.

I wondered if the man who hired me planned to meet here or if he even knew I'd arrived. I took out my phone, but of course there was no reception. I was holding my phone high and low, near the water and farther away—my private science experiment to test the bounds of Verizon—when Betsy Clench approached.

"No need to do that. You won't find much reception on the island. This community doesn't exactly prioritize cellphones. They leave too much of a paper trail."

She lightly elbowed me, chuckling to herself. "Someone should be here to get you soon. After all, there's only one ferry a day. Arrives at 11:15 A.M., departs at 11:45 A.M. If you miss the boat, you're outta luck for twenty-four hours," she said, turning to look out at the water.

"You know I've never spent more than thirty minutes on this island? Been doing this route for years," she said, almost to herself. "I've always wanted to stay over, just for one night."

"Well, if this guy ever comes to get me, I'll be sure to tell you all about it," I said.

"Would you?" she asked, putting her number into my phone. "If you want to reach me, make sure you're on the wifi! I've actually never even ventured past the downtown area! They make it pretty clear I'm supposed to stay near the boat."

I wondered why. But before Betsy could say anything more, a man wearing a baseball hat walked up to me.

"Luella van Horn, is that you?" he asked. "Sorry, I've lost my glasses. I can't see a damn thing."

"That's me," I replied. When I turned back to find Betsy, I saw she was already busying herself on the boat.

"This way," he said, leading us further inland. "I hope you don't mind walking. Usually I'd drive, but my wife's got the car today, and the other two are back in the city. Plus, like I said, I can't find my fucking glasses."

I picked up my suitcase and followed him. The man walked with a limp in his left leg and wore coral-colored shorts and a polo shirt. Despite the limp, he was fast and seemed determined to stay a bit in front of me. His baseball hat had an *E* just above the back strap. Maybe it was because I had Dave McCarthy on the brain, but that *E* looked like the Endeavors logo.

"I'm sorry, I didn't get your name," I said, but he ignored me. We passed the bistro on our left and continued along the sidewalk in silence.

As we ventured further onto the island, thick clumps of trees and hedges popped up along the path. I realized these likely signified property, giving the homeowners an extra layer of privacy from the road. From the pixelated maps online, I knew Murder Island was small and shaped like a kidney bean. Near the central narrow part of the bean was the island's bustling commercial area (the empty bistro, the closed swimsuit store). It was there I also spotted a general store selling a limited stock of the practical (toilet paper) and an abundant supply of the impractical (potted orchids, organic kefir, and artisanal biscotti). After that, everything seemed to be residential. Homes lined the exterior of the island, guaranteeing each one beachfront property. In the center of the island, just inland from the downtown area, was a large castle-like structure, mostly obscured by tall bamboo plants. When I asked about it, the man pretended not to hear me.

We walked south for about forty-five minutes, during which time the man in the baseball hat hardly acknowledged my presence. Finally we arrived at the client's house, surrounded by a wall of robust Italian cypress trees. My shoes were killing me and my stupid synthetic dress had me feeling and looking like a steamed sausage—the German kind that's sort of gray. I don't know the German word for it, but I'm sure it roughly translates to *dead man's penis.*

I looked up at the looming A-frame house nestled behind the cypresses. The shingles, the door, even the bricks were all painted black. It was stylish with a hint of the Addams Family. The man with the baseball hat opened the front door and gestured for me to enter.

The air inside the house was cool, and the place smelled like fresh roses. I noticed the interior was entirely white—the wood floors, the carpet runners, the walls. Even the framed portraits seemed muted and pale. The stairwell, the dining room, and the hallway that led to the kitchen were all some variation of white, as well. I couldn't believe it. All the money in the world and you design your house like an Oreo cookie.

I heard voices coming from somewhere in the house, maybe upstairs, but the man rushed me down the hall, through the kitchen, and out the back door onto the backyard patio.

"Sit," he said, gesturing to a chair at a white wicker table. The table was shaded by a cream-colored sun umbrella. I took a seat.

"Can we get some drinks out here!" the man yelled to someone inside.

"Coming, sir!" a raspy voice said from within the house.

I looked around. The garden was impeccably kept. A green, leafy archway near the back led toward a private beach. A dozen butterflies lingered around a clump of blue hydrangea bushes. I had no idea who this man was or what I was doing here, and as the anxiety bubbled inside me, I tried focusing on the butterflies. They probably knew more than I did.

The man with the baseball hat sat down in the chair across from mine. This was the first time I had a chance to really see his face. He looked like he hadn't shaved in a few days, but his jaw was strong and defined and his lips were full, almost pouty.

Another man dressed in tails stepped onto the patio, holding a tray with a pitcher of cold lemonade and two glasses. As he set it down on the table, the tuxedoed man and I made eye contact. It was Frank, from the boat! Frank and Yanni both worked for the McCarthys, so that meant the mystery guy across from me was associated with the McCarthys. And with that hat, there had to be a connection to Dave McCarthy. It was all too coincidental. I opened my mouth to say hello, but Frank shook his head ever so slightly, pouring a tall glass of lemonade for each of us. I wondered why he didn't want to talk to me. Was it because the hat guy was here? Or was something else going on?

"Frank, have you seen my goddamn glasses? I can't find them anywhere, and now I can't see five feet past my fucking face."

"I'm sorry, sir, I haven't. But I'll keep an eye out." Frank bowed and briskly walked back inside, leaving the two of us alone.

The man across from me sipped his lemonade, serenely looking out at the garden. I took a sip. This was the stuff made by squeezing a dozen real lemons over a cup of sugar. I could almost taste Frank's hands. By the time the man had finished his first glass, my chest was thumping. He still hadn't said a word. What was I doing here? Finally he turned to me, a gleam in his eye.

"Isn't it beautiful?" he asked, gesturing toward the garden.

"Gorgeous," I replied.

"But under all this luscious vegetation . . ." He trailed off. "You've gotta bury the bodies somewhere, I suppose."

Was this an expression or a confession?

"Luella van Horn, do you know why you're here?" he asked, smiling.

I shook my head. "I haven't the faintest idea," I said, trying a casual tone to cover my nerves. Even as I kept drinking the lemonade, my mouth felt like I'd just swallowed a handful of saltines.

"I've heard you're good at investigating, and I'm in need of a good investigator," he said.

Interesting he'd heard that. I hadn't worked in months, and I practically botched one out of every two cases.

"Tell me about the case," I said.

He paused, rattling the ice in his glass. He poured himself more lemonade and gestured toward me with the pitcher.

I shook my head. "What's the case?" I said.

"My wife's name is Caitlin McCarthy." My ears perked up. He continued, "She's been cheating on me, and I need to know who he is," he said. His pouty lips formed a small knot in the middle of his face. I'm not trying to be crass, but it wasn't *not* like a butt-hole. "If you're interested, this situation could be quite lucrative for you. Plus free room and board and all expenses paid."

The idea of room and board was so tempting I could cry. "Where would I stay?" I asked.

"With us. I'll tell my wife you're a distant cousin of mine staying here for a week or two—however long it takes. She won't suspect a thing. I have a large family, and several of them have visited us on the island. Your job will be to befriend Caitlin, go with her wherever she goes, and report back to me. I know how you women love to talk, and I'm confident you'll confirm my suspicions soon enough," he said, no longer looking at me. He'd turned back toward the garden, and his blue eyes followed a bright green grasshopper as it hopped near our table. Swiftly, he extended his foot and smashed the grasshopper to a paste.

"Whoa. Why'd you do that?" I asked, regretting the question even as I spoke. It just came out of me. He slowly turned to face me once again.

"It got in my way," he said flatly.

"I never got your name."

"It's Mark Fontaine. Now will you take the job or not? I've already wired ten thousand dollars into your bank account for your trouble today, and there's much more where that came from."

"How did you know my bank account?" I asked.

He chuckled, as if it was a stupid thing to ask.

"That ten thousand is yours regardless if you decide to take this case or not. But I'll warn you, the ferry doesn't go back until tomorrow morning, so at the bare minimum, you'll have to stay the night, and you might as well start the investigation. Trust me, it will be very worth your while."

I took another sip of the lemonade and swallowed too hard, causing me to choke. Mr. Fontaine sat with his fingers interlaced in front of him, blinking slowly, waiting for me to control myself. I stopped coughing and dabbed at my eyes, which had begun to water.

"So will you do it?" he asked, impatience creeping into his voice.

"All I have to do is lie and befriend your wife, find out who she's having an affair with, and then I'm done?"

"I want proof," Mark said, then added, "and then you'll have more money than you know what to do with." That little butthole mouth twitched.

I took a moment to realize who I was dealing with here. A misogynistic power player with mysterious access to my bank account, a man whose wife, Caitlin McCarthy, had to be connected to a crook I'd put in jail years ago. But really, what did I have to lose?

"I'll do it," I said. Mark Fontaine shot me a wide, toothy grin.

5

Mark Fontaine led me back inside and gave me a brief tour of the all-white first floor. I got to see the ecru living room, the cream dining room, the eggshell kitchen, the fresh snow sitting room, and of course, the milk-colored library. All the books on the shelves were pale. It was beginning to feel a bit 1950s insane asylum chic.

As we left the library, which I learned housed over sixteen hundred white-spine books—limited edition, thank you—we passed a closed door.

"What's in there?" I asked.

Mark stopped abruptly and turned to look at the door in question. "Oh. Um, that's just the basement. Nothing down there, and it's locked anyway. Let me show you the upper levels."

He quickly limped down the hall, leaving me to stare at the basement door. Once he was out of sight I jiggled the doorknob, which was locked as he said. Suddenly I got that feeling again, as though someone was watching me. I turned to see Frank standing in the kitchen doorway, staring. He put his finger to his mouth and shook his head.

"Luella! Please keep up!" Mark shouted from down the hall.

I jogged to catch up with him. We walked up the white carpeted stairs to a second level. The walls here were lined with family members' painted portraits. Well-dressed men and women, all with the same dimpled chin, holding tiny dogs or plates of fruit.

"That's Caitlin, when she was younger," he said, pointing to an oil painting of a ringleted young girl with her mother and father. "Those are her parents. Her mother died a few years ago. And her father . . . well, he's out of the picture. The McCarthys have actually had property on Murder Island since the 1950s. They were one of the first families to acquire land after the island went private. If you ask me, it didn't hurt that a McCarthy was the prison doctor at the penal colony back in the day, but no one asks me. I married in."

"Where's your painting?" I asked him.

"Haven't gotten one. Bloodline only," he responded curtly.

He led me up two stories to a locked attic.

"What's on the third floor?" I asked, curious why we'd skipped that part of the tour.

"Oh, that's Caitlin's floor. She prefers to keep that area private. I don't even have those keys." At that, Mark took out a large set of keys from his pocket and held them close to his face, struggling to find the right one. He eventually found it, opening the attic door to a spacious, light-filled room with a queen-size canopy bed and an en suite bathroom that were all various shades of white.

"This is where you'll be staying. Make yourself comfortable," he said, pocketing his key ring.

"Won't I need a key to go in and out?" I asked.

"Yanni will find you a copy. I need to keep this one, it's the master," he said, clearing his throat. "Frank will be serving lunch soon. You'll meet Caitlin then." Mark eyed me up and down. "If you couldn't tell, she likes white. Do you have anything white you could wear?"

I looked down at my sweat-stained leopard-print dress and scuffed black patent leather pumps. "I'll find something!"

The man turned to go, then paused in the doorway. "Let me know whenever you learn something about my wife. Even what you believe to be insignificant information . . ." Mark said, passing me a business card that had his name and that same E symbol from the back of his hat. It had to be Endeavors.

"What's the E stand for?" I asked.

His eyes darted away. "It's the family business," he said hurriedly. "See you at lunch." His limp made a heartbeat-like rhythm as he hurried down the stairs.

I set my suitcase on the luggage rack at the foot of the bed, hoping I'd brought something white with me. I'd packed hastily so there was a chance I'd accidentally thrown something in. Rummaging through my wigs and clothing, I thought about what Mark Fontaine had told me. He'd married Caitlin, who was almost certainly heir to a fortune. If she was having an affair and chose to leave him, he'd be out of the family and all the perks that came with it, including access to a summer manse on Murder Island. I wondered if he really loved her, or if it just came down to money. He mentioned he had a big family and that many of them had visited before. Was his family dependent on the McCarthys' wealth, too?

Finally I found a white T-shirt and some off-white bike shorts. Not exactly formal, but they'd do in a pinch. At least it'd look like I was trying here.

I thought about what else I knew of Caitlin McCarthy. She was extremely wealthy, she was likely having an affair, and her house was designed like America's Favorite Cookie.

On the dressing table, my phone buzzed. Service at last! Hallelujah!

But who could possibly be calling me? I thought. I looked at the cracked screen and saw an unknown number from New York. Fuck.

"Hello?" I answered. *Please don't be Taylor Bell,* I thought.

"Is this Marie?" a voice asked, cutting in and out.

"Who's asking?" I shifted around the room in hopes of improved service.

"Marie, dear, this is Joan Clyborne, from the library? I found some more information on Murder Island, and I wanted to share it with you."

"Joan! How did you get my number?"

"You signed up for a library card, dear. I know where you live and your mother's maiden name."

"Creepy," I said.

"All right, my mother's maiden name is Foreman, so now we're even," Joan said. What a little sparkplug! Was it normal to get such a glowing feeling from a librarian's cold call?

"You know, I'm actually on Murder Island right now!" I said.

"Isn't that wonderful!" she whispered. I pictured her calling from the main help desk, her reading glasses hanging around her neck, tangling with her long jewelry. "I'm calling because I've learned something that might interest you. For decades now—since it was privatized—Murder Island has been owned by just five families: the McCarthys, the Hunts, the Petersons, the Jorkavics, and the Tylers. But as of a year ago, the Petersons sold their land to the Hunts. So now the Hunts own more of the island than anyone else. What do you think of that?"

"Very interesting," I said. "I'm actually staying with the McCarthys now."

"Well!" Joan exclaimed in a stage whisper. "You know what I learned about the McCarthys? Their company is—"

But that's when the call cut out. I tried calling back, but my phone lost the brief signal it'd had. It had to be the Endeavors connection. But what did Dave McCarthy mean to these people?

Even if the call dropped at the most inopportune moment, Joan had done me a solid. The Hunts owning more property than any other family was a lead. I wondered if Caitlin's alleged affair could have anything to do with that.

I looked in the dressing table mirror, adjusted my wig, and put on a fresh coat of red lipstick. My bike shorts were already halfway inside me, but I could do this—make friends with a wealthy woman to prove an affair—for an unthinkable amount of money. Hell, I'd done much worse for less. It was summertime in New York, and I was no longer in my sweltering apartment. Instead, I was on the elite Murder Island for a cakewalk case.

Or so I thought.

6

I was relieved to find the attic door unlocked, and when I opened it, I smelled something glorious cooking downstairs. Something with lots of rosemary and yeast—possibly a fresh-baked bread? I realized I hadn't eaten properly in a long time. Before Murder Island, I'd been subsisting on bagels and cans of beans, and my digestive tract was not happy about that at all. This is too much information, but if we're laying everything on the table, I hadn't . . . *bowel movemented* in a regular way for a month and a half.

I walked down the white-carpeted stairs to the third floor, marveling at how they kept this place so clean. There were no spills, no stains, and no scuff marks. They must've had Frank and Yanni working around the clock. I wondered what Caitlin McCarthy did with that whole floor to herself. The woman surely had hobbies. I tried a door, but it was locked, just like Mark had said. *Why would the woman lock rooms in her own house?* I wondered.

Down on the second floor, I paused again in front of the painting of young Caitlin with her mother and father. There was a twinkle in her eye. The painter must've been quite smitten.

Suddenly I felt someone behind me and jumped.

"I'm sorry to scare you, Luella. I only wanted to know if everything's to your liking in your room." Yanni stood behind me, dressed in a well-tailored suit. He'd left two buttons open on his crisp white shirt, revealing a small forest of dark chest hair. I briefly recalled my last interaction with the topless Sophie and resumed eye contact. He smirked knowingly.

"It's all great," I said. "How's work today?"

"All fine," he said, nodding curtly and turning to go downstairs. "Come along, lunch is ready."

I got the slightest inkling Yanni had been sent to wrangle me.

Yanni led the way down and I followed, noticing the ornate details of the house. Original crown moldings glimmered around the ceiling's edges, carved into an intricate pattern of beautiful little logs. Little logs with berries? Wait.

Nope, those were penises. The wooden moldings had been carved into tiny, beautiful penises. And upon closer inspection, there were vaginas up there, too. The pattern was complex, but consistently, one part was going into the other one. I looked down the large hallway. The carvings were everywhere. The craftsmanship! It must've taken the artist years. And so many models . . . It was hard to look away.

"What's with all the crown molding genitalia?" I asked. Yanni kept his head lowered as he walked us toward the dining room.

"It's art," he murmured. "Hurry up, you'll be late for lunch."

We walked into the dining room, and again I was struck by the wonderful smells. The table was laden with white china platters, one piled with glistening roast chicken, another with sautéed broccoli rabe, and a third with a steamed salmon fillet that could feed ten. There were bowls heaping with rosemary roasted potatoes and leafy green salads. Steam rose off loaves of fresh-baked bread. My mouth began to water. Along with a blond wig and a red lip, fake white teeth had been an important component of the Luella van Horn look. I'd always been self-conscious about my chipped front tooth, and part of the Luella disguise was the perfect teeth I'd pop in whenever I was on a case. With the cash I earned on my last case, I got veneers, aka permanent big white chompers that I wore regardless of if I was Marie or Luella. Now I could eat on the job, which was basically a life changer in situations like this. My stomach growled and Yanni looked at me with mild disgust.

"Please sit!" he said. No one else was at the table yet, but I could hear people approaching. Mark Fontaine and a woman, their voices tense, possibly arguing. I pulled out a white cushioned chair and prayed I wouldn't spill anything on it for the entirety of the meal. Hopefully they wouldn't serve red wine.

Just then Frank came bursting out of the kitchen decanting a 1991 bottle of Malbec. Why did god play me like this? Mark and the woman's voices were getting louder, as if the argument was happening just outside the dining room door. I strained to hear what was said, but I could only make out one question from the woman: "Then why wasn't she at the wedding?"

Suddenly the door swung open and Mark and a woman with the same eyes and coloring as the little girl in the painting walked into the room. *So this is Caitlin,* I thought. Mark was still wearing his baseball cap. The woman looked flushed, her eyes slightly bloodshot, though she was still very attractive. She wore her shoulder-length chestnut hair in beach waves. Her large brown eyes were framed by long, curly lashes, and combined with her delicate features, she looked like a sexy quokka.

Caitlin's clothes looked expensive, all predictably in various shades of cream and white. I felt like some kind of monster compared to her, my body slowly consuming my bike shorts from above and below. But I tried not to dwell on our differences. It wouldn't serve a burgeoning friendship.

"Mr. Mark, Ms. Caitlin, Ms. Luella, luncheon is served," Frank bellowed, pouring the deep red Malbec into what looked like real crystal wineglasses. I wondered if it'd be gauche to ask for a straw.

Caitlin eyed me. "I'm Caitlin McCarthy," she said, briefly embracing me in her ropey Pilates arms. She stepped back and took me in. "You must be Luella van Horn. So nice to finally meet you."

"This is that cousin I was telling you about, honey. Didn't I mention she was coming?" Mark asked.

"You must've," Caitlin said. Her voice was even, her mouth barely upturned in a muted smile. This woman was hard to get a read on.

"I live in the city, and I've always wanted to see where Cousin Mark spends his summers." I wracked my brain for another safe detail I could share. "I'm the cousin with all the cats." *That's good,* I thought. *Let her know I'm insane right off the bat.*

"How many cats do you have again?" Caitlin asked.

"Just one," Mark said at the same time I said, "Five."

"Four just died," I quickly added.

"I'm so sorry," Caitlin said.

Mark shot me a look as if to say *let's move past the cats.*

"And how are you, Caitlin? Cousin Mark sends me updates every so often but not as much as I'd like. Catch me up!"

"We must've met before, but I can't remember the last time we saw each other," she said. "There's almost too much to catch up on. How about we ditch this stuffy meal and grab something in town? Just us girls."

Caitlin sauntered out of the dining room, and I stood there uncertain what to do for a moment. Mark shooed me off, mouthing *follow her!* I looked at all the beautiful food laid out on the table. It must've taken hours to prepare. I wondered what kind of person sees all that and decides to leave it untouched. Either Caitlin was extremely entitled, or perhaps she really needed to get away from Mark Fontaine.

7

I followed Caitlin out the front door. She clicked a key fob to unlock a white Range Rover parked out front and got into the driver's seat. I'd seen a blond woman driving a white Range Rover when I got off the boat this morning and wondered how many of these vehicles a private island could have. Maybe it was a status thing, like Birkin bags or well-placed filler.

I hopped into the passenger's side. Once I'd closed the door and buckled in, she turned to me with a big smile plastered across her face.

"You're going to love this place. It's got a to-die-for octopus salad."

I hadn't eaten octopus since I'd watched that documentary about them being smart, but a job was a job. I'd eat the geniuses if I had to. Anything to befriend this beautiful, impulsive woman.

She drove fast down the island roads, which were paved but only one lane. I kept thinking we'd crash into another white Range Rover speeding from the opposite direction, but we encountered no other cars on the road. Caitlin rolled down the windows and the breeze was delightful. On both sides of the narrow road there was lush vegetation, which was only occasionally interrupted by large gated fences. As we passed one, Caitlin murmured something.

"That's the Hunts' compound. Eight houses on that property, and that's not including what they snatched up from the Petersons. And rumor has it, they're after the Jorkavics' place next."

"Where did the Petersons move?" I asked.

"Oh, they still live here, they just pay rent to the Hunts. The Hunts are happy to have the Petersons live there. Don't get me wrong—it's not that the Hunts are generous. A tenant can be very lucrative."

"Sounds like a weird dynamic," I said.

"If it is, it's none of my business," she replied curtly, continuing with her tour. "Have you heard the island is shaped like a kidney bean?"

I nodded.

"Well, we're on the lower part with the Hunts, and the Petersons and Jorkavics live on the top part. With property on the top and bottom, the Hunts are not so subtly trying to take over the whole island. The fifth family, the Tylers, basically lives in the middle, near downtown," she said.

"They're the ones who live in that castle?" I asked.

"If you want to call it that, sure." She smirked. "I'm actually surprised Mark hasn't regaled you with all the Hunt property acquisition stories. It's basically the only thing he talks about these days."

I shrugged my shoulders. "We don't talk as often as I'd like."

"I hope you don't mind me asking, but what is it you do for your work again?" she asked.

"I train cats," I blurted out. That was a new one. "That's why I have so many . . . that have died. I pushed them too far."

"You train them to do what exactly?" she said.

"Well, I teach them to sit and stay, and of course, roll over. People think training is just for dogs, but cats can do it, too. They'll do anything for tuna." I needed to stop talking.

"Sounds interesting," she said with zero inflection.

"What is it you do? Mark must've told me a while ago, but I've forgotten," I said, desperately trying to turn this conversation around.

"Oh look, there's Bradford Tyler now!" she said, ignoring my question. She pointed toward a man walking down the left side of the road in salmon-colored chinos and a white polo shirt, periodically bending over to examine the ground. His sandy blond hair was tousled and he wore what looked like a Rolex watch and clear-framed glasses. I put him around forty years old.

"Bradford! Hello!" Caitlin yelled out the window as she slowed down the car. Bradford looked up, his glasses now askew on his broad, symmetrical face. You know the expression, *born with a silver spoon in his mouth*? This guy looked like he'd been born with a whole ladle shoved in there. He squinted at us as we drove closer.

"Caitlin, is that you? Forgive me, I was so enamored with this speckled toad. I've followed it from my front door all the way out here. It's green and smooth. All in all, quite charming!" On his palm, he held out a small green toad for our inspection.

"You're a delight, dear. Never change," Caitlin said. "This is Mark's cousin Luella. We're on our way to lunch, won't you join us?"

"Oh, I couldn't," Bradford said, wiping his brow with the toadless hand. "I have lunch plans with Mother in half an hour."

"Enjoy, dear," Caitlin said. "Ta!" She sped down the road leaving Bradford and his toad in a small cloud of dust. "Mother is what he calls his wife," she said, checking her reflection in the rearview mirror as we zipped along at sixty miles per hour. "That couple is doomed."

Was it possible Bradford Tyler was the man she was having an affair with? And if he called his wife Mother, what was Caitlin called? Sister? Auntie? I wasn't sure I wanted to know.

We continued down the one-lane road in silence. I could sense she didn't trust me, or didn't trust Mark, rather. Maybe my connection to him was a liability in her eyes. I'd have to find a workaround.

"I know it's strange, me showing up here unannounced. I don't even really know Mark. My mother, she doesn't talk to the rest of the family much, but I'm not one to turn down a free vacation," I said.

Caitlin looked over to me for a long moment, long enough to drive over a sapling.

"What was that?" Caitlin screamed as the sapling scraped the car's undercarriage.

"You might have just run over a tree," I said, turning to see the sapling spring up behind us, no worse for the wear.

"What?" Caitlin said, on the verge of tears or laughter, I couldn't tell. But she didn't slow down.

"It's fine," I said. "I see it back there. Young trees are buoyant. Everything's okay!"

Finally she screeched the car to a halt. Dirt from the road rose up in a cloud around us. The smell of burning rubber filled the interior, and Caitlin's shoulders heaved as tears rolled down her delicate cheekbones.

"Everything is *not* okay!" she sobbed.

8

When Caitlin's sobbing had subsided and her breathing resumed a normal rhythm, I asked her what was bothering her.

"I'm sorry. I know he's your cousin, but Mark is crazy."

"How so?" I asked.

"Oh, you know how he is," she said, blowing her nose on a tissue she'd pulled from her Louis Vuitton handbag.

"I sure do," I said. "Mark, uh, Mark can be . . . Mark." What I lacked in improvisational skills, I made up for in how many times I could say "Mark."

"Let's forget about him this afternoon. I'm famished, let's eat."

She pulled down her sun visor and looked at herself once more in the mirror. She shook out her brunette waves and wiped her eyes with another tissue. As she applied another coat of lipstick, a smile spread across her face, not yet reaching her eyes. She nodded to herself, flipped the visor back up, and pushed on the accelerator.

"To lunch!"

Ten painfully quiet minutes later, we arrived at her favorite lunch spot. It was Morgan's Bistro, the empty restaurant I'd seen when I first got in. The place was intimate—just twelve tables with white linen tablecloths. The ceiling and walls were painted a deep hunter green and the lighting was low. I could tell this was a spot where secrets were shared.

Our waiter was Caviar Guy, the gorgeous man I'd seen carrying the caviar crates from the ferry earlier that morning. He introduced himself as Paul and he smiled warmly as we sat down. "It's good to see you, Caitlin."

"You have no idea, Paul," Caitlin replied. "You're looking wonderful, darling."

"I try," Paul demurred. "And who's this? Your sister?"

Caitlin let out a slight gasp. "Absolutely not! This is Mark's cousin."

Paul winked at me, and I felt a drop of sweat roll down my back. All I wanted was one day without humiliation.

"Welcome to Morgan's, Mark's cousin," Paul said. If Caitlin wasn't having an affair with Caviar Guy, I would happily step up to the plate.

Paul knew Caitlin's specific lunch order by heart. Shrimp cocktail with mignonette sauce to start, then the octopus salad served as an entrée. To drink, an extra-dirty martini, three olives. I looked at the menu, which of course did not list its prices.

"I'll do the same," I said.

Paul gave us a little bow. "Anything else you need, please let me know." As he walked toward the kitchen, I noticed he had the most shapely ass I'd ever seen. Like, carved from marble. I looked to Caitlin. It seemed she, too, was appreciating it.

I cleared my throat. "So. Shrimp with mignonette sauce? I've only ever had it with cocktail sauce," I said, as if I was trying to end the conversation before it began. Caitlin looked from Paul's ass back to me, confused. I mean, truly, I wouldn't want to talk to me, either.

"Yeah, my father used to order it. Mignonette on oysters," she said in a faraway voice.

"Did he pass?" I asked.

"Oh no. But let's talk about something else, shall we?" Caitlin replied.

This was going nowhere. I didn't have any friends in the city, so why would I know how to make friends on Murder Island? I racked my brain trying to think of what women bonded over. Shared experiences? Common interests? I desperately needed an in. I tallied up what I knew about this woman so far: She could be having an affair with the hottest waiter I'd ever seen, or maybe with the man who studied toads in the middle of the road; she wasn't crazy about her husband/my fake cousin; and her father was off-limits. I decided to try the Mark Fontaine angle.

"Family is complicated . . ." I started, and what a start that was. "You know, my mother hates Mark."

Caitlin straightened her shoulders and gave me a sharp look. "Why?"

"She thinks he's controlling, a little sexist even. Oh—I hope I'm not offending you!"

Caitlin's brow furrowed. "Not at all. In fact, I understand where your mother's coming from."

"How so?" I asked. As she was about to answer, Paul set down our shrimp cocktails. Eight pink jumbo shrimp were placed in a circle around the tiniest bowl of mignonette sauce I'd ever seen. They looked like synchronized swimmers frozen in time.

"Will you beautiful ladies be needing anything else for right now?" Paul asked.

"We're all set, thank you, darling," Caitlin said as she gingerly dipped a shrimp into the vinegary sauce. She took small bites and chewed for longer than I thought was necessary. Almost as if she was avoiding any further conversation with me.

If this was shrimp-eating time, so be it. I took small bites, as well. With the permanent dental implants, I could chomp-chomp-chomp from morning till night. If I was on the clock, so be it.

I waited until she'd finished every last one of her shrimp, which took nearly half an hour. Paul came by and cleared our plates with a nod. There was no getting out of the conversation now.

"Are you happy with Mark?" I asked.

She blushed and took a sip of her martini to buy some time. "Of course! He's not perfect, but . . ." She trailed off as her eyes moved toward the front door of the restaurant. I turned around to see what she was looking at. Two women walked in, both clad in head-to-toe expensive-looking beige.

Caitlin waved to the women. "Carla! Lindsay!" The two women

looked from Caitlin to me, smiled, then made their way over to our table.

"Caitlin, honey, how are you?" The taller woman extended her hand to me. "Carla Jorkavic, nice to meet you. And this is our neighbor Lindsay Peterson."

The shorter one, Lindsay, held up her manicured hand in a half wave. "And you are?"

"Luella van Horn. I'm a cousin of Mark's, visiting from New York."

Lindsay raised her eyebrows as she exchanged a quick glance with Carla. "Well, I love your hair. Caitlin, how are you?"

"Amazing," Caitlin said just as Paul set down our second course—two octopus salads. Oh god, they looked so smart, even on Bibb lettuce. "And you?"

"Also amazing! We'll let you two get on with lunch," Carla said. "That salad is to die for, right?" She gently squeezed Caitlin's hand, then Paul escorted the two ladies to an outdoor table.

"Friends of yours?" I asked.

Caitlin forked a seasoned tentacle. "Depends what you consider a friend," Caitlin said. "Around here, you never know." She took two more small bites then wiped the corners of her mouth with her napkin. "Excuse me, I've just come down with the most terrible headache. I feel bad asking, but would you mind horribly if we went home? I've gotten these before and they only get worse if I don't lie down right away."

"Of course," I said, shoveling in a few bites of octopus. The brainiac was dead, and the least I could do now was appreciate its flavor with a citrus dressing. Caitlin flagged down Paul and he swiftly brought us the check. When he set down the leather bill holder, I reached for it, but Caitlin shooed me off.

"Please. You're our guest," she said, opening her Christian Dior wallet and placing her platinum card in the bill holder. While she had it open, I quickly scanned her wallet for anything indicating an affair, like a hotel loyalty card or condoms, though I doubted Caitlin would keep condoms anywhere near Dior.

There was her driver's license, a few more credit cards, and then I noticed a business card tucked into the top right pocket. There was that silver embossed *E* again. The same logo from Mark's hat and business card—Endeavors seemed to be everywhere. But what did that mean for Caitlin and Mark? Did they both work for Dave McCarthy? And what did the alleged affair mean for their working relationship?

Before I had a chance to study the business card more, Caitlin snapped her wallet shut, just as Paul returned with her credit card. She signed the check, tipping Paul two hundred dollars. No wonder he knew her order by heart.

Caitlin drained the rest of her martini before standing up from the table. It wouldn't be my go-to headache remedy, but maybe the upper crust had a different biology altogether.

"Shall we?" she said, already walking toward the door. Outside, Lindsay and Carla were just beginning their octopus salads. As we passed their table, Carla quickly dabbed at her mouth and sent her fork clattering. Lindsay's eyes narrowed as she took a long sip of her martini.

"Caitlin!" Carla called out, and Caitlin turned back. "I meant to tell you, Josh said he wanted to talk to you about something. He wouldn't say what. Could you give him a call when you get a chance?"

"What's your husband need to say to Caitlin?" Lindsay asked. She popped an olive into her mouth and chewed slowly. There was something distinctly feline about Lindsay. The woman had big cat energy, like she'd kill you for fun.

"Not sure," Carla replied. "Do you know what he needs to talk to you about, Caitlin?"

Caitlin shook her head. "I'm sorry, ladies, but I have a terrible headache. We have to get back. I'll call Josh soon."

As we walked away, I turned back to see Lindsay whispering something to Carla. A grin spread across Carla's face as both women's eyes remained on Caitlin. Then Lindsay caught my eye and winked. I was caught off guard and a little confused, so I hustled to catch up with Caitlin, who was already in the driver's seat. I jumped into the passenger seat and grabbed for my seatbelt when I realized the woman had just downed a martini and had a splitting headache.

"Would you like me to drive?" I asked. She looked at me, then her brow furrowed, considering something.

"Yes, actually, I'd love that, Luella. Do you mind?"

"Not at all," I said. I walked around the car and got into the driver's seat as Caitlin got into the backseat and lay down.

"Can you possibly take me to my doctor? He's just down the road," she said, rubbing her temples.

Her doctor turned out to live four miles north of the restaurant. His house was enormous—four stories at least. It was a classic colonial with red brick, black shutters, and a gabled roof. I parked the car and got out to help Caitlin, but she was already sitting up and opening her car door by the time I got to her.

"You can head back," Caitlin said. "My car is equipped with GPS, so it won't be hard to find your way. Our home address is preprogrammed in there."

"Don't you want me to wait for you? I'm happy to," I said.

"No, I'll be fine. My doctor will take me home," she said.

Caitlin slammed the car door then hobbled up the long walkway toward the house. As she approached, the front door opened, and a handsome man in his forties walked out and wrapped his arm around Caitlin's narrow shoulders. He was slender with a head of thick salt-and-pepper hair. He nodded in my direction, and I waved.

The doctor brought Caitlin inside and shut the door behind them. I stood watching for a moment then got back inside the car and started it up. The GPS system was preset, like she'd said. "Home" was in there, but so was this place. She'd labeled this one "Josh Jorkavic."

9

So Carla's husband, Josh, was the doctor Caitlin needed to see so urgently. When Carla mentioned at lunch that Josh had a question for Caitlin, it'd seemed casual, social even. Was Carla alluding to something medical? If so, that felt like a HIPAA violation.

I knew I was supposed to drive myself back to Mark and Caitlin's place, but here I was, and I couldn't shake the feeling something strange was going on. Why label a couple's house in your GPS with just the husband's name? It couldn't hurt to lurk, maybe snoop around a bit. No one was expecting me back at the house, and if Caitlin asked, I could tell her I had car trouble. I turned off the Range Rover and took in the enormous house. I started counting the windows. There must have been at least ten bedrooms inside.

The dining room was located to the right of the front door, and I could see movement in there. It was easy to make out Josh's salt-and-pepper hair and Caitlin's all-white outfit. Josh led her through the dining room. From behind, Caitlin's arms went around his chest, and he paused. Then he turned around and kissed her softly. Caitlin's hands went into his hair as he grabbed her ass, and it occurred to me that this was not at all a medical procedure. There was no way Caitlin had a headache.

I was starting to feel like the island pervert, watching these two going to town on each other in the darkened dining room. Soon her clothing was on the floor in a white heap. He ripped his shirt off, and she began unbuckling his belt.

Being a private investigator had its perks, but for me, this was not one of them. It's only so often you can watch infidelity in real time before you lose all hope in the institution of marriage, and I was jaded enough to begin with. But on the bright side, I'd accomplished what I was hired to do, which was to find out who Caitlin was having an affair with. It was Dr. Josh, in the dining room, with the fake headache treatment. Now I just needed some evidence. I took some photos with my phone, but they turned out blurry. For a photo that would stand up in court, I'd need to get closer, unfortunately.

I quietly shut the car door and crouched behind the hood, careful not to arouse the suspicions of any possible passersby. The house was surrounded by thick bushes, and across the street there was only forest. If someone was watching me watching Josh and Caitlin, they'd have to be in a tree, like Tony from *Survivor*. I took my chances and quickly made my way to the house.

To avoid being seen by Josh or Caitlin, I ran around the perimeter of the property, pausing to hide behind the shrubbery for moments at a time. The last stretch between the house's exterior and a large tree was about ten feet, and I decided to army crawl it. The window in the dining room was practically floor to ceiling, so the lower I was, the better my chances were of not being caught. I'd have to explain the full frontal grass stains on my all-white clothing at some point, but I'd figure that out later.

By the time I got to the house's brick exterior, I was gasping for breath. I must've swallowed at least three bugs and a handful of grass. I didn't even want to think about what had made its way into my wig.

I froze when I heard voices. Two of them, a man and a woman, presumably Caitlin and Josh, though I'd never heard his voice before. Both voices sounded tense, the woman's almost pleading. I couldn't look in the window without being spotted so I stayed flat on the ground while I listened.

"He's going to kill me if he finds out," Caitlin said.

"He'll never find out. Don't worry," the man replied.

"I should go," Caitlin said. "Can you take me home?"

"Sure, let me get my keys," the man said.

I needed to get the hell out of there with Caitlin's car before they left the house. I debated army crawling back, but I knew it wouldn't be fast enough, so I made a run for it, trying to stay as low and as close to the trees as I could. The branches scraped my bare arms, and my knees felt like they were about to give out.

I was almost at the car, but any moment now they could come out of the house and see me duck-running across the front yard. My heart was pounding as I gasped for breath. I shoved my hands into my pockets, found the key fob, and unlocked the car, hurling myself into the driver's seat. I started the ignition before I'd even closed the door, and the dashboard beeped angrily at me.

I put the car in drive and peeled out so fast the tires screeched against the pavement. Once I was nearly fifty feet away, I looked in my rearview mirror. Josh and Caitlin were just leaving the house. Josh was locking up the front door, but Caitlin glanced in my direction. I could've sworn she made eye contact with me, and I stepped on the gas.

I drove for a mile before I stopped to plug the *Home* address into the GPS. My hands wouldn't stop shaking. I realized that Caitlin would probably beat me to her house, but I'd prefer that to her and Josh tailing me the whole way back. It was possible she didn't actually see me, that I was just being paranoid. I'd have a laundry list of excuses ready either way. *I got lost! The car was confusing! I was taking in the island's sights and sounds!* Regardless, I needed to get back to the house as soon as possible. The GPS said it would be a twenty-six-minute drive. I'd do my best to make it in ten.

As I drove from Josh's house to Caitlin and Mark's, I passed an estate so large it could have been a K-through-twelve school. This must've been the Peterson lot. From the road, I spotted a swimming pool, a tennis court, and a moderate-sized golf course. It occurred to me that I had yet to see a single child on Murder Island. Was all this for adults? I was reminded of the adults-only couples resort my ex and I went to for our honeymoon in the Poconos. The place had basketball courts, archery, even a corn maze. At the time, I marveled how much one could do to avoid making love to the person they'd just married. I now knew of at least one extramarital affair on the island. I wondered if something similar was going on around here.

Once I got back downtown, I passed Morgan's Bistro again. The table where Carla and Lindsay sat was now empty. That must've been a quick lunch.

I whizzed by Bradford Tyler's castle, thinking about what a strange bird he was. Probably richer than god and spending his afternoon petting a toad. I guess that's what happens when your forefathers squeeze every drop of the American Dream into your bassinet. Lost in thought, I barely saw the strange shape in the middle of the road until it was almost too late.

I skidded to a stop, the wheels turning out from under me on the narrow one-lane road, causing the whole car to fishtail. A rush of adrenaline coursed through my body as I tried to process that I was still alive and the car was fine, albeit partially on the grass. But what was the Range Rover built for if not the off-road experiences?

I was pretty sure I didn't hit anything. I put the car in park and got out to see what I'd almost hit.

Bradford Tyler sat slumped over in the middle of the road.

"Bradford!" I said. "Bradford, are you okay?"

He looked up at me slowly. "Me? I'm fine!"

"I'm so sorry, I would've stopped sooner, but I hadn't seen you! It's not safe sitting in the middle of the road like this." I was flustered and beginning to ramble. "Would you like some help up? Are you sure you're okay? What are you doing here?"

He looked around, back toward his estate and then farther down the road.

"Sometimes we need to slow down. Too many people are rushing around. It's Murder Island. We all just need to slow down."

This guy was freaking me out. Although he was very handsome, something about him reminded me of the Monopoly Man if he did mescaline. I extended my hand and he took it. This guy needed to get off the road before someone else killed him.

"You've come at a bad time," he murmured as I hooked his arm over my neck and hobbled with him toward the entrance of his castle. "You've come at a very rushed, bad time."

"What do you mean?" I asked. Between the adrenaline and dragging the weight of this man, I was sweating buckets. It was hard to keep his arm from sliding off me, and I held on to the side of his textured polo shirt for dear life. Though it felt like we'd been walking for miles, we were still only a quarter of the way up his driveway.

"Everything was going smoothly for so long. The five families. Our parties. Of course, greed would get us in the end . . ." He trailed off.

I'd only just met this man today but I knew he was on something, though I couldn't say what. He was almost run over by a car, and all he could do was mumble incoherently. Did the obscenely rich have access to different drugs than us regular folks?

"What are you saying, Bradford?" I asked. We'd finally made it to his entranceway. Before he could answer my question, an older man in a tuxedo swung open the front door.

"Sir," the man said, bowing to a crumpled Bradford Tyler. He looked at me. "Ma'am. Thank you for your help. Have a blessed day." The butler, or whoever he was, scooped up Bradford Tyler like a baby and carried him back inside.

"Bradford, what do you mean greed would get you in the end?" I shouted after him, but the butler only nodded to me and gently shut the door in my face. I got back in the car and wondered what in the holy hell I had gotten myself into.

10

I pulled up to Caitlin and Mark's house twelve minutes later, slightly decompressed but not by much. Over the drive, I'd tried to wrap my mind around this messed-up place. The five families, the recent property acquisitions, the wealth, the claustrophobia of it all. But there was a silver lining. I'd confirmed Caitlin was having an affair with Josh Jorkavic. That meant the case was nearly closed. I could probably go home on the ferry tomorrow with more money in my account than I knew what to do with. I wanted to feel relief. Closure. But something nagged at me.

As I approached the front door, I heard footsteps on the gravel behind me.

"Come with me," someone whispered. But when I turned around, whoever it was had just run around the side of the house. With queasiness in the pit of my stomach, I followed their footsteps.

"Hello! Who's there?" I called out, walking past a wall of hydrangea bushes. Suddenly I found myself back in the garden area where Mark and I had sat with that pitcher of lemonade. Still, I saw no one.

"Frank? Yanni?" I said. "Mark? Caitlin?" Behind the ivied archway, I finally spotted her.

Caitlin looked grave as she silently motioned for me to follow her onto the beach. Just past the archway, the grass and flora were replaced by small white stones and broken shells. She walked up to the gray water, which lapped against the shore in gentle, foamy waves, and stared out at the horizon beyond. I walked across the rocky terrain with the dreaded knowledge that things were about to get more complicated. I joined her at the shore, but she didn't acknowledge my presence with even a glance.

"I know you saw us," she finally said in a low whisper.

"I couldn't start the car," I said, fumbling for my pre-rehearsed lie.

She laughed to herself. "Doesn't matter. But Josh and I—it's not what you think," she said. "It's not just a silly affair. It's different."

They all said that. *This one's different. This one's real.* I wasn't the best private detective, but I'd stopped buying the excuses years ago.

"Caitlin, I don't want to get between you and Mark . . ." I purposely trailed off.

"Mark can't know," she said.

"He's your husband. He's my cousin," I said with a little too much conviction. Maybe I should've joined my ex-husband in those acting classes.

"It's for his own good. Trust me. The less he knows, the better."

"I know it feels that way with affairs. That the longer they're kept secret, the less they can hurt the other person, but sometimes it's best to bite the bullet," I said. Internally, I cringed thinking how long it took me to tell Leslie I was moonlighting as a private detective.

Caitlin turned to me, her eyes brimming with tears. "I'm his wife. It should come from me. Just give me some time to think about how to say it."

I'm ashamed to say my thoughts went straight to the money. If I was depending on her timeline, when would I get paid? Sure, these people's domestic life was about to be blown up, but hey, so was mine. I couldn't tell my landlord, "It'll be a few weeks. Caitlin McCarthy's just trying to find the right words."

Briefly, I wondered if being broke had made me completely depraved, or if I'd been this depraved all along. Would having the kind of money that let you live on Murder Island make things easier, at least morally speaking?

"Let's go inside. Mark will be wondering why we've been gone so long," Caitlin said, already heading back toward the house.

"How's your headache?" I asked, struggling to catch up to her.

Caitlin paused. "Oh, much better, thank you. Josh actually is a doctor, I wasn't lying about that." She smiled at me—a tight, unhappy smile—and resumed her pace. We passed through the garden archway and across the backyard. Frank was there to greet us at the back door.

"Ms. Caitlin. Miss Luella," he said, slightly bowing his head toward each of us. I wondered how long he'd been waiting at the door, watching. Caitlin nodded to Frank then turned to me.

"See you at dinner," she said brusquely before running into the house. Moments later, I could hear her footsteps racing up the creaking stairs. This woman couldn't get away from me fast enough.

Frank invited me to sit at the kitchen table while he made afternoon tea. I obliged and took the chair facing the stove. The table was across from Frank's makeshift office—a wooden stool tucked into a nook papered with an open day planner and Post-its, reminders to call the plumber and numbers to call when the internet was acting up. A pair of broken glasses lay behind the day planner, and a brass dagger-shaped letter opener lay on a stack of unopened mail. Frank's keys hung on a ring just above the desk.

I turned back to Frank, who was gracefully maneuvering around several kitchen drawers and cabinets to make us a proper pot of Earl Grey.

Moments later, he set down the steaming pot of tea and a plate of what looked like expensive artisanal Oreos, irregular-shaped brown cookies sandwiching a cream filling dotted with tiny flecks of vanilla bean. As Frank poured the tea into our mugs, I picked up a cookie and took a bite. It tasted like air.

"Those are Ms. Caitlin's favorite cookies," he murmured.

Yeah, have you seen her house? I wanted to say. Instead, I responded, "They're light," brushing about a hundred crumbs off my shirt. Frank took the seat across from me and began doctoring his tea with milk and honey.

"Thank you for the tea," I said. "You've made this a lovely stay, but it looks like I'll be going home tomorrow."

Frank continued stirring but looked up. "What do you mean?" he asked.

"In so many words, I've done the job I was hired to do," I said, taking a gulp of the too-hot tea and scalding the roof of my mouth.

"I wouldn't be so sure," he said, his gaze settling back on the surface of his milky tea.

"Why is that?" I asked, now choking on what was left of the dry cookie. Eating and drinking were clearly still new to me.

Frank took a slow sip, then set his mug down and wiped the corners of his mouth with a white cloth napkin. "The terms of your employment are simple. You have to prove to Mark Fontaine, one, that Caitlin is having an affair and two, with whom Caitlin is having an affair. Do you have proof of either?"

I was so taken aback I set my teacup rattling in its saucer. "How do you know the terms of my employment?" I asked.

"I know everything that goes on around here. I don't want to make you nervous, but understand that the employees on Murder Island see every move. That's our job," he said, dunking a cookie in his tea.

"So why would Mark ask for outside help? Why wouldn't he just pay you a little extra to do his dirty work?"

He cleared his throat. "I don't work for Mark Fontaine, I work for the McCarthy family. And besides, no domestic employee in their right mind would try to disrupt the natural order around here. You won't get help from us."

"So let me get this straight. You're telling me to stay here longer, but you're not going to help me?" I asked.

Frank gave me a slow, passive smile. His eyes were wide, and his hands were now folded and still. I thought about his question regarding proof. Besides blurry photos taken from a distance, did I actually have proof to offer?

"Caitlin and I spoke. She's going to tell Mark tonight," I said, my voice coming out a little shaky.

"Why would she tell Mark? What's in it for her?"

"She knows I'll tell Mark if she doesn't," I said.

"Did she give you a specific time frame for when she would be telling Mark this information?"

"She said she needed to figure out exactly how—" I said as Frank cut me off.

"You're here as long as the job requires, and you have not yet completed the job. You will stay and continue to track Caitlin until she confesses or you hand Mark proof of the adultery." He took another long sip of his tea, finishing it.

I didn't like the idea of staying here indefinitely, but Frank was right. Caitlin could take as long as she wanted. It's not like I had much to get back to in the city, but something about this place creeped me out, like everyone was in on the same joke but me. Frank's behavior struck me as odd. I couldn't figure out whose side he was on, but I knew it wasn't mine.

He grabbed both cups before I could finish my tea and set them in the sink, turning his back on me as he ran hot water over the dishes.

"Why are you telling me all this?" I finally asked.

"Because leaving Murder Island is never easy. It's important to set visitors' expectations," Frank said before drying his hands on a dish towel. "Dinner's in an hour. Don't be late." He walked out of the kitchen.

Leaving Murder Island was *never easy*? Betsy Clench said the ferry came and left once a day. What wasn't easy about that? I would not be stuck on a private island where the average income was nine figures. There was no way. This was a free country. Of course I could leave when I wanted to. Frank was talking nonsense.

Maybe I could find Caitlin before dinner and convince her to confess tonight. Or if I couldn't find her, maybe I could find something to use as evidence of her ongoing affair with Josh Jorkavic. I left the kitchen and wandered down the hall toward the stairs. Then I heard creaking from the floor above me. Someone was walking up there. I quickly made my way up the stairs, and once I got to the second floor, I looked around but saw no one.

"Hello?" I yelled. "Is that you, Caitlin?" No response.

I stood still as I listened for any other sound, but I heard nothing else. There were four rooms on the second floor, three to the east of the stairs and one to the west, and all the doors were closed. Whoever it was had to be hiding in one of the rooms.

I tried the first door east of the stairs, but it wouldn't budge. It must've been locked. Briefly I imagined a world where I had so many rooms I could lock some of them and keep living normally in the rest of my home. No wonder it was weird here—these people had too much indoor space. If you put Bradford Tyler in a studio apartment, I bet he'd be a lot less interested in picking up toads.

Suddenly I heard the wooden floors creak again. The noise was coming from the only room west of the stairs. I tiptoed down the hall and put my hand around the knob. This one opened.

Inside the room it was dark. "Caitlin?" I called tentatively, but my voice came out hollow. My hand shook as I glided it along the cold, smooth wall until I found a light switch. Once my eyes adjusted to the light, I saw bookcases lining the walls. Set against the window was a large antique desk and matching chair. This was someone's office. I shut the door behind me then made my way over to the desk.

Up close, I saw the edges of the desk were carved in an intricate flower pattern. Not that I was about to lift it, but the desk must've weighed nearly a thousand pounds. Based on its age and bulk, I could assume there were at least a few secret drawers inside.

On top of the desk sat a nice fountain pen, a framed photo of Caitlin and Mark, a stack of papers, and a day planner opened to the current week. The handwriting on the planner was small and slanted, written quickly and without regard for legibility. I noticed I was in there. In blue ink on today's date it said: **11:45 A.M., PICK UP LVH.** This must've been Mark's planner. Under that, he'd put: **9 P.M., XXX.** I wondered what was happening tonight—whatever it was, it seemed ominous.

I looked closer at the stack of papers. Scanning the text, I quickly recognized the legal jargon. These were divorce papers. I read further; it seemed Caitlin was asking for a divorce from

Mark. So that's why he needed proof of the affair. This was about settlement money.

I heard the floorboard creak once more, then two times in quick succession, just outside the door. Those were definitely footsteps. Someone was approaching. I froze behind the desk as the office door swung open. The hallway was dark, but a figure slowly emerged. Once my eyes adjusted, I realized it was Mark Fontaine.

I caught my breath as he stepped into the room. I don't know why I felt so unnerved by his presence—maybe it was the fact that he still hadn't said a word, and that was pretty odd, to say the least.

"Mark?" I finally managed to say once he'd made it to the center of the room. But he said nothing in response. He was no longer wearing his baseball cap, revealing a bald spot surrounded by matted brown curls.

"Hey, Mark!" I repeated, the fear now audible in my voice.

"Yeah, yeah, yeah," he finally said in a monotone.

Mark stood still for a moment, staring at the floor. He then crossed the room to the desk, sweeping everything off with one arm. The pen, the frame, the planner and all the papers were sent clattering. I jumped back on instinct.

I called out to him again, but by this point I could barely speak. Mark was acting irrationally, as if he was sleepwalking. He didn't even seem to recognize me. I backed toward the door, watching him rummage through the desk. Even in his daze, he seemed to be laser focused on finding something in particular. He pulled a lever in the first drawer, which made a latch pop, and a small drawer emerged from the desk's surface. Not to say I told you so, but see, I knew that thing had secret compartments. He flung it open and rummaged around, finally pocketing what he'd been looking for: a pill bottle.

The whole situation felt like some kind of interactive play, and of course, I mean that in the bad way. You go to support your friend from college, but before you know it, a skinny Macbeth is insisting you clutch his breast while he whisper-sings, "Twinkle Twinkle Little Star," and then you go home and have sex nightmares. Just one of many reasons to keep actors out of your life. I had those sex nightmares every night for two weeks straight.

My heart thumped in my chest as I tried to settle my nerves with deep breathing. Just then, Mark stormed out of his office, holding a letter opener in the air like it was a butcher's knife. I couldn't tell if I should laugh or run.

Most days, my go-to state of being is *coward eating cereal,* but I was already so far outside my comfort zone that part of me wanted to know where Mark was heading with that letter opener. Staying a few feet behind, I followed him as he ran down the hall and up the stairs to the third floor. My footsteps were loud and fast, but he didn't seem to notice I was behind him. I realized it must've been only 5 P.M., so my sleepwalking theory was wearing thin. Mark's behavior had to be the work of strong hallucinogens. Or whatever was in that pill bottle.

He began muttering something. I couldn't quite hear what it was at first, but he repeated it over and over as if it was a chant. Eventually I was able to make out the words.

"He's a dead man."

Maybe he had concrete evidence about the affair after all.

As Mark made his way down the off-limits third-floor hallway, he slashed the letter opener through the air, lunging and jabbing with it, until he got to a bookcase. I noticed this floor was colder than the others. On all other floors, the doors had been left their natural wood color, but on this one, they'd all been painted off-white. A small red cursive *C* had been painted on the front of each one.

Mark stood in front of the bookcase and pulled on a tan-colored book, then the bookcase opened into some sort of passageway. This job was getting stranger by the second. Before I could follow him in, I felt two hands grab my shoulders.

I turned around to find Yanni giving me a disapproving look. His broad forearms wrapped around my shoulders as he ushered me away from the closing bookcase.

"I don't think you're supposed to be here," Yanni said with a teasing lilt.

"What's wrong with Mark?" I asked. "Did he take something?"

"Of course," Yanni said. "Always." *Always?*

"Was that a secret passageway he went through? Did you see the letter opener he was waving about? What was in that pill bottle?" I peppered Yanni with more questions but he wouldn't respond to any of them with more than a shrug or a small chuckle. It was just like Frank had said. None of the McCarthys' employees were eager to give me answers.

As we walked up the stairs, I realized Yanni was escorting me back to my room. He took out a large set of keys, opened the door, and gently shoved me inside.

"What are you doing?" I asked.

"Dinner's canceled," he replied. "I'll bring a tray up later tonight. In the meantime, you stay up here, you naughty girl."

With that, he shut the door in my face. I could hear the brief jingling of keys on the other side, then I jiggled the doorknob. Yanni had locked me in. I examined the only window, and just my luck, it was painted shut. I guess Frank was right about a lot of things. Murder Island was going to be harder to leave than I thought.

11

Time was moving slowly inside the locked room. For the first few minutes, I tried everything I could to pick the lock, but it was to no avail. That thing must have been really old or really new, and either way, it was beyond my skill set.

As I lay on the bed, I was hit with waves of emotion—anger led to fear, which led back to anger and then to helplessness. *Why was I locked in a room on a private island? How could I not have seen this coming when Mark was cagey about the keys when I first got here? What could I have done differently with my life to avoid this scenario? Was this all because I was a Sagittarius?*

I tried crying but no tears came out, and I just felt like a bad actor. Speaking of bad actors, I wondered how Leslie was faring. Once he realized all the trouble I'd gotten myself into, I hoped he'd be devastated he hadn't offered to help me. So far, this was the only light at the end of the tunnel.

Oh, Marie, I'm so sorry, he'd say. *Oh, Marie, here's a blank check, take as much of my money as you want, and please forgive me.* Then I'd be like, *Sorry, I don't need your help, I'm with Gael García Bernal now. You must've heard of him, he's a real actor?* Then Gael and I would hop onto a stallion and ride off bareback into the sunset. I guess that's the one positive thing about divorce. Whenever anything goes wrong in your life, it can always be your ex's fault.

My perma-shut window looked out onto the front lawn. As I watched the sunset spread reds and oranges over the cypress trees,

I thought about what I knew so far about Mark and Caitlin, the house, and the island.

Caitlin was having an affair with Josh Jorkavic, who was married to Carla Jorkavic, who was supposedly Caitlin's friend. Caitlin had served Mark divorce papers. Whatever was going on with Mark, I'd say the best-case scenario was heavy drug use. I didn't love the way he was brandishing that letter opener, and with all those "he's a dead man" mutterings, it was safe to assume he knew something about Josh. Then there were the three Xs in his calendar for tonight, though the what and why of that were still a mystery to me. So far I'd met the McCarthys, the Jorkavics, Lindsay Peterson, and Bradford Tyler. I still hadn't met anyone from the fifth family, the Hunts, although on the ferry, I had met Sybil, who worked for them. And the two people who worked for the McCarthys, Frank and Yanni, were only making things more difficult. See Exhibit A: me locked in this attic.

I thought about why Yanni would lock me up here. Perhaps there was something he didn't want me to know? Maybe he didn't want me to see his employer acting like that. But Yanni had said that behavior wasn't out of the ordinary. Mark seemed to know exactly where he was going, like it was a recurring ritual. I had to know where that passageway behind the bookcase led and why Mark was going in there.

I checked my phone, and by some miracle, I had a little service. I tried calling the one resource I had: Joan, the blessed librarian. I wanted public records of the property, if there were any. Maybe they could tell me something about that secret bookcase. Even though it was after hours, in my head, Joan lived at the library. I could just picture her in a little tent by the picture books, making Sleepytime tea in a nightdress and booties for her 6 P.M. bedtime. The phone rang for three minutes before I hung up.

I tried looking up the public records myself, but the service was so spotty nothing would load.

I couldn't pick the lock, I couldn't get my phone to work, I was alone and at the mercy of a muscly handyman named Yanni. What I really needed was a friend, and the closest thing I had was the phone number of a librarian who didn't even live at the library.

I lay back on the bed, exasperated. After a very strange day where the only things I'd had to eat were shrimp cocktail and octopus, my mind started to wonder why I was doing this.

I thought about how I was thirteen when I saw my first perp. School was letting out, I remember it was a Friday, and even though it was only 3:10 P.M., most students had already left. Usually I was gone by this time, too, but on that particular day, my math teacher, Mr. Elison, had asked me to stay after. I had failed my last two algebra tests, and if I didn't get my act together, I would have to repeat the class.

I shoved my heavy math textbook into my book bag, even though I knew I wouldn't open it that night. I'd been dragging my bag down the hallway, wallowing in self-pity, when I saw a sixth-grader get punched. I didn't recognize him, but I knew the bigger boy, the one who did the punching. His name was Stephen Breen, and he was in my grade. Stephen was known throughout the school for two things: one, having a short fuse, and two, reeking to high heaven. I didn't like Stephen Breen before, but now I hated him. And I knew that whatever that sixth-grader did, he didn't deserve to get punched. I watched him crumple as Stephen walked away.

Over the next few weeks, whenever I had free time, I followed Stephen Breen. I learned his daily habits. I knew he got to school at 8:32 A.M. I knew he ate a salami sandwich and Doritos for lunch. I knew he usually took a big shit in the middle of his sixth-period English class. So one Friday, as he was coming out of the bathroom, I punched him like he'd punched that boy. My now ex-husband, Leslie Jones, was watching from the drinking fountain. When Stephen Breen moved to hit me back, Leslie stepped in and threatened to tell the principal, and Stephen backed down.

That was the day I'd fallen in love with Leslie. I really needed someone like him now, but there was little chance of that.

I sat up, and in a moment of pure frustration, threw my phone across the room. It landed with a thud against the scalloped base molding. I walked over to pick it up and noticed on the hardwood floor there was a three-by-three-foot square that had a slightly different grain. Upon closer inspection, it looked to be a separate piece of wood from the rest of the flooring. A trapdoor? Perhaps a way out? I pried my fingers around the edges but couldn't get it to budge.

The tips of my fingers became raw and bloody trying to lift the piece, and I angrily slammed my fist down. Suddenly, the wooden square swung up half an inch. It must've been on a magnetic push latch. I lifted up the edge of the panel until it was perpendicular to the rest of the floor, then peered down.

The trapdoor opened onto a narrow, darkened, musty staircase. I contemplated going down there, but it didn't exactly look inviting. Remember that part about me being first and foremost a coward, with the cereal, etc.? Yanni had said he'd bring up a dinner tray, and what would he think if he brought it all the way up here to find me missing? Now I was coming up with excuses. I gazed once more into the darkness below, and my body got the message loud and clear: it was time to have diarrhea.

Twenty minutes later, I'd landed on a plan from the comfort of a heated bidet. After dinner, if I was still locked in—and I hoped that was a big *if*—I would wait until everyone in the house was asleep, then I would go down those freaky little stairs.

At eight o'clock, I heard someone heading up to my room. I watched the knob turn as the person unlocked my door. I stood up from the bed, ready to confront whoever it was. Especially if it was Yanni. I had words for that guy. Just because you're hunky and chiseled does not give you the right to lock someone in an attic.

The door opened, revealing Frank. His silver tray held my dinner and a bottle of wine. I don't know wine, but the label looked pricey. In those days, most of my wine came from a box.

"Frank, Yanni locked me in here. This is not acceptable. I'm not a prisoner here, I'm on a job, and furthermore—" I had more to say, but Frank set down the tray and held up his hand.

"I can't go into detail, but trust me when I say you're in here for your own safety," he said, his eyes direct and serious. "After tonight, everything will be taken care of, but until then, you'll need to stay up here with the door locked. As long as you're inside this room, you're as safe as you can be."

"What's going on out there? Is it Mark? Is he dangerous?" I asked. I suddenly felt a lump in my throat, making it hard to swallow.

"The less you know, the better," Frank said, already turning to go.

"Wait! You can't just leave me up here without a clue!" I said.

"Everything will come out eventually," he said, slamming the door behind him. I immediately pushed against it, but I could already hear him turning the key, locking me in again.

Dinner was leftover poached salmon and the roasted rosemary potatoes from lunch. The wine was a chilled Riesling from 2004, but I tried to go easy on it. Those stairs looked rickety and were probably as old as the house. I needed all the balance I could get.

I finished everything on my plate and looked at the time. It was only 9 P.M. No one would be asleep yet. I heard faint creaking throughout the house, so it was safe to assume people were still up and about. I drank my wine slowly as I tried again to load the history of the property on my now-cracked phone.

At last, success! I learned the house was built in 1953 by an architect named Dale Delacorte. The guy was known primarily for his optimization of interior space, and later, for forcing his assistants to sleep with him. Delacorte had built all the houses on the island, starting with this one. I wondered if it was Dale's idea to lock the attic from the outside. I wouldn't put it past him.

I tried looking up Caitlin McCarthy and Mark Fontaine, but it was taking forever to load another page. I looked at the time again—only 9:15 now—and I let out a frustrated sigh. The self-pity was creeping in. How long would I be stuck up here? And who's to say they'd let me out in the morning? I thought I must have someone I could call for help.

I scrolled through my contacts in despair, and the A's were already looking grim. Then I came across a name that gave me some hope. I dialed optimistically. After the first ring, she picked up.

"Hello? This is Betsy Clench."

"Betsy! Hi, it's Luella van Horn! Is this a good time?"

"You know it! I'm just hanging in lower Manhattan, nursing a beer at this surf-and-turf bar. Pretty low-key night. I think I have a canker sore, though, so that sucks. Can't eat oysters with a canker sore, am I right?"

"Totally," I said. This woman was something else. "Listen, I may be locked in the attic at the McCarthy house, and I just wanted you to know in case something happens or I never get out of here."

"Oh," she said. I could hear her taking a sip of beer. "You want me to come get you? I bet I could steal the boat!"

"Not just yet," I said, relief flooding through me. Here was someone actually willing to help, even if she was a few beers in and across the river. God, I loved Betsy Clench.

"Wait, what day is it?" she asked.

"It's Friday. I met you this morning."

"Uh-oh," she said, taking another sip.

"What?" I cried.

"I wonder if that's their day. The day they do their sex thing!"

"What sex thing?" I said, regretting every bite of the poached salmon. I thought about the XXX in Mark's calendar that was supposed to start at 9.

"C'mon, Lala, you really didn't know about the sex thing? Why else would you go to Murder Island?"

"Betsy, you need to tell me what the sex thing is!"

Betsy laughed out loud, and I could hear her murmuring to the person next to her, "She didn't know about the sex thing!"

"Betsy?"

"It's a widely known secret that all the couples on Murder Island sleep with each other. This has been going on since the families first built their houses there."

"Wait, so their parents and grandparents all had sex with each other and now their grandchildren are all having sex with each other? Aren't they worried some of them might be . . . related at this point?" I asked.

"Well, see, that's the thing. That's why none of the current couples on the island have any children. They're worried about the incest thing. 23andMe got 'em all spooked. These parties have been going on so long they don't know who's related to who at this point, and they're afraid of what's lurking in those tangled-up family trees. It's like that European family with the chin."

"The Habsburgs?" I asked.

"Oh, you know those guys?"

"Not personally," I muttered.

"Anyway, rumor has it they're trying to bring in new blood. The Hunts started buying up all the properties to lease them on a fancy Airbnb site, but the Jorkavics refused, so now their plan is cooked."

"Wait, if they're all sleeping together, what would the issue be with someone having an affair?" I asked.

"Well, it's all about designated nights. Because of that, any sex that happens outside of those special nights is particularly taboo. It's part of the bylaws, infidelity."

"There are bylaws?" I asked.

"What's an island without bylaws!" she yelled. "And you know where the sex party is happening tonight? That is, if it's to-night . . ."

"Where?" I asked.

"At the McCarthys', where you're staying! Man, what I wouldn't give to be part of that new blood. Can you imagine, going to town on Mark Fontaine while being railroaded by Lindsay Peterson with a strap-on?"

I could now.

"You really think it's happening here tonight?" I asked. I tried to picture Mark getting it together enough to participate in some sort of group sex. On the other hand, perhaps that was why he was so messed up. Maybe he'd pregamed.

"Pretty sure. They rotate houses, and it could very well be the McCarthys' turn to host." She paused to burp. "According to my source, the party would be happening in their basement."

Betsy was starting to creep me out. "Who is your source?" I asked.

"I've worked that ferry for fifteen years now. Miss Betsy Clench has *lots* of friends. Look," she said. I could hear her walking out-side the bar where it was quieter. "I know if they threw me in, I'd be dynamite. If any of those billionaires said to me, *Hey Betsy, what are you up to tonight?* I'd say, *Nothing much, just ovulating, ready to go!*"

"Ew," I said.

"Ovulating is hot, and you know it," she snapped. "Just do me a favor. If you sniff out any action, let me know. Because I'll bring the party. I'll find a way to get there."

I looked around. "I'm locked in the attic, Betsy. If the action isn't happening up here, I'm not going to see it."

"That's just a front! They're testing you! There's gotta be a way out. It's all part of their sexy mind games. I'm sure there's a hidden key or a trapdoor or something."

Aha. "Betsy, let me call you back," I said, walking over to the panel of hardwood flooring. There was no need to wait until everyone went to sleep if there was a sex party happening downstairs and this was all a test.

"If you make it to the party, don't forget about Betsy Clench!" she yelled as I hung up the phone. I banged on the strange floor square, and up sprang the trapdoor again. Peering down the narrow staircase, I could've sworn I heard music, maybe the murmur of far-off voices. Still, it was dark and musty, and I couldn't decide if I was being influenced by Betsy or this was actually the way to the sex party.

I stood up and put my foot on the first step. The wood wobbled and felt soft underfoot, and I paused. These stairs must've been ancient. And did I really even want to go to a sex party? I'd had quite enough with the *Sex Island* case. Reality TV stars competed to win one hundred thousand dollars by being the best at sex, and then one of them got murdered. It kinda put a damper on sex in general.

Bottom line, I didn't want to have sex, and I didn't want to watch others do it, especially not these people. But what was I going to do? Stay up here all night, when raucous debauchery was happening only a few floors below? Debauchery that could be leverage to get out of here for good. I owed it to myself as a private investigator. And as a divorcée! When you get divorced, you are legally entitled to go down a rickety staircase that leads to a rich person's orgy.

I'd sufficiently built myself up enough to climb down the dark, rotting steps. I turned on my phone's flashlight, then held the phone with my teeth while I placed my hands on either side of the narrow passageway. These new veneers were practically paying for themselves. After a few too many close calls, I stuck to the outsides of the stairs, avoiding the middle where the rot seemed to be more prevalent. I could feel parts of the old brick walls crumble under my damp hands.

The stairs alternated direction every eight steps. I'd only made it down fourteen steps (obviously I was counting every single one), but already my knees were shaking, my jaw ached, and I could tell I was starting to drool on my phone, which is one of the main things they tell you not to do at the Apple Store. Just based on jaw strength, I started to wish I was one of those inbred Habsburgs.

When I got to the sixteenth step, I knew I couldn't go on. I had cobwebs on my face and dust in my eyes, and though I could feel something crawling up my leg, I couldn't bend down and grab it without breaking the step below me. This was too hard. I was afraid both to go back up and to keep going down. What if I died inside this dark, nasty staircase? Would Betsy Clench tell them to look for me here?

That's when I saw the light. I double-checked—I wasn't dying, I literally saw light shining through in long slivers. I felt around the wall and finally located a knob. I was so excited my mouth opened, and my damn phone fell out. Based on how long I could hear it tumbling down the staircase, I gave up any hope of getting it back. But who needed a phone when you had a wall with a knob on it? I reached for the knob again, turned it, and a door opened, allowing the light to get so bright I could barely see.

I stepped out into the light, relieved to be on firm ground again, and when my eyes finally adjusted, I took in my surroundings. The door was covered in books. This had to be the same fake bookcase Mark had run through earlier this evening. That meant I was on the third floor. Caitlin's floor.

Suddenly I heard footsteps coming and I quickly ducked back into the dingy staircase, shutting the door behind me. I could hear the footsteps walk past, pausing only briefly in front of the book-case. I held my breath. Finally the footsteps moved on.

The way I saw this situation, I now had three options. One was to go back upstairs and curl up in bed. That was my favorite option. The other two were less favorable. Option two was to wander through the house somehow undetected and find evidence of Caitlin's affair, whether that be in one of her rooms or at the al-leged sex party. But I wasn't sure what the ramifications would be if they found me wandering about. Would I get dragged back upstairs and handcuffed to the radiator? I know that sounds hot for some people, but it's really not my thing. I prefer the kind of sex where my shirt's still on and my pants are still on and there's waffles and I'm just describing breakfast, aren't I?

Option three was my least favorite because it involved going down more of the dark, twisty stairs until I either (a) found my phone, (b) found the party, or (c) fell to my death. It was like my choices were to go to heaven, stay on earth where things weren't going great, or go directly to hell. But something told me once I saw that party, everything would make sense. And I knew deep down the secret staircase would be the most surefire way to get there without being stopped. Unless I died by falling down the stairs. Which also felt somewhat surefire.

I decided I'd comfort myself with some math, having gotten marginally better at it since I was thirteen. I'd gone down sixteen stairs to get to the third floor. To get to the basement, which was likely where the sex party was happening, I had three stories to go, which meant forty-eight more steps. I could do this, probably. Forty-eight was less than fifty, and much less than a hundred. As I began to walk down, I thought of what a small number forty-eight was. Forty-eight crayons was the smaller box! Forty-eight Q-tips was basically a travel pack. I could live maybe forty-eight more years if I didn't fall down these stairs.

By the time I'd gotten to what had to be the first floor of the house, I'd pissed off a lot of spiders and seen a rodent so large I prayed it was a cat. Parts of the wood stairs had softened with age, but I was getting the hang of this descent with the dregs of my adrenaline. The music got louder the lower I got in the house, but all I could focus on was the number forty-eight. Forty-eight sunny-side-up eggs. Forty-eight women named Janet. Forty-eight gumdrops in the sweaty palm of a mall Santa.

By then I'd lost track of how many steps I'd gone down. All I knew was that sweat was dripping into my eyes and it burned. I paused on a larger landing to catch my breath. That's when I heard a noise in addition to the music. A human noise, for sure, but haunting. Like a yell but longer and more pained. Perhaps someone was in danger? I heard the noise again. It was coming from below. Decaying wood be damned, I raced down the rest of the way. The noise got louder and the air became damper.

The last step I took was on a rotten plank, and I landed in a heap against a wooden door. My ankle began to feel hot as I put my ear to the door. I could hear people murmuring and the music was much clearer now—smooth jazz. These billionaires could throw a sex party but still manage to have no imagination when it came to a playlist. As the saxophone solo started to really take off, I felt above my head, finally locating a knob and turning it. What I had hoped was a pull was actually a push. The door opened out in front of me, and my body rolled into the newly open space. In the dim red light, I took in my new surroundings.

The human noises were clearer now, and I realized what sounded like shouting in the staircase was more accurately pornographic moans. Well, I had definitely found the sex party. I cringed as I sat up and dusted the cobwebs off my clothes. Even in the low light, I could see my ankle had already swollen to twice its size.

I had landed in some sort of antechamber. Whoever else was down here must've been one room over. Everything in the antechamber appeared to be red. There was a velvet armchair the color of merlot and an oxblood credenza. The only light came from a lit candelabra on top of the credenza, dripping pools of red wax that looked oddly like congealed blood.

I found I was able to stand if I put all my weight on my other foot, then hobbled over to the credenza. Next to the candles was an open guest book. In the candlelight I could barely make out the writing, but flipping through, I saw the entries went back to the 1980s.

A blindfolded woman staggered in, squealing. I held my breath. Her blond bob looked familiar. I'd seen this woman somewhere before. She was topless but wore lacy black panties and thigh-high snakeskin boots. Her breasts bounced as she clomped further into the little room. My mind flashed back to Sophie. Unfortunately, that image was never going away.

Suddenly the woman let out a giggle. She breathed through her mouth, listening for her pursuer. When no one came, she frowned, put her arms out in front of her, and felt her way back through the archway.

I could hear her boots click-clacking on the wooden floor, but the sound got farther and farther away. Betsy Clench was right. This had to be their sex party night.

Someone put their hands on my shoulders and I jumped, causing my ankle to make a very painful popping noise. I couldn't turn around, but still got a look at the hands. They were large and callused.

"Luella, you're not supposed to be down here," a raspy voice said before a blindfold was put over my eyes. The last thing I knew, I smelled rubbing alcohol and was thrown over somebody's shoulder like a sack of potatoes.

12

I woke up in a dark room with my ankle feeling heavy and itchy. It took me a minute to realize I was back up in the attic. Somehow I'd been tucked under the covers. When I pulled back the sheets, I noticed I was wearing an ankle brace. Someone must've carried me up several flights of stairs, put me in bed, and tended to my injury. On instinct, I reached for my wig. It felt matted, but at least it'd stayed on.

My memory was fuzzy, and I wasn't sure what time it was. Maybe someone had used ether on me? Whatever it was, it must've knocked me out for hours. I looked around for a clock, but of course I found none, and my phone was long gone. From where I lay on the bed, I could see the moon bright and full outside my window. Based on its position in the night sky, I figured it was either 10 P.M. or 2 A.M.

I thought about the voice and hands of the person who'd confronted me in the basement. Their voice was raspy, and their hands were rough. Whoever it was didn't want me going into that party, but somehow knew exactly where I'd be and cared enough to fit me with an ankle brace. All signs pointed to Frank.

I thought about the moans I'd heard, the secret staircase, the blindfolded topless woman hoping to be chased. What was this place? Betsy Clench could have the sex parties all to herself. I was hired to find evidence of an affair, which seemed simple but was proving more challenging with every step. Sure, I could make more money than I'd ever made on a single case, and sure, that raised some red flags, but what was I supposed to do? Say *no thanks, I'd rather starve in the big city than enter your world of wealth and debauchery for a couple of days?* I don't think so.

A sudden noise startled me out of my shame spiral. There was a creak in the floorboards, just outside my door, then footsteps, light and fast, running down the stairs. I sprang out of bed and hobbled over to the door, which of course was locked. I looked down at the floor. An envelope lay on the ground that hadn't been there before. I bent down to grab it and saw it was addressed to Luella. On a whim, I sniffed the envelope—it smelled like roses.

I flicked on the light and opened the letter quickly with my thumb. Inside was a small card with scalloped edges. It said:

Watch out for Mark Fontaine.

Why? Because of his drug use, or the way he bandied about a letter opener, or just his general unpleasant demeanor? But Mark was the one who had hired me. I was supposed to report to him. This case was becoming messier by the minute. The real question was: Was it worth the fat paycheck? Yes. Probably. Hopefully, yes.

Somehow with all of that swirling around my brain, I still managed to fall asleep for a couple of hours, because the next thing I knew, sunlight was streaming through my window and miraculously, the attic door was open. My prison sentence was seemingly over. I could use the normal stairs again!

I put on a fresh wig, a pair of leather pants, and just enough makeup to go downstairs and see what the day had in store. My ankle throbbed as I walked down to the third-floor landing, then I heard what sounded like muffled sobbing. The closer I got to the first floor, the louder and clearer the sobbing became. It was coming from the dining room.

I hobbled down the last staircase to the main floor and peered into the dining room, where Mark Fontaine sat huddled with Caitlin. I'd never even seen them touch before. Mark looked up at me as I entered the room and his brow furrowed. He seemed sober this morning. But there was nothing on his face that resembled remorse or regret—maybe he'd blacked out the night before. Caitlin's shoulders heaved, but she kept her head pressed against Mark's chest.

"What's wrong?" I asked.

"He's dead," Mark croaked. "Josh Jorkavic."

"What happened?" I asked as I joined them at the dining table. Frank entered the room, quietly placing a steaming cup of coffee in front of me and laying a napkin in my lap. I get that it's fancy, but it's never not going to be weird for an adult to put a napkin on my lap. That's the hill I'll die on.

I took a sip of the too-hot coffee as I waited for someone to answer me. I added a follow-up. "And when did he die?"

Caitlin let out a loud sob and excused herself, leaving Mark and me at the table and Frank quietly standing against the wall holding the coffee urn.

"Come with me, I'll show you," Mark said, pushing his chair out.

He'd show me? Oh hell. I gulped down the rest of my coffee and followed him out of the dining room, down the hall, and toward the basement door. Mark pulled out his keys and unlocked the door with a click. The coffee churned in my empty stomach. As if he were reading my mind, Frank came up behind me with a basketful of muffins.

"Fresh blueberry muffin?" he said solemnly.

It was definitely not a time for fresh muffins, but I grabbed one anyway. It was warm in my palm, and I took a large bite, crumbs trickling onto the floor. It was moist and buttery, and its sugary top balanced the tartness of the blueberries. If someone at that moment asked if I knew the Muffin Man, I'd say, *yes, it's Frank*. Mark was already halfway down the stairs. I shoved the rest of it in my mouth and hurried after him. Frank and his muffins followed us down.

The lights were off, but in the morning light, I could see the walls were red, as was the carpet on the stairs. The air in the basement smelled different from the rest of the house. Like human sweat and spilled liquor. Underneath, there was something incensey, long since burned.

That perfect muffin was already sitting like a rock in my stomach. I followed Mark into the basement's main area, nearly toppling over three different low velvet sofas. Why did rich people love a low sofa? It's like they were saying, *Look how much we paid for something so close to the floor. You think you can sit here? Squat for it.*

"This way," he said, leading us into a dim hallway. Frank and I kept close behind as the hallway opened into the same antechamber I'd been in the night before. The only light still came from the lit candelabra. Its bloodred pools of wax were six inches deep this morning.

In front of the credenza lay a very still Josh. As I knelt closer to his body, I noticed his face was permanently grimaced. I felt my own face form a similar grimace. Overnight, this had become a murder investigation. My mind flashed to Taylor Bell's wife's fingers in the garden, David G dead in my bathtub. Those cases almost broke me. I was starting to wonder if I shouldn't just stick to lost dogs. Too late now.

Josh's arms were crossed over his chest, and his throat had a thin gash across it, but there was no blood anywhere. I yanked a candle out of the candelabra and brought it closer to Josh's body. I knew the carpet was red, but there was not a drop of blood around him. This meant his body would've had to be moved post-mortem and posed how he now appeared. Whoever did this was trying to send a message. But what message, exactly? His crossed arms and bloodless slit throat suggested a certain flair for the ritualistic. Almost like he'd been sacrificed.

There was a chalky blue residue on his fingertips, in particular the right thumb and forefinger. I didn't take Dr. Jorkavic for much of a pastel artist, which left the possibility of drugs. If he had been holding a pill, those two fingers would be the ones to do it. Maybe he was prescribing himself something on the side.

"What kind of doctor was he?" I asked.

Mark snorted. "He wasn't that kind of doctor. I think he had a PhD in reading. Literature of the Croatian diaspora, something like that."

Ah. That meant Caitlin was lying to me even after I found out her secret. I thought back to our conversations. She'd definitely alluded to Josh being a medical doctor, but had she said it outright? I knew she was in a tough situation, but something told me I couldn't trust her. Could I trust anyone in this house? I thought about that card I got late last night telling me to watch out for Mark Fontaine. Who would've had more of a reason to kill Josh Jorkavic besides him? What could help now was a timeline.

I lifted Josh's leg to check for rigor mortis. It was very stiff. That meant he had to have been killed at least twelve hours ago. If that *Forensic Files* narrator was to be believed, rigor mortis reached its peak between twelve and twenty-four hours after death. I asked the current time. Mark checked his watch and said it was 11 A.M. That left the time of death sometime before 11 P.M.

"I think he may have been murdered," Mark said. "His throat is slit. That's, uh, that's crazy."

"No shit," I said. For the amount I was being paid, I knew a simple affair was too good to be true.

13

By the time Mark had made this amazingly astute discovery, Frank was already halfway up the stairs.

"Where are you going?" I called after him. But Frank continued up the stairs without looking back. The basement door shut quietly behind him.

"He's probably going to check on Caitlin. She's not built for stuff like this," Mark said. "Anyway, this isn't your problem. We'll involve the police once we get back to the city. There's no police on the island—it's all part and parcel of the privatized land deal. The NYPD assumes we're fine, and the five families pool together a generous donation to the New York City Police Foundation every year, just in case situations like this pop up. I'll call today."

"If this isn't my problem, then why are you showing me Josh Jorkavic's body?" I asked.

Mark sighed, looking up toward the ceiling. "I know Josh was having an affair with Caitlin."

I froze. "Then why did you have me investigate?"

"Well, I wasn't sure, until now." Though Mark's eyes were sad, the corners of his mouth were upturned in a sickening smile. "I can't believe somebody slit his throat," he said, then swiftly made his way up the stairs.

I was now alone in the basement with Josh's dead body. I still held the candle, and I winced as some hot wax rolled onto the back of my hand. If Mark already knew about the affair, why was

I brought here? Maybe he knew Josh was going to be murdered. Which meant, either he killed him, or he knew who did.

People often say a detective and a murderer are playing cat and mouse, but I couldn't help feeling like this was a game of cat and yarn. I was the yarn, obviously, which was not ideal. What kind of person commits murder under the scrutiny of a private detective? Whoever it was, I knew at least one thing: they were certainly bold.

I sifted through Josh's pockets for anything out of the ordinary. I found his keys, half a pack of Listerine breath strips, his wallet, two condoms, and his phone. I helped myself to a Listerine strip, which was so minty my eyes watered, then I studied his phone. It was password protected, but he had two visible text notifications. One was from Caitlin, and it said, we're being watched. The other was from an unknown number. All it said was meet me in the antechamber.

Everything seemed to be falling into place rather nicely. Too nicely. Here was Josh, dead in the antechamber. And the last text he received was from someone telling him to meet in the ante-chamber. So was I supposed to believe whoever texted him killed him? In order to text on this island, you had to be on wifi. So whoever killed him was clearly a friend of the McCarthys', and at the very least invited inside. I thought of the mysterious topless blond woman I'd seen the night before.

Who would want Josh dead? If Mark knew about the affair, it had to be him, or maybe Josh's wife, Carla? Both had motive, but the way his throat was cut indicated experience as a killer, or a surgeon, or a kosher butcher. Whoever it was, they knew what they were doing.

Just then, I heard a scream from the top of the stairs. I moved as fast as I could out of the antechamber and up the staircase in time to see Caitlin, still screaming, pounding her fists against Mark's chest. Midscream, she and I made direct eye contact, then she ran. Mark's face twisted in anguish, and he sent me dagger eyes before running after Caitlin. I heard someone yank open the front door, then there were more pounding footsteps.

Out of breath after hobbling up the single flight of stairs (I'd get a gym membership one of these days), I turned down the hall to see the front door swung wide open. Out front, Caitlin was climbing into her white Range Rover, but Mark had nearly caught up to her. Stitches formed in my sides as I hurried after them. I'd just made it to the front walkway when Caitlin peeled out, tires screeching, leaving Mark chasing after her like an angry junkyard dog.

Caitlin's car sped up and finally Mark gave up the chase. He limped back toward the house and up the walkway, passing me like a ghost.

"Mark?" I said. "What happened?" But he ignored me, shuffling back into the house. I followed him in, watching as he made his way up the stairs and into his office on the second floor. I heard the door shut and the lock click.

I stood there dumbstruck. Josh had been killed, Caitlin had driven off, Mark had locked himself in his office, and Frank and Yanni were both mysteriously absent. Technically I had done my job and I could go home. Would go home. Should go home.

But I couldn't help but feel like someone was leaving me breadcrumbs, enticing me to stay. *You figured out that affair pretty quick, but do you have what it takes to solve a murder?*

It was very likely the murder and the affair were connected. Caitlin cheated on Mark with Josh. Then the sex party happened. Josh ended up with his throat slit and no blood to be found. Where the hell was all that blood?

I decided my best plan of action was to find Caitlin. She was emotional and raw, and if I could talk to her now, she might let her guard down enough to give me something to go on.

On foot, I set out toward the downtown area. Since Josh was dead now, I had a feeling she wouldn't go back to his house, and Morgan's Bistro seemed to be a place of comfort for her. That was the direction her car went, anyway. Besides, where else could someone go on this damned island?

With the majority of weight on my good ankle, I walked along the road, marveling at all that was Murder Island. Passing Bradford Tyler's enormous estate, I wondered what part of the penal colony it was before. Was that where they kept the prisoners or the warden?

I was peeking through the cedars at the Tylers' private golf course when someone tapped me on the shoulder from behind. I was so startled that I screamed. I hadn't seen or heard anyone near me on the road.

Despite being in his sixties or seventies, Bradford's butler's posture was ramrod straight, as if an invisible string kept his head at a perfect ninety-degree angle to his square shoulders.

"You scared me," I said.

"My apologies. Please come with me, ma'am."

14

Bradford's butler walked directly behind me. Considering he was the only one who knew where we were going, it felt like a power play. When I asked where we were headed, he said, "Just around the corner, ma'am." Out of the corner of my eye, I scanned for a gun, but he held his hands behind his back. Classic butler shit.

Somehow he steered me around to the Tylers' pool deck. This was not the time to appreciate the patio decor, but that deck was truly stunning. Bright red tropical flowers accentuated these big olive-green tasseled sun umbrellas. The loungers were all upholstered in coral, and the tables in between were polished teak. I don't claim to have any taste when it comes to design, but this place looked like it was straight out of a magazine.

Bradford lay sleeping on the farthest lounger, his face pointed directly at the sun. That white man was going to wake up crispy as a hash brown potato.

"Is he okay?" I asked.

"He's fine," the butler said. "He's best when he's napping."

If anyone ever described me as "best when napping," it'd be time for some drastic personality changes.

The butler beckoned me toward the tennis courts just past the pool.

"How much more are we walking here?" I asked, wincing. "My ankle's not in great shape."

He stopped in the center of the court, and we stood on either side of the net. We could both still see Bradford's sleeping figure from there.

The butler leaned close to speak. "This place is not what you think it is. If you're not careful, Murder Island will trap you here."

"You're not the first person to suggest that," I said, trying to force out a chuckle. "But what the hell do you mean?"

"Answer this question: why are you here?"

"I'm here for a job," I said.

"And is the job complete?" he asked.

"Yes, but—" I said. Just then, Bradford must've stirred awake because we both heard him screaming.

"What's that noise? Who's there?" Bradford yelled. The butler ran back toward the pool, and I limped close behind.

"Sir, will you be needing your afternoon spritz?" the butler asked Bradford while waving me away. *Leave,* he mouthed to me. I quickly hobbled back toward the road.

I couldn't shake the creepy feeling that butler gave me. *Why was I here? Was I being trapped? Why did he keep calling me "ma'am" when I was only thirty?* It felt like everyone on this island had read the same playbook, and it was called *How to Lose Friends and Unsettle People.* Without a phone, I looked up at the sky to see where the sun was. I guessed it was roughly noon. Josh's murder be damned. In less than twenty-four hours, I would be on the next ferry out of here.

Despite my ankle being the size of a melon, I made it downtown in record time. There was something about this island that kept me moving. Like if I stood in one place for too long, a sniper's laser might appear on my forehead. I'd nearly sweat my wig off when I spotted Caitlin's white Range Rover parked in front of the closed swimsuit store. I felt the hood—it'd cooled considerably. That meant she'd been here for a bit. I walked to the bistro where the sexiest man alive was outside refilling ice waters for two women I didn't recognize.

Paul's arm muscles glistened in his rolled-up shirtsleeves, and I noticed one of the women lick her lips suggestively as she ogled him. As I approached, the lip licker glared at me. I thought of what the Tylers' butler would say. *No need to glare, ma'am.* I hoped her oysters contained just the tiniest bit of E. coli.

"Are you interested in a table? I'm happy to serve," Paul said. *God, was he baiting me? Did he talk like that on purpose? Focus, Luella, focus.*

"Um, have you seen Caitlin McCarthy around here recently?" I asked him in a low whisper.

"No, I haven't," he said, then looked me up and down. "Is she okay?"

Before I could respond to Paul, I heard someone yell, "Lolly!"

I turned to find Betsy Clench walking toward me with her arms wide open.

"Lolly van Tiesel!"

"It's Luella van Horn," I said as Betsy embraced me in a bear hug. She could mess up my name all she wanted. Betsy Clench was a one-woman oasis.

"What are you doing here?" I asked.

"Captain called me this morning, said we needed to head back to the island for an emergency transport."

"Could you take me back to the city?"

"Not this run, unforch," Betsy said. "Captain's on the boat, and he gave specific instructions to let no one leave the island."

"Do you know what the emergency transport was for?" I asked. This had to be for Josh Jorkavic's body.

"They just loaded up whatever it was. That's why they told me to take a breather in here."

I looked out the window but couldn't see any action happening around the boat. Betsy had a few minutes before she needed to head back. Without a clue to where Caitlin could have gone and the emergency boat transport being a new piece of this puzzle, I figured a drink with a friendly first mate could be just what I needed. Betsy said she'd be willing to have one, if it was on me. A girl after my own heart.

Turns out Betsy Clench was a gal who loved a morning shot, or rather, shots. After we each downed three tequilas, I had already forgotten about my ankle pain and Betsy was only getting started.

"Hey, what do you know about Mark Fontaine?" I asked.

"Mark Fontaine," Betsy repeated, clapping her hands. "Mark Fontaine!"

I tried to shush her, and she cackled. The lip licker looked up at us from her undressed salad. *Ma'am, please. You may have been exposed to E. coli. Your time is limited.*

"All right," she said in a stage whisper. "Here's what I know. He used to work for Caitlin's dad, Dave McCarthy. That is, before Dave got arrested."

Finally somebody said it. Everything was starting to click.

"You see the statue where we first docked? That's Dave McCarthy's grandfather, Bill McCarthy. He was the first one to buy property here, and he was the one who got the five families together. I used to know all their names, let's see . . . there's Frederick Peterson, then . . . what was Jorkavic's first name? It's on the tip of my tongue."

"Betsy, did you know Josh Jorkavic well?"

"Of course," she said. "I know everybody on this island."

"He was killed last night."

"Oh, that is a real shame," Betsy said, clicking her tongue. "Why do all the sexy motherfuckers have to die young?"

"Do you know anyone who might have wanted him dead?" I asked.

"Paul, did you hear this?" she yelled out to him. He set down the two identical plates of miniature crab cakes he was holding and hustled over to Betsy's side.

"You hear Josh Jorkavic was murdered?"

Paul put his hand over his mouth and staggered back like an old Hollywood starlet. "It's crazy you asked about Caitlin McCarthy. Before yesterday, the last time Caitlin came in here, she was with him."

"Did things seem tense between them?" I asked.

"No, not at all. They actually seemed quite smitten with each other. They sat at that table over there for almost three hours," he said, pointing to a table in the back corner of the restaurant. "They only left because she finally looked at the time and then rushed out. I remember he paid. He wasn't a good tipper like she is. Left ten percent, before tax."

"Who do you think killed him?" Betsy said, licking the inside of her shot glass.

I held up my hand to ask for another round. "I don't know yet," I said.

"Paul, did you kill him because he's such a bad tipper?" Betsy asked.

Paul looked at her with a furrowed brow and put his hand on his chiseled left pec. "I would never kill anyone, even if they didn't tip me at all."

"That's nice," Betsy said, smiling a dopey smile. Her phone buzzed and she looked at the time. "Damn, Captain's asking where I am. I should get back. Thanks for the drinks, and good luck with . . . whatever it is you're doing here!" She staggered off her barstool, burped twice, pounded her chest, then straightened her sailor hat and walked out of the restaurant, erect as a soldier.

I paid my tab, making sure to tip well in case Paul was, in fact, the murderer, then hobbled out of the restaurant to see if I could catch any action around the boat before it took off. That's when I saw that Caitlin's white car was no longer parked nearby. But we were near the water, which meant the roads were sandy and would easily show tire tracks. There was only one set of tracks, and it showed someone had pulled out from that spot and driven north. It had to be Caitlin's car.

The sand extended onto the island for about half a mile. I noticed the car's tracks had a unique pattern—the tires were wider than average and it seemed there was a rock or something lodged in the back right tire. I followed the tracks as long as the sand allowed, and when I looked up, I recognized the path. She had been heading toward Josh Jorkavic's house. Ankle brace be damned, I began the long trek on foot.

As I neared the Jorkavics' house, I saw multiple cars parked along the road, including Caitlin's Range Rover. The front door was open, and hearing voices, I let myself inside. People were gathered in the living room, dressed in fashionable black clothing, sipping cold white wine and snacking off delicate china plates. Large white flower arrangements had been placed everywhere.

As I entered the living room, the small crowd turned toward me and quieted. An unsettling feeling, to say the least. I recognized some faces—there was Carla Jorkavic and Lindsay Peterson huddled by the fireplace, both holding nearly empty glasses. Bradford Tyler sat by himself on a low cream-colored sofa, eating caviar with a celery stick. A truly odd man at every turn. And there was Mark and Caitlin, holding hands near the buffet next to a woman with a blond bob. I squinted, certain I recognized her, too. Was that the woman from last night's party? It had to be.

"Luella," Caitlin said, breaking the silence. "Thank you for coming to Josh's vigil. Everyone, this is Mark's dear cousin. She briefly met Josh, and she wanted to be here for him." Caitlin was covering for either me or herself.

People solemnly nodded, and Carla walked over to me, her toned arms extended. She embraced me, lightly grazing my cheek with a dry kiss. "Thank you for being here. Josh would appreciate that you've come." She smelled like cigarette smoke and jasmine.

Bradford looked up from his caviar, made eye contact with me, and shook his head. *The butler was right. He is better when he's napping,* I thought. With her ice-cold hand, Carla took mine and escorted me to the bar, where she refilled her glass and poured me a fresh one.

"To Josh," she said, lifting her glass. The room joined her in toasting, then resumed their subdued conversations. Carla clinked glasses with the nearby woman with the blond bob, then turned to me.

"Come," Carla said, leading me down a marble hallway toward a bright and airy kitchen. In here were more white lilies in vases. The refrigerator had a see-through door, and inside, all I could see were rows of nonfat Greek yogurt. I counted three sinks and two stoves, and I'd bet anything these people didn't even cook.

Carla opened a drawer to the right of the fridge and pulled out a stack of papers. She held them to her taut frame and stepped closer to me, until I could smell the chardonnay on her breath.

"I'm so sorry for your loss," I said.

She gave me a tight smile. "Thank you. Now can I ask you something about Mark?"

"Sure," I said, no clue where she was going with this.

"Do you think he plans to sell? I got my offer from the Hunts' lawyer this week, but no one else has mentioned receiving theirs, so I wasn't sure how to proceed. If you see any offers lying around the McCarthy house, would you be a sweetheart and let your friend Carla know?"

The woman's husband just died, yet real estate was at the top of her mind. I supposed grief comes out in mysterious ways.

Just then, a woman yelled from the hallway, "Luella? Where did you go?" I recognized Caitlin's voice. Carla shoved the stack of papers back into the drawer, held her finger up to her mouth, the universal signal for *our little secret,* then darted out the door on the other side of the kitchen.

Caitlin appeared in the doorway we'd come in from with her hands on her hips.

"What are you doing here?" she asked.

"I've been trying to find you," I said. "You didn't tell me your father was Dave McCarthy."

Caitlin's brow furrowed as she walked further into the kitchen, pausing near a platter of spring rolls. "What's that got to do with anything?"

"I'm not sure," I said. "But don't you think it's a strange coincidence? I worked with your father's business partner before, and out of all the . . . cousins Mark chose to bring out here . . ."

She shook her head. "My father is complicated, but he deserves to be in jail. I didn't put the pieces together until now, but I've always been grateful for the private investigator who put him away. So thank you. And I know you were here to prove Josh and I were having an affair, but now Mark is out of control. I think he killed Josh, and I'm scared. I don't know what he'll do next."

"Then you need to get away from him," I said.

Just then, Mark popped his head into the doorway. "Everything all right in here?" he asked, looking only at Caitlin.

"We're fine," Caitlin said. She nodded at me, then walked out of the kitchen, leaving Mark and me alone. He moved closer to me.

"Be out of our house by sunrise and I'll still pay you in full." Then he walked out of the kitchen. I stood there dazed for a moment, then hobbled down the hallway. I was trying to sort out my thoughts when, from a darkened doorway, someone held out a small plate piled high with caviar. I nearly ran into it. *What a metaphor for my time on Murder Island,* I thought. *Crashing into a plate of caviar.*

"Excuse me," I said to the plate, craning my neck to see who was behind it. But the plate holder remained hidden behind the doorway.

"Take the plate and eat the caviar," a man's voice said.

"What? Why?" I asked.

"Just look busy. I need to tell you something," he said. It almost sounded like Bradford Tyler, but this guy's behavior was nothing like Bradford's.

I took the plate and began eating heaps of the caviar with a tiny spoon. It was salty and slightly fishy, and with each bite, I imagined how much money was going down my throat. The lady with the blond bob glanced at me from the living room, then averted her eyes.

"Beware the bat and the rooster," the man said.

"What the fuck does that mean?" I asked between bites. When he didn't respond, I turned and looked around the doorway where he'd been hiding. The man was gone.

Mark reappeared at the far end of the hall. Quickly, he walked toward me and grabbed my arm.

"We're leaving. You've got something on your . . ." He trailed off, gesturing all over his face. I brought my hand up to my chin and felt it dotted with little bits of caviar. *You can take the girl out of Staten Island,* I thought.

"Don't forget. Out of our house by sunrise." Mark limped out of the hallway, and I tried to swallow the lump forming in my throat. Did he kill Josh Jorkavic? Did he plan to kill Caitlin tomorrow? What could I do here?

I was just about to walk out the Jorkavics' front door when

Carla intercepted me. "You're leaving so soon? Remember our little chat. If you see any papers around . . ." she said. "And thank you for coming. It means a lot. Josh's memory is a blessing." She put her manicured hand on her heart and frowned as much as the Botox allowed.

"Sorry again for your loss," I said. Just then, I heard Caitlin honk the car horn several times. "My cousin's my ride. Sounds like they're ready to go."

"Let's talk later," she said. "Hope you enjoyed all that caviar."

"It was delicious," I said. "You'll need to send me the recipe!" I called as I walked out the door.

"It's just caviar, dear. There is no recipe," Carla said.

Kill me.

15

Caitlin drove us back to the house in near silence.

"The caviar was nice," I said, just for something to say.

"Oh, it was far too salty," Caitlin said.

"Right, that's what I meant," I said.

When we pulled up to their house, Caitlin announced she needed to lie down, and Mark said he'd join her. They went upstairs together, and I realized this gave me an opportunity. It was all adding up, I just needed to find proof that Mark was the killer.

"Frank?" I yelled. I needed to make sure the coast was clear. "Frank, are you home? Yanni?"

When they didn't respond, I snuck toward Frank's kitchen nook and grabbed his keys to the basement. With no one around, this was my chance to reexamine the crime scene. This time I'd have no one hovering over me.

The Dave McCarthy angle was becoming clearer in the light of day. Did Mark know who I was, and did he want to punish me for what I'd done to his father-in-law? It didn't seem like they were close, but with all those sex parties, maybe they'd formed a special bond? Nah. Sleeping with the daughter and the father was bold, and if I was being honest, it didn't seem like Mark's MO.

I called out for Frank once more to make sure he wasn't lurking nearby, and when I heard nothing, I snuck around to the basement door, which was locked again. After three or, if I'm being realistic, twelve tries, I finally found the key that worked. I was in. That stale incense smell lingered and it was easily five degrees cooler down here. The lights were off, and past the first few stairs, the basement looked like an abyss. Making sure the coast was clear, I closed the door behind me and began my descent.

I tottered down as quickly and quietly as I could, hyper aware of every Velcro scraping sound my ankle brace made. The third to last step creaked under my weight. I winced, frozen to the spot. I counted to sixty, and my eyes began adjusting to the darkness. I waited to be caught, and when no one came, I breathed a deep sigh of relief. I hurried down the remaining two stairs into the darkened basement.

With the door shut, I figured no one would know if I turned on the lights. I felt around on the wall for a switch and eventually found one to the left of the staircase. When the lights came on, I realized I hadn't ever seen the place like this before. Now everything was in full view. And it was nasty.

There were whitish stains everywhere. They were all over the low couches, splotched on the Persian rugs. I shuddered realizing that this was all dried semen. Then, with my good foot, I stepped on something that squished. When I lifted it, I saw a used condom had stuck to my heel. I shook my shoe to get it off, and it turned out it was actually two used condoms. Before I could stop myself, I was hurling up all that caviar. It was pound for pound the most expensive vomit I'd ever produced.

With all the caviar evacuated and my shoe finally condom-free, I took a moment to collect myself. I wiped my mouth and adjusted my wig in the mirror behind the bar, when something caught my eye. On the shelves behind the bar, above the high-end liquor bottles, crystal rocks glasses were lined up in neat rows. Each one had an identical etching. I grabbed one to get a closer look. There was that Endeavors *E* again. This place had Dave McCarthy's prints all over it.

Even if he was in prison, Dave McCarthy had to be the reason I was here. This was no coincidence. But I'd never even met Dave, and I'd only spoken to his partner on the phone. It occurred to me then—was Mark Fontaine that partner? The man had called himself F on the phone—was it possible F stood for Fontaine? Re-

gardless, I couldn't just be a sitting duck. I had to get to the bottom
of this.

I wandered around the rest of the basement, now extra careful
of where I stepped. The remnants of group intercourse were on
every surface. No wonder they lit so much incense, it smelled like
a teenager's laundry down here.

There were three hallways extending off the main room. I knew
the one that led to the antechamber I'd been in last night and this
morning. The other two were anyone's guess. I walked down one
and found it led to a room with a king-size bed and a sex swing
installed above it. Most unnerving, the sex swing swung lightly back
and forth, as if a ghost had been trying it out. Was someone else
down here with me? I listened, and hearing nothing, limped back to
the main room to try the second hallway. Halfway down the hall,
the red carpeting stopped, revealing concrete flooring, which led
into a dark concrete room that smelled like pennies. I tried the light
switch on the wall but nothing happened. With no windows and
the hallway light already dim, I couldn't make out much.

I walked back to the main room and grabbed the smallest candelabra, which probably weighed forty pounds, and lit it with a
matchbook from Morgan's Bistro. Holding the candelabra in one
hand, walking toward the cement room, I felt like a thirty-year-
old Nancy Drew. I briefly wondered if Nancy Drew's ex-husband
would also have tried to be an actor, or if she'd ever find herself in
a rich people's sex dungeon. Probably not.

Inside the cement room, the penny smell was overwhelming. I
set the candelabra on the ground, and in the flickering candlelight, I could see it was a square room, approximately nine feet
long by nine feet wide. There was no furniture to speak of, and
nothing adorned the walls. It was no bleaker than your typical
unfinished basement, so I decided to head back to that antechamber, see if there was anything I missed. I picked up the candelabra
and was starting to leave when I felt something drip onto my shoe.
The same shoe that had stepped on two condoms. Lowering the
candelabra, I examined the drip in the candlelight. There was no
mistake—this was blood. That was it. These shoes would be getting incinerated.

My hands shook, and I nearly dropped the forty-pound cande-labra when I saw the drain. A small metal drain had been installed in the middle of the room where the cement floor slightly dipped. A clump of salt-and-pepper hair sat matted on top, and around the drain there was a shallow pool of blood. That looked like Josh's hair and was most likely Josh's blood. So he'd been murdered in this room, bled out, then dragged into the antechamber and posed there.

Just as I began wrapping my mind around why, someone came for my wig. I screamed and swatted behind me, but there was no one there. Then I felt my wig lift off my head. Was this the ghost from the sex swing? I grabbed the bloodied candelabra and held it up, frantically looking around for whoever took my wig.

Then it came for my face.

16

It was small and shrieking and it had stolen my wig. I was completely out of sorts, but I needed to see to whatever demon this was. First I saw its beady little eyes, then its leathery wings, and in its nasty claws, my wig. I couldn't believe it. I was dealing with a fucking bat.

The creature shrieked again and dove toward me, and I helicoptered both my arms as self-defense. With my right hand, I made contact. I felt the little thing smack against me like a paper airplane. The bat fell to the ground and lay still. *Oh god, I killed it,* I thought. I hated it and I feared it, but I didn't mean to kill it. I wondered if this is how Mark Fontaine and Taylor Bell must've felt.

The bat lay in a heap in the corner of the cement room. I took the candelabra over and looked at it. *Poor thing,* I thought. He was so small. This hadn't been a fair fight. I didn't know why he'd scared me so badly. In the candlelight, I could see he was the size of a saltshaker.

My wig was still in his little claws, so I reached for it. But that's when the demon came back to life. With his teeth bared, he flapped his wings and flailed toward me like a drunken sailor. I'd heard somewhere that once bats got grounded, they couldn't fly up—something about their wings allowed them only to fly down. But that biological rule didn't seem to apply to this little motherfucker.

I scooted away from him, tripping over myself and feeling

something wet under my palms. The blood; I'd forgotten about the pool of blood. I was living in a nightmare. The tiny freak was coming at me with a vengeance, and I'd somehow backed myself into the far corner of the cement room. I tried to tell myself that this thing was minuscule, that I could take it, that I'd already killed it once, but its hissing and screaming and flapping had me terrified. My knees wouldn't stop shaking, and my body felt cold all over as I huddled there. Then that little bastard dropped my wig into the blood puddle.

I don't know what came over me then. You know those moments in ESPN documentaries where the star athlete says he found a reserve he didn't know he had and that's how he got the spare in the bowling championships or whatever? That's how I felt. I let out a war cry from deep within my soul and straightened myself to my tallest height. I squared my shoulders. This thing was going down or buying me a new fucking wig, whichever came first.

Luckily my victory was swift, though in no part thanks to me. At first, all I saw was a lacrosse stick swiping across my field of vision. Someone behind me swiftly swung it down, and the bat was trapped in the small space between the net and the cement floor, where it flapped and flailed in desperation. I watched my beautiful blond wig become a sacrifice as the bat evacuated its bowels in the bangs. A single tear rolled down my cheek. Rest in peace, guano wig, you gave it your all.

Wearing only my wig cap, I turned to face my savior in the dim light, but whoever it was had already started running away. I followed the sound of their footsteps down the hallway toward the main basement room. I eyed his tuxedo tails midway up the basement stairs.

"Hey!" I yelled. "Frank, stop!"

Frank paused on the stairs, though he remained facing forward. His upper body heaved from running, and one hand held the flapping bat in the pocket of the lacrosse stick.

"You weren't supposed to see that. You aren't supposed to be down here," he said, his voice gravelly.

"I know, I'm sorry," I said. "But that room—that's where Josh was killed, isn't it?"

"That is not your business here, and if I were you, I would steer clear. Now you'll need a rabies shot. Dr. Tyler can administer it. Let's go."

"Bradford Tyler is a doctor?" I asked, incredulous.

"No. Dr. Tyler is his wife," he said. "Haven't you heard that old riddle?"

"Thanks, Frank. Very helpful, as always. But are we talking a medical doctor or a doctor of Croatian literature?"

Frank only continued his climb up the basement stairs. "Your hair is gone. You'll need to fix that before we go."

At this point, I was covered in human blood and bat shit, I was limping, and I'd stepped on two used condoms. I must've smelled like a run-down zoo. If Luella had ever been considered glamorous, I had no memory of that.

I ran upstairs to put on another wig and change clothes while Frank grabbed the keys to Caitlin's car and called Dr. Tyler to let her know we were on our way. When it came to rabies shots, Frank said it was "now or never." Much later, I realized this was not the case. In fact, many doctors say until you're foaming at the mouth, you can still get an effective rabies shot. I know now Frank just wanted me out of the McCarthys' house.

Once I got to my room, I checked myself for bite marks. I couldn't find any, but with all the adrenaline coursing through my veins, I was paranoid. *Where the hell did that bat come from?* I wondered. Suddenly, I remembered what Bradford Tyler had warned me about before I left Josh Jorkavic's memorial. "Beware the bat and the rooster." Had he meant a literal bat? Did that mean there was a rabid rooster just around the corner? I honestly didn't know how much more I could take. And that was all before I got a rabies shot in the ass.

17

The old butler answered the door at the Tylers' property, and he and Frank exchanged a quick glance before escorting us into the foyer.

The Tylers' castle was enormous, making the McCarthy place seem nearly middle class. Upon entry, twin marble staircases met at a platform midway up, then split off again, leading to the east and west ends of the house. The floors were adorned with ancient rugs I felt I shouldn't be walking on. Of the art hanging in the front hallway, I recognized two Picassos, a Monet, and a Basquiat. The Tylers appeared to be Daddy Warbucks–level loaded.

The butler led us past a living room, a dining room, a sunroom, a family room, a music room, and a meditation room, all on the way to the doctor's home office. We were still miraculously on the first floor.

"Dr. Tyler's office," he said, leaving Frank and me alone to wait. The room was decorated in various hues of dusty rose and cream. Four low sofas were positioned around a coffee table that looked like it was once an important part of a sequoia tree. I'd had enough of these little fuckin' sofas. I'm sure they were all custom-made by sadistic Europeans with perfect joints. Listen, I don't care how much it costs. If you have to grunt to sit down, the sofa is too low.

Frank and I were both grunting our way down when Dr. Tyler entered the room. With more grunts, we hoisted ourselves back up to greet her. My ankle ached, and heat radiated up my calf.

"Sit down," Dr. Tyler said, so Frank and I grunt-grunt-grunted our way back down. We each landed on our sofas with a thud. Dr. Tyler delicately perched on a third sofa.

"What seems to be the trouble today?" she asked.

"Dr. Tyler, Luella is a dear cousin of Mark Fontaine's visiting for the week, and she was most unfortunately attacked by a bat this afternoon."

"That is most unfortunate," she said, adding, "Please, call me Debra." She smiled warmly at Frank, then me. "I'm sure you'll be fine, but just in case, I'll give you a rabies shot. It's one in a series of four, so I'll give you the first one and your general practitioner will have to follow up with the rest. Now take off your pants."

"What?"

"Many doctors use the upper arm as an injection site, but I much prefer the buttocks."

"No," I said. Out of the corner of my eye, I could sense Frank smiling. *The sick fuck.*

"Yes, I'm afraid so. Now lie down, lower your pants, and we can make this quick."

"Could we try the arm—" I said, but she cut me off with a small shake of her head. "Oh, also my ankle might be twisted, maybe we start with that?"

Debra Tyler glanced at my ankle, then gave me a tight smile. "You've braced it up well! You've done all you can do. Now, let's see that buttock."

I let out a deep exhale, tracing the steps of how exactly I got here. I was broke with no support system, I took this job by mistake, then I got attacked by a bat. There were so many places to reverse course, and yet.

Dr. Tyler prepared the syringe, which was humongous, by the way, practically a bubble tea straw. Much later, I would learn that most if not all doctors use a small syringe for rabies shots, like the kind they use for insulin. Not Dr. Tyler, though! She was special.

I was instructed to lie on my stomach and lower my pants until "the cheek was out."

"Frank, can't you go somewhere else?" I asked.

"Where shall I go?" he asked.

"Stay, Frank. It'll be over before you know it," Debra said.

I closed my eyes tight, willing Debra to be right about that.

"Mother, did you ice the champagne?" a man asked from just outside the room.

"What's that?" Debra yelled, as I imagined the syringe was hovering just above my ass.

"Mother! Did you *ice* the *champagne*? I don't remember if I did!" the man yelled. I craned my neck to see Bradford Tyler walking into the room.

"Oh, I'm sorry, Mother, are you in the middle of something?"

"What did you ask me?" Debra said.

"I wanted to know if you'd iced the champagne," Bradford said.

My ass was out. A syringe was hovering above it. And Bradford's mother was his wife.

"I haven't. Did you ask the butler?" Debra said.

"What's that, madam?" the butler asked. Oh great, the butler was back.

"Bradford was wondering if someone's iced the champagne for tonight's party yet," Debra said.

Clearing my throat, I asked, "Excuse me, Dr. Tyler, could we finish this please?"

"Oh yes, of course. My apologies." Then she stabbed my ass with the bubble tea syringe, and it was so painful I couldn't stop myself from yelping.

"There, there, all done! One of four treatments, that is. I should say, the first one's the easiest."

"Well, I guess I have absolutely nothing to look forward to," I said, shimmying my pants back on before turning to sit up.

"No, don't sit, you need to let the medicine dissipate," she said.

I lay back down, this time on my side.

"Now don't be so glum. You know, we'd be honored if you could join us for this evening's festivities. The more, the merrier, right, Bradford?"

"Of course, Mother," Bradford said. "She'd be a lovely addition."

"Then it's settled. We'll see you tonight. And do yourself a favor: avoid sitting for the next four to five hours."

I gently rolled off the couch onto the floor, where I got onto all fours and slowly made my way up to standing.

"Thanks for the shot," I said, nodding at Dr. Tyler.

"Next one goes in in seven days!" she said cheerily as Frank and I took our leave.

"Bradford, is this what you meant by warning me about the bats and the roosters?" I asked.

Bradford's face went ghost white, and his blue eyes bulged. "I don't have the faintest idea what you're talking about."

I looked from Bradford to the butler to Debra, then to Frank. Bradford glared at me, while the rest of them glared at Bradford. All of them looked quite contemptible.

Dr. Tyler cleared her throat. "I forgot to mention—tonight's party is themed. It's Cock and Balls Night!"

18

My ass was sore, my ankle was huge, and my brain was fried. If I stayed on this island long enough, I was pretty sure it would end me. Something seriously evil was simmering on Murder Island. Josh Jorkavic had just been killed, but that hadn't deterred tonight's "Cock and Balls" party, whatever that meant. Between Bradford, Dr. "Mother," and Mark Fontaine, there wasn't a normal person among them.

Frank drove us down the one-lane road back to the McCarthys' house, while I lay in the backseat. We were surrounded by tall trees, and the air smelled green and alive, but none of that helped. The rabies shot felt like my ass cheek had eaten a golf tee.

Frank finally spoke. "It's not a normal party."

"I figured as much," I said.

"I'm sorry you came here. It wasn't supposed to be this messy," he said, pulling into the large circular driveway in front of the McCarthy house. I looked up to my little attic window and wondered how many people had been trapped there before me.

"You'll need a costume for tonight," he said, though he wouldn't make eye contact. "I'll find you some options." We headed inside, and Frank ran upstairs, leaving me alone in the white foyer. The house seemed empty. I thought about the cement room in the basement, and Josh Jorkavic's blood likely still pooled there. I wondered where Mark Fontaine was at this moment, and for that matter, Caitlin. If there was a party tonight, both of them would be expected to be in attendance. So if Mark was the killer, when would his next move be? At the party? And what if Mark wasn't the killer? Then what?

Back when I was a social worker, I used to administer these career aptitude tests. My clients were fresh out of jail, and most were eager to start a new chapter. A lot of them hadn't loved the jobs they'd had before they were locked up, so the career test tended to come with promise. It offered clear-cut proof that they were destined to do something besides criminal activity. It was almost always an uplifting session.

Then one day, I decided maybe I should take it. It'd been a bad week. A client was back in jail and besides that, my whole agency was a bureaucratic mess. It was amazing any of us accomplished anything. So during my lunch break, I gave myself the career aptitude test. When I looked up the results, I laughed out loud. It said I should be a private investigator. That I was independent and resourceful and curious, and that I was comfortable with the unknown. *Me, comfortable with the unknown!* I married my high school sweetheart, I lived ten blocks from where I grew up, and I didn't even like to switch yogurt brands. For over twenty years, I'd been a Yoplait purist. But something clicked when I read those results.

For the first time in my life, I realized I'd been seen the way I wanted to be seen. I *wanted* to be comfortable with the unknown, I *wanted* independence and adventure. This test said I was meant to be a private investigator, like Sherlock Holmes or one of those guys wearing a cheap suit on *Forensic Files*.

I'd packed a lunch that day. It was the same lunch I'd packed every day: a turkey sandwich on wheat with mustard and lettuce, barbecue chips, an apple, and a couple of those Pirouette cookies that always ended up broken at the bottom of my lunch bag. But that day, there was one still intact. I pulled it out and stuck it into my mouth, puffing on it like I was an old-timey private eye smoking a cigar. *A private investigator,* I thought. It gave me such a thrill.

Luella van Horn started making appearances soon after that lunch. I remember my first official case. There was this beagle who'd been lost for two weeks. A family dog. The children were inconsolable, so the parents were desperate and had put fliers up on every lamppost. I'd stapled bacon up and down the insides of my pants and walked around the family's neighborhood for three nights. On the third night, I heard yips. I found the beagle with a litter of puppies in a neighbor's shed. The puppies pissed all over me and the mama beagle nearly ripped my pants off trying to get some of that stapled-on bacon. I brought her and the puppies back to the family that night, and the smile on the little girl's face when she saw her dog again . . . I know it's sappy, but it was sweet, and it felt pure. I was hooked.

My mind often returned to that moment when I hit a rough patch in a case. *Imagine what could be waiting for you if you solve this thing,* I'd think. But who was going to be that relieved if I solved Josh Jorkavic's murder? Carla Jorkavic or Caitlin McCarthy? I guess time would tell.

It might've been the overwhelming presence of extreme wealth, but I was having trouble sympathizing with these people. Did they ever find themselves with no support system or safety net? Were they ever on the verge of eviction? Likely no. These people had everything they ever dreamed of and more. And one of them was a murderer to boot. Was I just going to let them get away with it? Taylor Bell was enough of a mar on my résumé. I was here until tomorrow morning. There was plenty of time to catch a killer. There would be no more Taylor Bells. If Mark Fontaine was my perp, he was going down.

My first step would be to return to the crime scene. There had to be something I missed before. With seemingly no one else around, I patted down my pockets for the basement keys I'd stolen, but they must've fallen out when all that nonsense happened with the bat. I walked to the basement door and jiggled the knob, on the off chance that it had been left open. No such luck. The door was locked. I'd need to get those keys again. In the meantime, I would get ready for this elusive Cock and Balls party.

When I got up to my room, I found Frank had laid out a catcher's uniform for me, complete with a face-covering helmet, pads, and cleats, plus a brand-new ankle brace. So the Cock and Balls theme was a sports thing. What a relief. Though a catcher's uniform was not my typical party attire, I liked that the helmet provided some anonymity. I would make this party work for me. I was going to get some answers out of these rich creeps whether they liked it or not.

Turns out Frank knew what he was doing. When I got to the Tylers' that night, I discovered that everyone was dressed like either a catcher or a pitcher, except for Bradford, who greeted me at the door dressed like a rooster, quite frankly looking ridiculous. All that talk about "beware the rooster," and he's the damn rooster. He wore a brown feather suit, with long gray tail feathers and a red comb wobbling on top of his head. He wore no beak, and it's like, if you're going to commit to butt feathers, at least go 100 percent.

"Welcome to Cock and Balls," he said. "I can't tell who you are."

"It's Luella," I said, lifting up my catcher's helmet to reveal my face.

"Aha! Come in, come in, Mother's expecting you! Let's get you something to drink! How are your buttocks?"

"A little sore, thanks for asking," I said, following him inside.

"So you're a catcher," he said with a smirk.

"Yeah," I said.

"You know what that means, right?"

I shook my head. He turned to me conspiratorially. "Catchers want to get it. Pitchers want to give it."

"Ah. Great," I said. "I don't want to get it, though."

"Then you should've been a pitcher," he said, his butt feathers swaying as he walked. It was official: I hated these fucking people.

The castle was decorated in a style I'd describe as rich person's bachelorette. There were penises everywhere. I saw phalluses made of glass, silver, iron, and jade. There was even one made from an amethyst geode that must've been six feet tall. I spotted drippy penis candles, dozens of sparkly crystal testicles, and an extremely veiny ice sculpture that was embarrassing to look at. It only got smaller as the night went on. *Why would someone carve this in a melting medium?* I thought. It felt almost feminist.

There were twenty or so people milling about in the dim light of the castle's parlor. Among them, I was pretty sure I recognized Carla Jorkavic (a pitcher), Debra Tyler (a catcher), and that blond woman with a bob I kept seeing everywhere (also a catcher). By the time Bradford had mixed two French 75s, at least three catcher-pitcher duos had paired up and made their way into the adjoining living room, where there was slow dancing, back massaging, and neck kissing happening on the one-inch-off-the-ground couches. Someone was playing smooth jazz on surround sound. I'd actually landed myself at another Murder Island sex party, and this time I'd been invited.

I'd never seen anything like it. You'd think a sex party would evolve, take some time. But this all happened so fast. I blinked and then there was loosening belts, ripping off shirts, pants dropping to ankles. The pitchers were thrusting and moaning and pegging, while the catchers were sucking and moaning and receiving. I couldn't take my eyes away, even though I wanted to very, very badly.

"Typical Cock and Balls party," Bradford said, handing me one of the French 75s. "You want one?" He held out a pill case with seven blue capsules inside. "Makes the party more fun." I shook my head while he swallowed one with a gulp of his champagne cocktail.

"What are those?" I asked.

"Special medicine," he said coyly.

We both watched as Caitlin pegged somebody who looked nothing like Mark over a glass coffee table. But where was Mark?

"So . . ." I winced, trying to look away. "Is this party in Josh's memory?"

"Who?" Bradford said.

"Josh Jorkavic. The man who was murdered last night," I said.

"Was it murder?" Bradford asked. "I hadn't heard that. How

awful. I can't imagine anyone who could've done such a thing!" He stared intently at me then. "Murder? Really?"

"I'm afraid so," I said. "He was found—" Then I heard through the moans and groans someone whisper the words *shut up*. "Did you say something?" I asked Bradford.

"Murder? You really do think so?" Bradford replied, lost in his own world. "How odd."

"Shut up," someone whispered again. I turned around, looking for the source. Everywhere I looked, there were genitals flapping against each other. Sure it'd been awhile, but if I never had sex again, I decided that'd be just fine. If that's what everyone looked like doing it, no, thank you.

"Who said that?" I asked, but Bradford was already being whisked away by someone wearing a Roger Clemens jersey.

I stood alone at the sex party, watching the penis ice sculpture drip onto the seafood tower. Somebody needed to get those crab claws far away from there. I wondered how I'd get information out of all these people mid-coitus. I was scanning the room, making myself a little nauseated, when I spotted two eyes staring at me from inside a darkened doorway just past the living room.

Making my way through the mass of gyrating bodies required some skill, especially with a bad ankle. Luckily, Frank had equipped me with the catcher's helmet and chest pad, which gave me a little more oomph busting through the evolving duos and trios. I gave these folks about fifteen minutes before it became a full-on orgy. I was nearly at the doorway when someone pulled me back. There were two hands on my hips and another grabbed on to my elbow. I could still see the shining eyes in the darkness ahead, but they were no help, they just continued to stare.

"Excuse me," I said, prying myself away. I felt someone sucking on my pinky finger, and I yanked it back so fast the person's mouth made a popping noise. Finally I turned to face the people who'd been grabbing at me. Carla Jorkavic and Debra Tyler. I quickly pushed them together, and they began kissing, leaving me free to reach the doorway.

I paused just in front of it, now somewhat hesitant to enter the dark hallway. Then I felt someone's bare foot rub up the back of my thigh, and that gave me enough of a jolt to run into the unknown. Very little light from the living room bled into the hallway, and I held out my hands to feel for the walls when I made contact with someone's face. They had a strong, stubbly chin, a Roman nose, and full lips.

"Please stop that," the person said around my fingers, and I pulled them back quickly.

"I'm sorry," I said. "Were you the one who's been looking at me? Who said to shut up?"

"Yes," the low voice said. "If you want answers, you're going to have to listen more and speak less. Do you understand?"

"Wait, who are you?" I asked.

"Listen more, speak less," the voice said again. "It's clear who your killer is, if only you pay attention."

"Do you know who the killer is? Is it Mark Fontaine?" I said. Then I heard them walking away from me. "Stop! Come back!" I yelled, but I could tell they were already too far. I felt the walls, trying to follow them, but whoever it was must have known this house well, for there were unpredictable twists and turns to that hallway. I kept banging my knees into walls I didn't realize were there. I felt like a lab rat in a maze.

Walking along the dark passageway, I was relieved to see a beam of light coming from the far end. I followed it to a large eat-in kitchen that smelled like sage and melted butter. The floors were black-and-white tile, and the appliances glimmered, they looked so brand-new. On the kitchen island, trays of catered food had been placed over Sterno burners to stay warm. There were meatballs, escargot, and a couple varieties of flatbreads. Before this night, I never thought of flatbread as a sex party food. Until now, I'd only associated it with Panera, which is no shade to Panera. It's just the opposite of a sex party. Well, except for their mac and cheese.

The person I'd followed here had left the kitchen one of two ways. There was one door past the refrigerator and one on the other side of the breakfast table. First I tried the door past the refrigerator, but this turned out to be the biggest pantry I've ever seen in my life. It was quite literally the size of my studio apartment, and I couldn't even afford that. Rows of olives, gherkins, cocktail onions, fancy jars of tuna and trout in Spanish olive oil. There were French jams and honeys, chocolates, nuts, and marzipans. One shelf had matching glass jars of different flours, then a row of spices, salts, and chilies. Nothing was out of place. To be honest, it looked a little like a grocery store in there, and that's not a good thing. If your pantry looks like the grocery store, it's time to donate to people in need.

I heard footsteps and ducked inside, gently closing the pantry door behind me. I left it open a crack so I might see or hear who'd walked in.

The Tylers' butler entered behind Bradford, whose feathered costume now hung open around the crotch area.

"I warned you not to say anything to her. I've got this."

"I was only telling her to stop running her mouth," the butler said.

"Trust me when I say you shouldn't get involved. What she does and doesn't know has nothing to do with you. Don't make me send you back where I found you."

"No, sir, that won't be necessary. My apologies. Please resume your group intercourse. I'll get Bertha to set out more crab legs. The ones on the table have become damp."

Bradford Tyler shook his head in frustration, his rooster crown wobbling above him. He stormed out of the kitchen, leaving the butler alone. His eyes followed Bradford Tyler down the hall then lasered in on the pantry. I slowed my breathing as his eyes bore into mine. I could hear his footsteps getting closer and closer to the pantry door. My heart thumped in my chest as I prayed for him to turn around, for something to fall, for the partygoers to demand dry crab legs stat. I watched in horror as the pantry doorknob turned and the door swung open. The butler stood before me.

"Just remember: Listen more than you speak, and try not to speak at all." He spoke in a low, steady voice. I nodded, shivering from a chill that ran down my spine. "Go back to the McCarthy house. You may find what you're looking for."

I darted out of the pantry, heading toward the dark hallway that led back to the living room.

"Good luck," the butler said. "It's that way." He gestured to the third door with his eyebrows. "Run!"

19

The island was dark and quiet and the air smelled sweet as I shuffled back from the Tylers' castle toward the McCarthys' place. Something rustled the leaves behind me, and I couldn't stop myself from shrieking. I still hadn't seen Mark Fontaine that night, and I was afraid he might be following me.

I looked around the nearby trees, and when I found no one there, I realized the rustling must've just been the island breeze. Everyone was most likely still at the Tylers' having sex with each other. Who'd want to leave that to go stalk down a private detective with an ankle brace who knew close to nothing? I took a deep breath and limped faster toward the McCarthys'.

As I followed the road heading south, I thought about what the butler had said about listening and not speaking. I couldn't tell if he was threatening me or trying to help. What was I supposed to be listening for? A confession? And whom was I supposed to be listening to? It felt like everyone on this island had signed the same oath. "On my honor, I will be cryptic to outsiders. I vow to be freaky all of the time."

Even with a direct path, I was relieved to get back to the McCarthys' house. I tiptoed inside. It was late and I wasn't sure if Frank and Yanni were still awake. I shut the front door quietly.

"You're back," a scratchy voice said from down the hall. I jumped as my veneers snapped against each other. They might've been too big for my mouth, but they looked fabulous, so what.

"Frank?" I called out. "Is that you?"

From the foyer I could see a light switch on in the kitchen, and I moved toward it like a moth. In his little nook, Frank was sipping a cup of tea. A plume of steam rose off his cup.

"Tea?" he asked, already pouring me a cup from his white ceramic pot. I sat down, removing my catcher's helmet, and took a small sip. It was a soothing peppermint, herbal and fragrant.

"Heard you were poking around the Tylers' back hallways." He clicked his tongue disapprovingly. "A little sloppy, even for you."

"What do you mean?" I asked, taking a larger sip.

"Why you were brought here and what you're doing now are very different tasks. A murder is more involved than an affair. Are you looking into the murder?" he said.

"Maybe," I said.

"You know there is more power concentrated on this island than you could ever imagine. These families control the money, the government, the whole country. Even if you solve this, you think you'll be able to bring your findings to light? They'll be buried. Doesn't that bother you?"

"Well, sure," I said, unclear where he was going with this.

"So leave well enough alone. Sure, Josh was murdered. But he's a rich, entitled prick just like the rest of them. Besides that, he was single-handedly breaking up a marriage. You think he deserves justice?" Frank stared at me, his hazel eyes unblinking.

"Of course he does," I stammered. "Murder is a crime."

"Good girl," Frank said, taking the last sip from his cup and pouring himself a fresh one. "I knew you'd be perfect. You and me, we're the same. They're the ones who are different." He gestured to his surroundings.

"What exactly are you—" I said, but he cut me off.

"I know you're broke and desperate, and you may be in way over your head. You know what they do to outsiders? They'll slaughter you and think nothing of it. You're nothing to them. An ant. A crumb."

"Who will?" I asked, but Frank only shook his head. I continued. "Mark Fontaine? He can't get away with this. People can't kill each other and go on like nothing happened."

"Like Taylor Bell did?" he asked, smiling.

"What do you know about Taylor Bell?" I asked.

"All I know is he's looking for you. You really want to add a bounty to your head by solving this one? It'd be an unlimited bounty, so you're clear."

"I've survived this far," I said.

Frank's eyes twinkled, like he was suppressing a smile now. "You know I've worked for these people most of my life? And who would you think is the worst of them?"

"Who?" I asked.

"It's not the family. The family has their quirks, but you get used to them. It's the ones who marry in, who see it as a cash grab."

"Like Mark Fontaine," I said.

"I've worked for Mark and Caitlin for years now. Mark doesn't even know my middle name."

"What's your middle name?" I asked.

His mouth formed a straight line and his nostrils flared as he said, "Franklin."

"Your name is . . . Frank Franklin Fisher?"

"Yep."

"That's a lot of F's," I said. I thought back to my first encounter with Endeavors. "You ever come across a guy who goes by just F?"

Frank smirked. "Let's go look at the basement one last time." He grabbed his keys from the hook. The same ones I'd stolen only hours ago had made it back there. I wondered how.

Frank headed straight toward the basement door. Looking at me conspiratorially, he unlocked it and held the door open. "Ladies first," he said.

I walked down the basement stairs with the enthusiasm of a cat going into a bath. At that moment, I wasn't 100 percent certain I'd make it out of that basement alive. I couldn't decide whether Frank's intentions were good or evil.

The basement had the same stale incense smell, and so late at night the air down here was ten degrees cooler than the rest of the house. We paused at the bottom of the stairs to listen for footsteps above us but heard nothing. We were alone in the house. *Where was Yanni?* I wondered. Frank and I proceeded into the cement room where Josh had been murdered.

"What are we doing here?" I asked.

"I know your type. You won't give up until you've gotten your answers. Well, I found something today that might help."

He flipped on a stark overhead light that made me realize how grungy the cement was—in contrast to the rest of the house. I figured Caitlin didn't go in this room too often. Neither of us stepped inside, both preferring to peer in from the doorway. I pointed to a pile of what looked like bat dung on the floor.

"Is that guano? Should we be breathing this?"

"You'll be fine. Just be quick," he said. "We don't want another bat coming after you, do we?"

I held my breath and dashed in, looking closely at the drain in the center of the room. Josh's blood was still pooled there, and I noticed this time, a clump of medium-length blond hair. I was almost positive it hadn't been there before.

"Another victim?" I asked.

"There are no other victims. I'm sure that's a clue to your murderer. Baggie?" Frank said, handing me a Ziploc bag. I turned it inside out to grab the blond hairs from the drain. Inside the bag, they looked like a gnarled blood clot.

"Who's blond?" I asked Frank, running out of the room and taking in a big gulp of air from the main area of the basement.

"Who isn't?" Frank said. "There's Lindsay Peterson, Carla Jorkavic, that woman staying with the Hunts. And of course, there's you."

So much for my Mark Fontaine theory. "Maybe Carla knew her husband was having an affair, so she killed him," I said.

"Wouldn't that be a little too convenient?" he said, making his way over to the stairs.

"Who's the woman staying with the Hunts? Did she have a reason to kill Josh Jorkavic?" I asked.

"She was the last person to sleep with him, so depending on how bad of a lay he was, maybe?" He chuckled to himself and began heading back up the stairs.

"Frank! We're not done here."

"We are. I've been very helpful. Too helpful. Now the McCarthys will be home any minute. I've got to prepare their postcoital snack tray. Hopefully the medical examiner will have some insight soon. Ferry brought his body over this morning."

It occurred to me Frank was right. He *was* being too helpful. And why now?

Just then we heard footsteps above us.

"Shit!" Frank said, dashing upstairs with me close behind.

By the time we got back up to the first floor, Caitlin and Mark were already seated in the dining room. At least I could now confirm Mark's whereabouts. Frank ran to the kitchen and threw open the refrigerator doors, removing jars and Tupperware with precision. I watched in awe of how quickly he was able to pivot.

"Frank! Where are the snacks?" Mark yelled from the dining room. "We've gone over this! When we get home from a party, we like to have a plate of—" But his tirade was interrupted by Frank bringing out a tray piled with chicken salad, olive tapenade, salami, Gruyère, Parmesan, crackers, and a boule of crusty bread. From the kitchen, I saw their hands snatching slices of meat and cheese before Frank could even set the tray down on the table.

"I'm sorry, Ms. Caitlin, Mark. Next time, I will be more prompt."

"What were you doing?" Caitlin asked between bites of chicken salad. "You weren't in the basement, were you?"

Frank shook his head, his eyes quickly but perceptively darting back to me in the kitchen. Caitlin didn't seem to notice but Mark did.

"Who's in the kitchen?" Mark asked.

"It's just me," I said, walking into the dining room. Mark's eyes flickered between me and Frank.

"Oh good. I was wondering where you were. Won't you join us, cousin Luella?"

20

I sat with Mark and Caitlin and watched as they gorged themselves with a hunger only hours of group sex could fuel. They seemed eerily at peace with each other. I wondered if they'd also taken those blue pills that were being passed around, and if so, what exactly were they?

No one spoke. The only sounds came from their voracious chewing and swallowing over the steady ticking of the grandfather clock. I decided to break the ice.

"How was the rest of the party?" I asked.

Caitlin looked up from her hunk of bread and tapenade. There was mayonnaise on her chin (I hoped to god it was mayonnaise). "Therapeutic," she said with her mouth full.

"What have you been doing around here?" Mark asked, reaching for another slice of salami.

"Frank served me some tea. That's about it," I said.

"Please, have something to eat. You must be hungry. Let me pour you some wine. We have a 1982 Château Lafite I've been dying to open, and this is just the occasion, don't you agree, Caitlin?"

Caitlin nodded while swallowing.

Mark continued. "It's your last night, let's make it count." He excused himself to the wine cellar.

Caitlin cleared her throat. "You're going home tomorrow?"

"I suppose so," I said.

"That's too bad. You'll miss all the fun."

"What do you mean?" I asked.

"Oh, just that tomorrow will be a lovely day. Sun's supposed to be out."

"Caitlin, I hope you don't mind me asking, but I'm curious about Frank. How did he start working for your family?"

A chunk of Parmesan stopped midway to her lips. She looked at me quizzically. "Why do you need to know about Frank?"

"I just—" I redirected. "He's a fascinating man."

"Oh Frank's terribly boring. He's worked for my family since before I was born."

If Frank was the elusive F I'd coordinated with to put Dave McCarthy in jail, he must've recommended me to Mark for this case. But then why did Frank act like he was meeting me for the first time on the boat?

Mark came back with three glasses on a tray. Each was two-thirds filled with a deep burgundy-colored wine. He set down a glass in front of each of us, then proceeded to regale us about the qualities of the Lafite. I zoned out after he said the undertone was "earthy musk." He sniffed his glass, groaning and rolling his eyes in pleasure. It was a little much.

"Let it breathe," he said. "At least for a moment or two. The Lafite needs to get acquainted with its surroundings." I gave him a tight smile. This whole process was giving me a headache, and the last thing I needed right now was a glass of red wine.

Caitlin's eyes were closing. I looked at the grandfather clock in the corner of the room. It was nearing 3 A.M.

"A toast to you, Luella. Your presence here has helped in innumerable ways." Mark lifted his glass and clinked it with mine. Caitlin had fallen asleep sitting at the table. He clinked his glass to hers regardless. I took a sip of the 1982 Château Lafite. I know you're going to think I'm Staten Island trash, but this wine tasted like foot.

"Mmm," I said.

"Do you taste the earthy musk?" Mark asked, his eyebrows raised.

"Is that what I'm tasting? It's a little . . . fungal?"

"The wine might be a tad moldy," he said. "But stay focused on the deeper notes. Take another sip. What do you taste?"

I sipped the foot wine, struggling to think of any description that sounded remotely wine adjacent. "Oak . . . maybe cherry . . ." I said. Mark nodded encouragingly.

"Anything else?"

"Chalk? Bee pollen? Dusk?"

"The time of night?" Mark asked.

"Yes," I said, doubling down. "I definitely taste the dusk."

Mark took a long sip. "Ah, yes, now that you mention it, I, too, taste the dusk. What a refined palate you must have."

I only eat cereal, I wanted to scream. *To me, this tastes like piss!*

"What else?" Mark asked again. I took another sip.

"Grape?" I said, feeling my limbs go slightly numb. I tried flexing my feet under the table, but couldn't seem to do it. "Do you taste the grape?" I asked, feeling suddenly loopy. My vision doubled and my tongue felt like sand against the roof of my mouth. "Mark, I'm sorry, I don't feel very well."

"That's too bad," he said. "You were enjoying the Lafite so much."

My head felt light, like it might soon float off my neck.

"Frank, get in here! Take care of Luella and Caitlin. I need to attend to some things," Mark said.

The last thing I remember is a sense of déjà vu as Frank hoisted me over his shoulder and carried me up a flight of stairs.

21

I woke up in the attic bedroom sprawled on top of the duvet. The sun was shining outside my perma-shut window. I was still wearing my wig and my catcher's uniform from the night before. I felt hungover as I wiped the sleep from my eyes and sat up in bed.

What had I done the night before? I wondered. So much of it was blank to me. I looked out the window. It had to be midmorning, at least. I had a vague memory of having to do something this morning. What was it, though?

While stretching, I noticed a small off-white card with scalloped edges on my nightstand, just like the one that had warned me about Mark Fontaine. This one said: *Ferry leaves at 11:45 a.m. You can stay until then but no later.* With no real sense of what time it was, I got out of bed and began looking for my clothes, but my suitcase was nowhere to be seen. It wasn't under the bed or in the closet. And the clothes I had hung in the closet were missing, too. Part of me felt I should be alarmed, or at the very least, anxious about the time, but I couldn't muster either feeling in the deep haze in which I'd woken up.

I heard movement downstairs and figured maybe someone down there could provide some clarity. With nothing to change into, I fluffed my wig and tried the door, which I didn't remember closing. Again, I found myself locked inside.

For several minutes, I banged on the door and yelled for someone to open it, but no one seemed to hear me. Defeated, I sat back down on the bed, mentally preparing myself for another journey down that horrible secret staircase. I kept picturing my body doing what my cellphone did. I'd ricochet off the moldy stairs until I landed with a thud at the bottom with my screen cracked, and by screen, I mean my skull. Then I heard the door click.

I quickly hobbled over to the door. When I turned the knob, the door swung wide open. I peered around for who might've unlocked it, but no one was there. However, in their haste, they'd left their keys in the lock. I pocketed them and walked downstairs in my catcher's uniform. There was no one on Caitlin's floor as far as I could tell, so I went down another flight of stairs to the second floor, where I heard noise coming from Mark's office.

Mark was seated at his desk typing rapidly on his laptop when I knocked twice on the open door. He looked up from his work with a toothy smile.

"Luella! Good morning! I was just about to wake you! Glad to see you're up. The ferry leaves in half an hour. Remember you were supposed to be out by sunrise? Lucky for you, I'm feeling generous today. All ready to go?"

"Have you seen my suitcase?" I asked. "And did you write that note?"

He shook his head. "I had Frank pack you up this morning. You're quite the heavy sleeper!"

"Ah," I said, considering this information. I'd never been a heavy sleeper, even as a teen. "It's strange, I have no memory of last night after we drank that wine together."

Mark chuckled. "Sounds like you might've had a little too much. And that 1982 Lafite ain't cheap, so you're welcome!"

"I thought I only had a glass," I said, starting to put the pieces together.

"Well!" Mark shut his laptop. "You'd better be going! Don't want to miss the only ferry out of here, now do you? You've already overstayed your welcome."

As I walked down to the first floor, I couldn't stop thinking that Mark might've put something in my wine last night. I thought about that blue pill Bradford Tyler had offered me, and the blue residue on Josh Jorkavic's fingers, and I wondered if that was also what Mark had taken a couple of days ago. Had he given me the same thing? Just then, someone cleared their throat. I looked up to see Frank standing by the front door with my suitcase.

"It's time to go, Luella."

"Frank, what happened to me last night?"

Frank gave me an appeasing smile. "You remind me of those monkeys."

"What monkeys?" I asked. *Was it so much to ask to wake up and not be compared to monkeys?*

"You know the ones. 'See no evil, hear no evil, speak no evil.' Last night was a lesson in that." He paused, lifting my suitcase and opening the front door with his other hand. "You could always just do as the monkeys do . . ."

If one more person told me a vague riddle on this fucking island, I was going to explode. Frank took my suitcase out to Caitlin's car and got into the driver's seat.

"Where's Caitlin?" I asked as I hopped in the passenger's side. "I'd love to say goodbye."

"She sends her love, but she had a previous engagement this morning. Yanni accompanied her." Without another word, Frank started the car and we drove in silence to the ferry dock while I tried to understand all that had gone down in the last twelve hours. One: Murder Island was an incestuous pool of people with too much money. Two: there were blond hairs in the bloody drain and Josh's body had been sent to Manhattan. Three: Frank was most likely F, which meant we'd worked together before. Four: for some unknown reason, last night I was drugged. And five: this morning, Caitlin was mysteriously away, and the last thing she told me in private was that she didn't know what Mark Fontaine would do next.

As we passed the Tylers' castle, I thought about Occam's razor, and how the simplest explanation was usually the truth. So what was the simplest explanation for all of this? Mark learned Josh was having affair with Caitlin, so Mark killed Josh. Frank helped Mark with the dead body. Then Mark killed Caitlin. It didn't explain the blond hair in the drain, nor did it make sense why Mark and Frank would be working together. Frank seemed to actively resent

Mark Fontaine. Did Frank write both of those scalloped-edge notes to me? And was Frank definitely F, or was there still a possibility F was Mark? I knew more than I did two days ago, so how was this case getting harder?

Frank pulled over near the ferry dock and turned off the ignition. He made no move to leave the car so I remained in my seat.

"Well, thanks for the ride," I said.

"Some mysteries aren't as complicated as you think."

My mouth went dry. "Why do you say that?"

"Think. Why would someone murder Josh Jorkavic?"

"That's what I've been trying to figure out," I said, my voice coming out all froggy. Frank shook his head in disappointment as he unbuckled his seatbelt and stepped out of the car to retrieve my bag from the trunk. I followed him. He handed me my suitcase, but his gaze remained on the choppy gray water lapping against the dock just a few feet from us.

"Ferry should be here any moment now," he said, then got back into the car and started it.

"Wait," I said, bending over the back left tire. I dislodged a small stone from the tread. "Is there something you're not telling me? Do you know who did it?" I asked.

"Of course not," Frank said, then made a clean U-turn and sped off in the direction we'd come from. The gravel popped up like popcorn under the speed of the spinning tires. Dust clouds formed in the car's wake, and I began to cough. The inside of my brain felt a lot like those dust clouds. *Some mysteries aren't as complicated as you think,* he'd said. Frank knew something I didn't. And if Frank knew something, other people had to know, too. It really wasn't that big of an island.

I peered in the windows of Morgan's Bistro where I could see Caviar Guy busying himself chopping lemons and limes into identical thin half-moons. He paused to admire his own pectoral muscles. The ferry horn blew announcing its arrival, startling both of us. I crouched down as fast as I could but I had a feeling he'd seen me. He kept looking out the window. For the second time this week, I found myself duck-walking to avoid being seen.

Just then I spotted Betsy Clench mooring the ferry to the dock with swift efficiency. She wore cutoff jean shorts with her sailor hat. Once she'd secured the ropes, she called out to me.

"Ahoy!" she said. This woman really lived and breathed *boat*.

"Ahoy," I said, trying it out. Land wasn't going so hot for me at the moment. Maybe I could also be *a woman of the sea*. I approached the deck and was about to step on board.

"Ah, ah, ah! We're not boarding yet!" Betsy said, shooing me a few feet away. "I've still got some cargo I've gotta unload." She called to somewhere inside the boat. "Come on out here!"

From inside the ferry came the most beautiful sight I've ever seen. Of all people on god's green earth, out stepped the stunning middle-aged librarian, Joan Clyborne.

"Joan?" I said, hardly believing my eyes.

"Marie!" she said, running toward me. We embraced on the dock as Betsy looked on approvingly. "I was so worried after I couldn't reach you. I've been trying to call!"

"You have?" I asked. "But what are you doing here?"

Betsy cleared her throat and shook her head ever so slightly. Joan winked at her. Something was going on.

"You shouldn't talk here," Betsy said, scanning the horizon. "Let's get something to drink." She hopped off the boat and strutted toward the bistro, with Joan and me trailing behind her like ducklings.

"But the ferry—doesn't it leave soon?" I asked.

"Ferry's not going to start itself, now will it?" Betsy said, jingling the boat keys then shoving them into her back pocket.

As we walked into Morgan's, Paul had moved on to refilling the bar's olives and pearl onions. Betsy held up three fingers, and he nodded back to her, a big, broad smile across his face.

"Sit anywhere you like!" he said, his voice cracking midway through. His cheeks turned pink as he quickly resumed spooning more pearl onions into a short glass jar. He seemed nervous. *Had he been talking to Frank?* I wondered.

The restaurant was empty save for us. Betsy chose the table in the far back corner—the same one Josh and Caitlin had shared days before he died—and positioned herself in a seat that would allow her to look out on the entire twelve-table restaurant. Joan sat to her left, and I sat across from both of them.

"How do you two know each other?" I whispered, but Betsy shushed me since Paul was already approaching our table.

"What can I do for you ladies?"

"I don't know about you guys, but I'm not super hungry," Betsy said. "How about three cheeseburgers, a round of dirty martinis, oysters Rockefeller for the table, and two orders of the fried calamari? We'll start with that, see how it goes."

"Coming right up," Paul said with a smile. He sauntered away, pulling his pants tight across his ass.

"He is earning every *cent* of his tip today," Betsy said, licking her lips.

"Oh my word, that is quite the caboose!" Joan said, scooting her glasses further down her nose.

Once Paul had gone back into the kitchen, Betsy leaned toward the two of us.

"Okay, we're in the clear. Joanie, spill your guts."

Joan took a deep breath. Now that she was outside the library, I noticed her skin was dewy and bright, and her signature long braid was more silver than gray.

"Betsy snuck me onto the island. This place isn't open to visitors—you have to be on the first mate's list. Lucky for us, the first mate is open to a little adventure," Joan said, winking again at Betsy. *Were they fucking? What was happening?* I didn't want to get testy with Joan after she'd come all this way, but my patience was thin and I was going to need answers real soon.

"Why are you here, Joan?" I asked. "I was just about to leave."

"I don't think that's a good idea at all," Joan said. "There's so much to do before we get off this island. See, when I couldn't reach you, I tracked down a copy of that book by Walter Stanford. Remember it was the only book about Murder Island, and it was mysteriously missing when you came by the library? Well, I found it. It'd been misshelved in the fiction section." Joan rolled her eyes. "And some people have the nerve to call themselves librarians!"

"Joanie, honey, back on track," Betsy said.

"Right," Joan said, lowering her voice. "Well, it seems before writing that book, Walter Stanford had written a series of flops. Mostly paperback murder mysteries. Pulp. Long story short, he needed money bad, then he caught a lucky break and married into the upper echelon of New York society. That gave him the opportunity to attend several functions on Murder Island."

Betsy picked up the story. "Back in the day, the roster of who traveled to and from Murder Island wasn't nearly as secure. You'd just sign your name when you boarded the ferry. I helped Joanie go through the archives. That's how we first met. She approached my ferry and asked for a little history lesson, and let's face it, she came to the right place," Betsy said, tipping her sailor's hat to each of us. Joan the librarian, Betsy the sailor, and Luella the private investigator. What a strange trio we formed.

The table went quiet as Paul came by with a tray of ice-cold martinis and two plates piled high with crispy golden calamari. As he set everything down, he knocked Joan's fork to the ground. "I'm so sorry about that," he said, slowly bending down with his perfectly round ass right next to the calamari. Normally I'd say that was a health violation, but with Caviar Guy, it felt like an act of service.

"I'll be right back with a clean fork. Enjoy, ladies," he said, turning slightly pink again. Betsy shook her head approvingly.

"That man deserves to go to heaven," she said. She took a sip of her martini and groaned. "Damn, I love breakfast!"

Paul came back with a new fork for Joan, and as he set it down, his hand lightly brushed Betsy's. They made brief eye contact, then Paul looked away. Maybe he really didn't know anything about the murder. Maybe he was acting nervous for an entirely different reason.

"Where were we?" I asked.

"Oh, right!" Joan said. "So Walter Stanford married a woman named Rose Marie Peterson, who was a first cousin of Mary and Frederick Peterson, who owned a house here."

"Still do!" Betsy said. "Well now their grown kids live there, but it's still in the fam!"

"So Walter marries Rose Marie," Joan said. "And soon after he starts attending these parties, he gets inspired to write a book. At this point, he's lost the faith of his publisher after none of his other books sold, so the publisher says this is his last chance. If this flops, he's done in the book business. He convinces the publisher this one will be a hit. It's called *Murder Island,* and it's all about the secret lurid lives of the richest of the rich."

Joan briefly paused her story as we both turned to Betsy, who was loudly crunching on calamari tentacles.

"Sorry, you gotta try these," Betsy said with a full mouth.

Joan continued. "Once the book was published, it did briefly become a hit. It was a bestseller before it got pulled from the shelves. Of course, the island's well-connected families wouldn't stand to be made a mockery of. The book ruined Stanford's social life. Rose Marie divorced him, and he was banned from ever going to Murder Island again. After that, the publisher dumped him. He had no career, no family, no friends. He lost everything for that book."

"What was so controversial about it?" I asked, dipping a calamari ring into marinara sauce.

"Apparently, he wrote about these tunnels that go between the houses on the island," Joan said. "Digging below an island, even if it's private, is something you need permission to do. Island construction can drastically alter the surrounding waterways, affecting boat traffic, water quality, and wildlife. Plus I'd imagine they weren't claiming that square footage on their tax returns."

Paul swung by our table again, this time with a tray of three gleaming cheeseburgers. He set one in front of each of us.

"I told them not to cook yours for too long," he said to Betsy. "I know you like it bloody."

Betsy bit her lip. "Thank you, Paul." Paul sauntered away again, this time even slower.

"Okay, Betsy, it's been a long week," I said, reaching my breaking point. "Just tell me: are you having sex with Paul or Joan, or both?"

Betsy and Joan looked at each other and began cackling. They laughed so hard tears streamed down Joan's face, and Betsy wouldn't stop slamming the table with her palm.

"Louise, will you relax?"

"It's Luella—" I said.

Betsy continued. "This is what happens on Murder Island. Everyone has too much money, so sex is the only currency that counts. For decades, Murder Island has been *the* elusive destination for the sexually depraved rich. It's a hotbed of the amoral activity du jour where the laws don't apply."

"When in Rome . . ." Joan said.

"Thanks, Joan. That's helpful," I said, taking an enormous bite of my cheeseburger.

If Betsy got hers rare, mine was cooked beyond recognition. I spit some gristle into my napkin. Maybe Betsy was onto something with this sex-as-currency theory.

"You know financially they're all part of this group called Endeavors," Betsy said.

"That's Dave McCarthy's company!" I said. "And now his daughter, Caitlin, is missing. And her lover, Josh, is dead. And her house has a bat infestation. I've been here for days and that's about all I've figured out."

"Well," Joan said, lifting her martini glass. "It seems we've come at just the right time."

22

Tell me if you've heard this one. A librarian, a first mate, and a private investigator sit in a bar. The first mate orders a second round of martinis. The librarian says, "It's barely noon!" So the first mate says, "Then we've got some catching up to do. Another round, bartender!" The private investigator sits there quietly, marveling at how she went from zero friends to two.

As we sat finishing our cheeseburgers and second martinis, Betsy, Joan, and I came up with a plan. We were all a little tipsy by then, but the plan was mostly coherent. Betsy was to go back on the ferry while Joan and I stayed on the island and tried to solve this case once and for all. Somehow.

Betsy would return with the ferry in twenty-four hours, and even if we hadn't solved it by then, we'd go back with her to Manhattan and be done with this lecherous place. Betsy said it was such a good plan we should do the "sailor's shake" on it. We all clasped left hands, and then over that, we clasped our right ones. I'm sure we looked ridiculous, and afterward, Betsy revealed in a fit of laughter that she'd made the whole thing up. This woman was unbelievable.

Betsy looked at her watch and stood up from the table, stretching.

"I gotta get back. You guys know how you're going to get to the bottom of this?"

Joan and I looked at each other, and though neither of us spoke, we both nodded, first at each other, and then at Betsy.

Joan's cheeks were rosy from the booze as she ate cold french fries off Betsy's plate. Betsy left damp cash on the table to cover the bill and a generous tip for Paul, then saluted us and strutted out the door with my suitcase, which she'd agreed to take back to the city. I needed to be unencumbered for what came next.

"Thank you!" I called after her, but she was already gone.

Joan took my hand in hers, and her kind gray eyes looked deep into mine. "So, Detective . . ." she said. "What do we do now?"

This case felt like a tapestry, and if we only pulled the right threads, the whole thing could come undone. But what were the threads, exactly? Well, Mark Fontaine was bad news. That much I knew. Then there was the issue of Endeavors, which was at one point run by Dave McCarthy and F. And if what Betsy said was true, Endeavors was the financial engine of this place. I'd put Dave McCarthy in jail after learning he'd embezzled funds, but whom had he screwed over the most? Did the murder of Caitlin's lover have something to do with revenge? And where was Caitlin now? I wondered if I had any old Endeavors information packed up in my apartment.

I asked to use the restaurant's landline and called the one person who I knew could help.

She answered on the fourth ring. "If this is a spam call to take advantage of the elderly, I will kick your ass all the way to Canada."

"Hi, Sophie," I said. "It's me."

"Where the hell have you been? I've been calling you for days, and it goes straight to the message machine. I left so many messages it said your mailbox was full. Your cats are ruining my life!"

Joan could hear Sophie's ranting from where she was sitting, and her eyebrows raised. *Everything okay?* she mouthed. I nodded.

"How exactly are they ruining your life, Sophie?"

"They follow me everywhere. They watch me eat. They watch me sleep. They follow me into the toilet room and watch me taking my poo-poos. They're worse than the KGB!"

"Sophie, that means they love you! I wish they followed me around like that! I've left the bathroom door open, but they won't go near me. Consider yourself lucky. How are they doing? Is there an underlying sadness in their eyes? Are they eating?"

"Are they eating? They've finished the cat food! I've had to give them my good sardines! When do you get back?" Sophie said, hacking. "Have I told you I thought I was allergic to cats? I am now positive I am allergic to cats."

Joan looked at me quizzically from across the table. I rolled my eyes.

"Thank you, Sophie, sounds like you're taking good care of them. Listen, I'll be back tomorrow, but I was wondering if you could help me with something first."

"More help?" she screeched. "Your cat is sitting on my foot, and you want more help?"

"I swear I'll make it up to you. Can you go into my apartment and find just one file?"

Sophie grunted into the phone as she stood up. Her footsteps were heavy on the linoleum floor. I heard one door close, keys jangling, then another door open.

"Oh my god!"

"What's wrong?" I asked. "Are you okay?"

"The cats!"

"What's wrong with the cats?" I asked.

"They followed me in here!"

I rubbed my temple with my free hand. Why had I entrusted my babies with this unwell woman?

"Lord, it's hot in here. I feel like I'm melting!"

"Sophie, this will be quick. I just need you to open a box labeled *Office 2.* There's going to be a folder in there, and the folder is going to say *Endeavors.* Do you see it?" There was more grunting, then came the sound of rustling papers. "Did you find it?" I asked.

"Yeah, yeah," Sophie said. "It's a bunch of bullshit."

"I know that, I'm in the process of moving out, give me a little leeway," I said, trying to disguise my mild annoyance.

Sophie snorted. By now I could actually tell the difference between her snorts. There was the standard loogie snort, the loud early-morning/late-night snort, and then my favorite, the outrage snort. This, I could tell, was an outrage snort.

"What is it?" I asked. "Did you find the file?"

"Reading it now. It's a shell company, no integrity, that much is clear." She took a moment to read. "Well, that's something."

"What is?" I asked.

"Back when I was a paralegal for Don Ustan, aka the shittiest estate lawyer in New York City, I'd see companies like this all the time. They're scammers. Bernie Madoff shit. People put in money thinking they're making a profit, but the guy's just juggling cash around. To the untrained eye, you would have no idea, but once you know where to look, you can spot these gangsters a mile away. *Endeavors.*" Sophie groaned. "These companies are always named something like that. Don Ustan's business was called Solutions Inc. And that man was an idiot."

"So what are you saying?"

"I'm saying Endeavors is a load of shit, and I'd imagine it's left a trail of very angry people." Sophie cleared her throat. Standard loogie. "Anyway, in twenty-four hours, I expect you to be here! These things' piss turns into clumps of sand! It's witchcraft, is what it is!"

"Bye, Sophie, take care now." I said, quickly hanging up before I got another outrage snort. The phone had grown hot against my cheek. Of course Endeavors was a scam. I knew it at the time, but somehow the details had grown fuzzy over the years. I thought about the Endeavors baseball hat Mark Fontaine wore when I first met him. I couldn't say if it was new, but it certainly didn't look vintage. Even if Endeavors had filed for bankruptcy back when Dave McCarthy was put in jail, there was a possibility it was back up and running now. I needed to find Caitlin, hopefully alive. I needed to know what she knew.

Morgan's Bistro was starting to fill up with the early lunch crowd. I recognized a few faces from the memorial and the Cock and Balls party. The woman with the blond bob sat at a table near the window with a man twice her age. I still hadn't learned her name, so I figured this might be the time. We'd been at the same parties. I was 99 percent sure she was the woman in the antechamber the night Josh Jorkavic was killed. Plus there was the issue of the blond hair in the bloody drain. Maybe she knew something I didn't.

Joan and I walked over to her table, and as we got close, the woman quickly buried her face in her menu.

"Excuse me," I said. "I wanted to introduce myself. I'm Luella and this is my friend Joan Clyborne. Haven't I seen you around?"

The older man looked both of us up and down, stunned by our apparent boldness. He had a comb-over made with precision. The thin gray hairs on top of his head lay perfectly perpendicular to his bushy side tufts. Meanwhile the blonde remained engrossed in today's specials.

"We don't mean to interrupt your lunch. My friend just wanted to say hi," Joan said, but the blonde refused to look up.

"Would you mind leaving us alone?" the old man said, his chin raised high. "We're trying to have a date."

Joan was visibly taken aback. "Let's go," she muttered, then turned on her heel and hightailed it out the door. This woman had worked at the New York Public Library for decades, but this is what shook her? Everyone had their limits, I guessed.

I followed Joan out of the restaurant, and for a moment, we both stared at the gray water. Betsy Clench's ferry was already far from shore, a speck floating near the horizon.

"People like that guy, they make me sick to my stomach!" Joan said, her voice tight with anger.

"Well, you'll never guess what kind of people live on Murder Island!" I said.

"These people make me want to join an anarchist collective."

"Wait, Joan!"

"What?"

"You haven't even seen the properties."

"Are they disgustingly ostentatious?"

"The most disgusting! The most ostentatious!" I said.

"I can't wait! Let's do a tour!" Joan said, clapping her hands together. To find another person who was equally repelled and intrigued by extreme wealth almost brought a tear to my eye.

Joan and I started walking down the road that led to the Tylers' castle (she was going to lose it when she saw that one) and were about twenty feet away from the restaurant when we heard footsteps behind us. We both turned to see the menu-faced blonde running toward us at full speed.

"Stop!" the blonde said. "Please stop! I need to speak with you!"

Joan and I looked at each other. The woman was tall, maybe five-ten, with the kind of long legs that made running look lackadaisical. Her hair was perfectly coiffed, and I noticed in the sunlight she had large green eyes and a mole above her right cheek. She could've been anywhere between thirty and forty-five years old. That was the problem with these über rich people—you couldn't tell how old anyone was unless you saw their hands. Their faces were pulled tight in the exact same way, like they all shared a surgeon.

The woman towered over me and Joan.

"I couldn't say anything around my boyfriend, but I know you're trying to find Caitlin. I am, too. I was part of that little prank, remember?"

"What little prank?" I asked.

"Never mind, it's a long story. But see, my man—he's an associate of the Hunts. I've been to Murder Island so many times over the years, but this was my first time staying as a guest." She blanched. "A guest of the Hunts, I mean. And well, this morning, the help was acting strange."

"The help?" Joan asked, her eyebrows raised about an inch.

"What little prank?" I asked again, but she brushed me off with a flutter of her long fingers.

The tall woman continued. "I don't remember this woman's name, and I don't know what she does. She might be a cook or a maid or something. But this morning, she was acting so suspicious. She had a tarp and was heading toward the river."

I thought about the woman I'd met on the ferry who said she worked for the Hunts. Sybil Williams. "Are you talking about Sybil?" I asked.

"Yes! That's the girl's name. I'm sure whatever she's up to, it'll lead to Caitlin."

"Sorry, what is your name?" I said.

The woman looked side to side, then leaned in closely. "Most people recognize me. Caitlin actually gave me this wig for discretion while I'm visiting," she said, lifting the blond bob half an inch, revealing curly red hair underneath.

Joan's gasped. "You're Lenore Fisher. You were in that movie . . ."

"You must mean *March of Thieves*. I'm always honored to meet a fan." Lenore extended her hand to Joan in such a way that Joan's only course of action was to kiss it, which she did reluctantly.

"Sorry I couldn't speak in the restaurant. My man hates when I get recognized in public. I should get back to him. Best of luck." She ran off like an antelope and hollered, "Don't forget to look for that Sybil woman!"

Once she was out of earshot, I asked Joan, "Was *March of Thieves* any good?"

"Horrendous start to finish," Joan said. "But she's very pretty. You know, besides the height difference, you two sort of look alike."

"It's just the hair," I said.

We continued our Murder Island walking tour toward the Tylers' castle. Joan was interested in the local flora, and as she passed each new plant or tree, she would mutter the Latin name to herself in awe.

"*Cedrus, Quercus bicolor, Agastache foeniculum . . .*"

"Joan, are you okay? You sound like a wizard."

"I'm better than okay! Look! *Asclepias tuberosa!*"

"Oh, I love a good *asclepias tuberosa* this time of year," I said. Joan shook her head but continued rattling off the island's native plants under her breath.

When we got to the Tylers' castle, Joan took a moment to marvel before becoming sickened by America's wealth disparity. Despite my ankle situation and Joan's queasiness, we were moving at a good pace. We stood in the shade just south of the Tylers' property to catch our breath. From there, we could see their pool and tennis court, where I'd spoken to their butler.

"That Lenore Fisher . . ." Joan said. "Do you think there's any weight to what she said?"

"You think Sybil might actually be involved in Caitlin's disappearance?" I asked.

"Well, I don't know Sybil or Caitlin, but a lead's a lead, right?"

"Joan! An hour in and you're already quite the PI."

"All day I look for answers to people's questions. I hunt down overdue library books. I figure out who's watching porn on the public computers. A librarian is basically a detective, Marie."

"Fair point," I said. "Maybe next you can get to the bottom of that prank she mentioned. That's been bothering me ever since she said it. But first, let's find Sybil!"

Sybil Williams worked for the Hunts, and they shared the southern half of Murder Island with the McCarthys, so we'd need to be very careful. For all the McCarthys knew, I was halfway across the East River by now. It was important that they believe they'd gotten rid of me. If I had to pin these crimes on one person, it'd be Mark Fontaine, and I had a feeling he'd act very differently with the private investigator out of the way.

I tried to avoid any paths that looked familiar so we wouldn't accidentally find ourselves back at the McCarthy residence, but soon we were walking in circles in the hot sun. My ankle throbbed each time I put weight on it. Joan was kind enough to find me a large walking stick, which helped.

"If only we could walk in those tunnels Walter Stanford wrote about," Joan said, wiping sweat from her brow.

"Joan, you're brilliant!"

If there was a tunnel system, there had to be entrances hidden throughout the island. Then we could also travel while avoiding being seen. I instructed Joan to look for anything that might be a way in.

"Maybe it's an area covered in fresh grass, or an especially thick tree, or—" I stopped in my tracks. Further into the woods, I could make out the mouth of a cave. That had to be the way in. How else would a bat have gotten into the McCarthys' basement? And if all the houses were connected, then any tunnel could eventually lead us to the Hunts' place.

Joan looked where I was looking. "Or a cave?" she asked.

"Exactly," I said.

We both slowed our pace as we neared the mouth of the cave.

It was dark inside, and the closer we got, the heavier the damp, cold smell became.

"What's the Latin name for cave?" I asked.

"*Antrum,*" Joan said. "The poets also used that word to describe the stomach."

"The stomach, huh?" I said, my eyes searching the dark abyss just ahead of us. "Hope nothing's too hungry in there."

Joan looked at me. She was chewing the tip of her long silver braid.

"I know this seems terrifying, Joan. It's a dark cave. We're on a scary island owned by the rich and powerful. We're both possibly still a little tipsy from day drinking."

"I'm not supposed to be here. I'm a librarian."

At this point, I think it's pretty clear I am not a brave woman. Almost any skill that private detective work requires, I do not have. I am not stealthy, nor am I physically strong. What I do have is perseverance, stamina, and a few wigs. And when I need to, I can convince people to do things they really don't want to do. That was half the battle of being a social worker.

"Okay, listen, Joan. Do you see these teeth?" I flashed her my big pearly whites. "Would you believe these are veneers?"

"Of course. They're enormous. You look like a weather girl."

"Well, do you know how one gets veneers?" Joan shook her head, so I continued. "The dentist files down each of your teeth into little nubs, which is very painful and slow and sounds like death itself. Then over the course of *several* long appointments, he glues on your new porcelain teeth. After the first appointment, most of your teeth are nubs, your tongue is dry, and you realize you've made a huge mistake. But what do you think I did?"

"Well, you obviously went back, because you have a mouthful of gigantic fake teeth now."

"That's right," I said. "I didn't give up then, and I'm not giving up now. Joan, what are librarians?"

Joan's braid fell out of her mouth as she mumbled, "Librarians are detectives."

"Hell yes, they are! Now let's go!" I stormed into the mouth of the cave, really hoping this was the entrance to the tunnels.

Inside, the air was cool. The cave was at least ten feet tall by five feet wide. I could hear rushing water somewhere deep within, and in what little light seeped in, I could see glittery crystalized stalagmites rising from the ground. I really didn't want to look up. If I didn't see any bats, then there weren't any bats there. My ass cheek ached just thinking about them. I thought again of that bubble tea straw syringe and winced.

But that didn't stop Joan. "Oh look!" she whispered. "*Myotis lucifugus!*"

"Please Joan, speak English."

"Little brown bats! Did you know that *Myotis lucifugus* is the most common—"

"I did not know that, and I don't want to know *anything else* about the Lucifer fungus bats."

"Well, then, I won't tell you that there are several hundred hanging from the top of this cave, and that we should probably run because if we inhale any more of their guano, we will be extremely sick."

We were on the same page about getting away from those devil fungus bats. "Okay, okay!" I tried to think, and fast. "Running water would form tunnels naturally, right? So let's go toward the sound of the water!" I said.

At a certain point, no more light entered the cave, and soon we were immersed in total blackness. We decided against using Joan's phone flashlight so as not to alert anyone (bat or human) that we were in there. I led the way, moving as fast as I could with my walking stick. First I hit my head on a stalactite, then Joan ran face-first into a cave wall, then we collided into each other, where my veneers must've sliced through her cheek because Joan screamed and I tasted blood. We'd been on the move for ten minutes and were both already groaning in pain. It was feeling a bit like the Three Stooges in there. A lump had started to swell on my head.

"I know you don't want to know anything about them, but if we make too much noise, the bats will wake up," Joan said.

"You're the one who screamed!" I whispered.

"You're the one with the giant teeth!" she whispered back.

"Well, we can't keep going like this. We're about *this* close to getting impaled on matching rock formations."

"Wait! I have an idea!" Joan said, reaching for my elbow in the dark and hooking hers through it. "Let's do this like a three-legged race. That way we don't bump into each other, and we can each have one hand out to keep us from running into another cave wall."

The woman was a genius. It was much smoother sailing after that. I found myself giggling at how much ground we could cover together and how in sync we were. Even though I was likely surrounded by bats, I couldn't stop smiling. It was like we were Laverne and Shirley if they did the opening credits from inside a dark cave. But the fun stopped suddenly when we both heard footsteps echo not far from where we were.

"Did you hear that?" I whispered. "Someone's here."

The footsteps were getting closer by the second.

"Let's get against a wall," Joan said, and we scrambled backward until our backs were touching one side of the cave. We became quiet as we listened for the direction of the footsteps. Whoever it was had come from deeper inside the cave, and they were fast approaching. On the bright side, that meant we were likely heading in the direction of the tunnels. At least this wasn't all for naught.

The steps got louder, and it sounded like the person was only twenty feet away from us now. I held my breath, and I noticed Joan did, too. We both heard a click, then saw a beam of light shoot out. The person had turned on a flashlight and was using it to light the path in front of them. They walked with urgency but stopped right in front of us. I could hear Joan breathing again and I grabbed her hand tightly so she'd quiet herself.

The person must've sensed us. The flashlight shone on the ground to the left of us and then on the opposite wall. Then we heard a single drip plop onto the ground. I feared it was blood from Joan's cheek. We both froze as the flashlight panned over the ground in front of us, which confirmed the drip was blood, then up to our terrified faces.

"What are you doing here?" a woman's voice said. "Who are you?" Her voice sounded vaguely familiar. I could rule out Caitlin, but I had a feeling I'd met this woman before.

"We're trying to solve—" Joan said, but I cut her off. This was no time for honesty. We didn't know who we were dealing with yet.

"We're guests of the island. And frankly, we're disgusted how long it's taken to get proper medical attention!"

The woman's flashlight went from Joan's face to mine. "Don't I recognize you?"

"Of course you do," I said, without a clue who the hell I was addressing. "I am a close cousin of Mark Fontaine's. And when he hears how we've been treated . . ."

The woman with the flashlight steadied the beam on my face. "Wait a second. I know you. We met on the boat. You're that private investigator, Luella van Horn. Frank told me all about you. And who are you?" The flashlight moved to illuminate Joan's face.

"I'm a librarian. My name is Joan."

The woman took a long sigh, then held up the flashlight to her own face. "It's me, Sybil."

Joan couldn't help letting out a small gasp. "Sybil, we were in here looking for you!"

"You were?" Sybil asked nervously. "What—why?"

"We were told to find you—that you might have some answers to our questions," I said.

The flashlight moved off her face and toward the ground, but not before I could detect a hint of defeat in her expression.

"Come with me. It's not safe here."

23

We followed Sybil's flashlight deeper into the cave. As we walked, the rocky, uneven terrain was eventually replaced by a path made from smooth wooden planks. The cave itself became narrower, and we found ourselves having to walk in single file to fit. With Sybil in front, I marched right behind her, and Joan was third. The sound of rushing water was getting closer, and the air began to smell more like salt than mammal, for which I was extremely grateful. It seemed as though we'd passed the bat phase of the tunnel experience.

"Seems like everyone here knows you as Luella van Horn," Joan whispered. "I've been calling you Marie."

"It's a long story," I whispered, feeling my face flush.

"Did you know the origins of the name Luella? It means famous warrior."

"I've heard as much," I said. *When you're picking out a name for yourself, why not go for gold?*

"Well, it's fitting," Joan said, and I couldn't help but smile. To have someone see you the way you want to be seen, even if you are limping in a damp tunnel, well, it's pretty great.

Sybil stopped, and we came face-to-face with a heavy wooden door. She felt around for her keys, then unlocked it with a clanking sound that echoed past us. The door opened to a dimly lit hallway with ancient dark wood floors. The walls were lined with red wallpaper with an intricate gold design on it. Upon closer inspection, it was a repeated pattern of different animals—there was a rooster and a bear, but I couldn't make out the others. I thought about that flag I'd seen on the ferry and wondered how it was connected.

Sybil turned her flashlight off, and now the only sources of light were sconces dotting the walls every few feet. Inside the hall, the air smelled sweeter, like pipe smoke and vanilla extract. As Sybil plodded in front of us, I snuck a look over at Joan. Her eyes went wide. I'd gotten used to the hell that was this island, and until I saw Joan's face, I forgot we could be in real danger. We were following a suspect through a strange passageway, and no one on earth knew where we were. *Right, of course, danger. Danger, danger, danger.*

The hallway eventually led us to two more heavy wooden doors. Each had a solid gold letter bolted to it—the one on the left had an M and the one on the right had an H. Sybil took out her heavy key ring once again and opened the door marked H.

This door led to another hallway with more modern recessed lighting, a gold-tiled floor, and walls painted cornflower blue. When I tried sniffing this hallway, the only thing I noticed was the lack of any smell. Not even antiseptic. Like air purifiers had been going all night.

At the end of the hall, there was a closed steel door. Sybil turned around to face us. "All right, we're entering the Hunts' house now, so don't speak until I give you the signal it's safe. I know I sound paranoid when I say this, but they've got sound recorders everywhere."

"Why?" Joan asked.

"Why does anyone do anything on this island? Blackmail ammo," Sybil said. That certainly put all these sex parties in a much different light.

Sybil held her ID over a sensor discreetly blending into the cornflower wall, and the steel door opened. Once inside, Joan and I both took a moment to take in our surroundings. The room we entered was junglelike and huge, with high ceilings, forest green walls, and floor-to-ceiling windows on one side. This had to be the Hunts' solarium.

Large sprawling plants climbed out of pristine white ceramic pots. Plush white chairs surrounded a beautiful indoor swimming pool. From where I stood, I could make out a mosaic of some famous art piece on the bottom of the pool.

"*The Battle of Anghiari*," Joan whispered, pointing to the mosaic. "Originally painted by Leonardo da Vinci."

"You are a walking encyclopedia," I muttered.

"Usually yes, but this time there's a plaque," Joan said, pointing to the brass label affixed to the wall in front of us.

"Typical librarian . . . brags about reading," I said, and Joan smirked.

"Be quiet, and keep up!" Sybil whispered.

Past the solarium, we walked through several rooms, including a sauna, an indoor basketball court, a man cave with four big-screen televisions and a leather sectional couch that could fit twenty, then a huge room with a bunch of suits of armor in it, just like they have at the Met.

Once we'd passed the suits of armor exhibit, a hallway led us to a white wooden door. Sybil scanned her ID again, and the door opened to a small, dark apartment, complete with a kitchen, a bedroom, and a sitting room. Sybil had taken us to her apartment.

Joan and I sat next to each other on a pink overstuffed couch (of regular height, it's worth noting). Sybil grabbed three bottles of beer from the fridge. She sat across from us on a white leather BarcaLounger. She popped the caps off with one of her keys and handed us each a bottle.

"So, how much do you know?" Sybil asked.

Joan opened her mouth to speak, but I held my hand out. "We'd like to know what you know first," I said. Joan quickly nodded in agreement.

Sybil took a long swig of her beer. "Look, I try to keep my head down. The less I know around here, the better. But if you were sent here looking for Caitlin, I might know where she is."

"Is she alive?" I asked.

Sybil shook her head slightly. "Probably not."

I swallowed the lump in my throat, determined to put on a brave face in front of Joan. "Well, where is she?" I asked.

Sybil took another swig of beer. "Usually I just do what I'm told and don't ask questions. But when they ask me to wrap something heavy in a tarp and toss it into the river, I start to get curious."

Joan cleared her throat nervously. "What do you think was in the tarp?"

"Well, I can't be sure. It was heavier than I thought Caitlin would be. Maybe it was all that Pilates muscle. The whole thing came to me covered in a black plastic bag. I never opened it to check if a body was in there or anything. Like I said, most things that go on around here, I don't want to know. So I just dumped it like I was told."

"But there was a problem. Lenore Fisher saw you," I said.

Sybil nodded, her eyes filling with tears. "I didn't kill Caitlin! I can't go to jail, but I can't lose this job, either. If I talk"—she looked around to be sure, then lowered her voice to a whisper—"and it turns out someone from this family killed her, they'll make sure I never work again. Or worse."

Joan shook her head in disbelief. I wanted to believe in Sybil's innocence, but I couldn't be sure.

"Who exactly told you to dump the . . . package?" I asked.

"Mrs. Hunt. She left a note, I'll show it to you." Sybil got up from her recliner and rummaged through some papers on her desk. "When I got finished with work last night, I found the thing all wrapped up outside my door on one of those foot trucks. This was pinned to it." Sybil handed me the note.

I held it between Joan and me so we could both read it. It had scalloped edges, and there was no hole at the top where it would've been pinned to a bag.

Take this to the river. Do not say a word.

"How do you know this is from Mrs. Hunt?" Joan asked.

Sybil looked at Joan like she was the dumbest woman in the world. "She's who I report to. I do what she tells me to, and no one else would dare."

Joan nodded. "Of course."

"Where's the pinhole?" I asked, holding up the note.

"What?" Sybil asked.

"How would the pin attach the note to the body bag if there isn't a hole?"

Sybil hesitated. "Must've been taped then," she finally said.

All I thought was *lie, lie, lie*. Sybil knew more than she was letting on.

"Why do you think Mrs. Hunt killed Caitlin?" I asked.

Sybil polished off her beer, then let out a long and low belch. "Maybe she was jealous. Or maybe she was looking to buy another property on the island and Caitlin was standing in her way. There are any number of reasons why someone would want to kill that woman."

Joan and I looked to each other. "You think that's a common feeling around here?" I asked.

Sybil put both hands on her knees and leaned into us. "That's not what I meant, and you know it."

Joan stood up then, dusting off her hands like she'd just finished a chore. "Well! I say we go down to the river and see if we can't find that body! I'm sure it couldn't have traveled far, with the river being at low tide. Luella, are you in?"

"Oh certainly!" I said, rising from the couch. Why hadn't I worked cases with a partner before? This was invigorating. No wonder Isles went seven seasons with Rizzoli.

Sybil looked from Joan to me, though she stayed seated. She took a deep breath. "I don't know if that's a good idea. You haven't even finished your beers." She gestured to the two nearly full bottles sweating on her coffee table.

Joan smiled at her. "I came all this way to Murder Island, and I won't be going home until I see a dead body!" She walked across the room to Sybil's front door then turned back. "Coming, Sybil?"

As she stood up from her chair, Sybil looked a little green. She clearly didn't want us to find Caitlin's body. Because if we did, that meant trouble for her. She walked us out then paused. "Actually, I'll be out in a minute. Just gotta use the john before we go."

Outside the white wooden door, Joan and I could hear the rustling of papers and a crash of furniture inside. Sybil let out a string of obscenities, then there was more crashing. She was up to something in there, that was for sure.

Joan gestured for me to come closer to her. She whispered in my ear, "Are you thinking what I'm thinking?"

"That there's something fishy going on with Sybil?" I asked quietly. Joan nodded. "Hey, Joan, have you ever watched the show *Rizzoli & Isles*?"

But before Joan could answer, Sybil yanked open the door and began walking down the hall in the opposite direction we came from. We followed her closely as she led us up gray marble stairs. I still had my walking stick, and the thump of the wood on marble was so loud it sounded like a bass drum.

"Auditioning for the reboot of *STOMP* back there?" Sybil asked, the acid brimming in her voice. I tried leaning on the walking stick more gently after that.

The stairs brought us up to a hallway, which seemed to be the main thoroughfare of the house. On our right we passed a dining room and a sitting room, and on our left, a breakfast room and a parlor. A few staff members busied themselves with cleaning, though I noticed none of them acknowledged Sybil's presence, nor did Sybil acknowledge theirs. I wondered if there was tension among the staff. Some of them looked much stronger than Sybil, so why had Sybil been the one chosen to dispose of the body? She had to be Mrs. Hunt's right-hand woman.

We walked out the Hunts' front door, which was surrounded by bougainvillea and pansies. How do I know this? Joan's whispers. I don't think I'll ever get the phrase "bougainvillea, nine o'clock" out of my head for as long as I live. If we were going to be partners, I'd need her to get over this plant fetish.

The front walkway led to a roundabout where three cars were parked. Sybil stared at the cars with a furrowed brow.

"What's wrong?" I asked.

"Mrs. Hunt must've gone out," she said. "Her car's a hunter green Mercedes. It's not here."

"Is that a problem?" Joan asked. Sybil shook her head, smiled at us absently, and continued walking toward the main road. I turned back once to take in the grandiosity of the house. From the front, it looked more like a college campus than a home where two people lived. It was five stories tall and must've been a city block wide. And I was here because I couldn't pay the rent on a studio apartment. Ah well, at least I never had group sex with my possible cousins.

We were walking north on the main road when we heard a car heading our way. We all shifted wordlessly to the left side of the road so we might see who was coming. When the car got nearer, Joan grabbed my elbow. "Hunter green Mercedes," she murmured.

I looked to Sybil, who realized too late it was her employer currently driving toward us. Mrs. Hunt slowed her car and pulled up next to us. She wore large tortoiseshell sunglasses and a Fendi bucket hat. She lowered the passenger-side window.

"Sybil, what are you doing walking down the middle of the road? And who are these people?"

Sybil straightened her posture and her mouth became serious. "I was just taking these visitors on a walk to the river."

"The river? Why would you do that?" Mrs. Hunt asked.

"They asked to see it," Sybil said, lowering her gaze.

Mrs. Hunt shook her head dismissively. "The river is disgusting. Take them on an architectural tour of the lovely homes."

"Okay, ma'am, I'll do that."

Joan nudged me and I nudged her back. We were on the same page. Sierra Hunt was either an incredible actor or she didn't have a clue why we'd go to the river. I doubted she was the one to write that note. Plus there was the fact it was written on that paper with the scalloped edges.

"Actually, would you get in the car? I'm so tired of driving," Sierra Hunt said.

Sybil glanced at us then nodded at her employer. Mrs. Hunt kept the car running as she got into the passenger side. Sybil dutifully sat in the driver's seat.

"Go see the houses. They're divine," Mrs. Hunt said without looking at either one of us. "Just follow this road. You'll pass some lovely architecture."

"Thanks," I said. From the driver's seat, Sybil looked at me with a fire in her eyes. *Wait for me,* she mouthed.

"Let's go, Sybil! My blood sugar is low, and you know that means I need to eat sashimi in the next ten minutes." With that, Sybil drove off, back toward the Hunts' residence, leaving Joan and me in the dust.

"What now?" Joan asked, clearing her throat.

"Let's see if we can't find Caitlin's body."

24

wanted to locate Caitlin's corpse for two main reasons, and neither was because I was a sick fuck. Reason one: I wanted to see if she was killed in the same way Josh was killed. If her throat was also slit, that pointed to the killer's MO, which could shed insight into who they were. Reason two: I'll admit it, I was confused. Either Sybil Williams was lying to us or Sierra Hunt was, and finding Caitlin's body could clear up who was protecting whom. What's more, we were on a time crunch. Betsy Clench was picking us up the next morning whether we solved this case or not. Sybil's warning be damned . . . We were going to the river without her.

When I put all my weight on my walking stick my ankle didn't bother me as much, so we made good time, both feeling a sense of urgency and dare I say excitement at the prospect of a meaty clue. As we passed the bistro, I looked for Paul wiping down the bar, ideally with his sleeves rolled up and a lock of hair in his face. Maybe he'd look at me with those smoldering eyes and slowly pop a maraschino cherry into his mouth. To be clear, this did not happen. Paul was nowhere to be seen. There were a few customers seated at tables, but they had already been served. I wondered where Paul was.

When we finally got to the river, I scanned the gray waves, but nothing looked out of the ordinary. At least there were no dead bodies bobbing like buoys. Joan began taking off her shoes and socks.

"What are you doing?" I asked. She'd already moved on to cuffing her pants.

"I'm going into the river!" Joan said. And that's when I realized Joan was a transplant.

"You're from the Midwest, aren't you? What is it, Michigan? Chicago?" I asked.

"I'm originally from Minneapolis, why do you ask?"

"Because no New Yorker in their right mind would ever step foot in the East River. Do you know what's in there, Joan? Toxic sludge, human waste, disintegrating dolphins. You don't go in the river. Even if Caitlin's body is floating in there. The last thing I need is you becoming a Teenage Mutant Ninja Turtle."

"That's not how they became . . ."

"Yes it is, Joan. Don't fight me on this. Maybe we can get a net or something. Fishing gear. Check for Caitlin's body that way . . ."

"Don't bother," a man's voice said behind us. Joan and I turned around to find Paul standing there, his arms crossed. While the sleeves were rolled up and the muscles were bulging, there was unfortunately no maraschino cherry. Still, he looked damn good.

"I've been watching the riverfront all day. Whatever Sybil dumped in there is long gone by now. The tide was supposed to be low, but the current is strong with the heavy winds. It's Sybil's lucky day."

"And apparently Caitlin's unlucky day," Joan murmured.

"You saw Sybil dump something? Do you remember what time? Or any details about it?" I asked him.

"It looked like a body wrapped in a black trash bag. It must've been around 5 A.M. this morning," he said.

"Why didn't you say anything when you saw us at the restaurant earlier?" Joan asked.

"I didn't know you wanted to know," Paul said, winking at her. "If you spend enough time on this island, you can see a whole lot. Especially if you work here. Then you're practically invisible."

"I doubt that," Joan said, eyeing Paul from top to bottom.

"Joan, you have a husband, don't you?" I said.

"We've been talking about opening up our marriage."

"Have you now?" I asked.

"Ladies, please. I know why you're here and I want to help you. Both of you," Paul said.

"Why do you want to help us? What's in it for you?" After the Sybil episode we just went through, I was hesitant to trust anyone else, even Paul.

"You two are lovely, but I was wondering . . . If I help you, could you put in a good word with your friend Betsy? I can't seem to build up the courage to ask her out."

"Of course we will!" Joan said, clapping her hands together. I didn't think we needed to be *that* enthusiastic about it, but I mean sure, I was down to help. Of course Paul liked Betsy Clench. Who wouldn't? Somewhere deep down, I was happy for her.

Paul looked around. With the coast clear, he continued. "Before every sex party, most people take this little blue pill, scopolamine. You can get it over the counter to help with nausea, but it also makes you black out. The Hunts have a huge supply, since their family is in pharmaceuticals. A lot of people take it so they don't have to remember the sex parties, then they can resume their normal lives afterward."

So that must've been what Mark Fontaine was on that time I saw him wandering the halls of the McCarthy house. And what Bradford offered me. And the residue Josh Jorkavic had on his fingers.

"If Sybil was sent to dump Caitlin's body, that means the Hunts probably had something to do with Caitlin's death," I said.

"Well, you have to be really careful with scopolamine—take too much and you can overdose," Paul said.

"What if someone gave Caitlin too much? Maybe the Hunts got rid of the body so there wouldn't be any connection back to them," Joan said.

"Interesting theory," I said. "But how do we prove it?"

"I think I'm getting an idea. You're really going to help me ask out Betsy Clench?"

"Yeah, Paul, we're on it," I said. "Now tell us, what's our next step?"

Paul thought for a moment. It was actually a few moments—approaching too many moments. I thought I might've broken Paul. The beautiful ones are fragile.

"Paul?" I said. "What's the next step?"

"Okay, I got it! There's another party tonight. If you can sneak in, you could see who's acting suspicious. If someone killed Josh and Caitlin, I can't imagine they'll stop there. This island is too small. Someone has to have seen something, and they'll be killed for that."

"Why do you say that?" I asked.

Paul's phone buzzed once in his pocket and he took it out to read the message.

"Who's texting you?" I asked.

"People are freaking out about Caitlin's disappearance, and they're trying to decide whether it's safe to still have the party. Since no one got killed at Cock and Balls, my money's on it still happening with heightened security. That means you guys will need to keep a lower profile. Best bet will be the interhouse tunnels."

Joan squealed. "We know all about the tunnels!"

"Where's the party tonight?" I asked.

Paul scrolled through his phone, then looked up. "It's at the Hunts' place."

I weighed my options. We could attend a sex party via underground tunnels, where people would be administering and using that blackout pill, which meant people's guards would be down, and they might do something like admit to a crime. Or we could just wait out the next twelve to fifteen hours sitting quietly on the beach. Josh was dead, Caitlin was likely dead. Could we really stop a third murder from happening? The beach option was sounding better and better.

"Joan, can I have a word with you?" I asked. Paul stayed put. "Alone?" I said to him. He raised his eyebrows and walked a few feet away. Out of respect for Betsy, I only looked at his ass for a second or two.

Once he was out of earshot, I whispered, "Joan, why are we doing this?"

Joan flipped her long silver braid and straightened her shoulders. "Of course I can't answer for you. But for me, this is the greatest adventure I've ever had, and I've come this far, so why stop now? Why do you think you're doing this?"

"Because you are," I said. I hadn't meant to be so blunt, but that's what came out of my mouth. "The thing is, Joan, I don't think we're going to solve this one. These people have more power and political sway in one pinkie than we do combined. And if they don't want these murders to come to light, they won't." I thought briefly about Frank shipping Josh Jorkavic's body to the medical examiner and wondered if the murderer knew about that.

Joan's brow furrowed as she looked at me with a sadness I hadn't seen from her before. She put her hands on her hips and puffed out her chest. "Do you know what I do when people don't return books?" she asked.

"Fine them?" I said.

"I send them a letter. And if they don't respond to that, I email them. And if that gets no response, I'll call them on the phone. And that's for an overdue library book. So if you think I'm just going to let you give up this Murder Island case, you've got to be out of your goddamn mind."

"Joan—" I said, gearing up to complain about the rabies shot I'd gotten in the ass, my twisted ankle, and all that billionaire group sex I had to watch, but she cut me off.

"I know we can do this, Marie. I'm excited, and I haven't been excited like this in years. I've never met anyone like you. You're a real, live private detective."

"I'm still not licensed," I said. "I used to be a social worker. I should've probably stuck with that." I kicked some sand around with the toe of my shoe.

"No. You're a private eye through and through. I've been watching you work. You ask the right questions. You listen. You follow your instincts. You know exactly what you're doing," Joan said. I felt my cheeks, and they were wet. Crap, was I crying? I sniffled and tried to save face. Paul looked over at us, but I hoped he was far enough away not to see me blubbering.

"I know you wear a wig, and those teeth are fake, and to be

honest, I don't know what to call you. Are you Luella van Horn or Marie Jones? I am an intelligent woman, and I'm confused. But you could take all that stuff away, and you'd still be my most exciting friend."

I sniffled again, trying to wipe away the mascara that had run down my cheeks.

"Come here," Joan said, wrapping me up in what I'll call a "librarian hug." As she held me tight in her arms, I smelled books.

"What do you say? Should we solve this case?"

I took a deep breath. "Yeah, and I think I know just where to start."

25

f I was a broken-down Chevy, Joan's little pep talk worked like a full tank of gas and an oil change. I was back up and running, at least for the next few hours. How had I done this job before Joan? I'd been so alone. My entire social circle was two cats. I know, I know, cats can be friends. But let's be real—if I said to someone, *Hey, want to meet me and my friends for dinner?* and that person said okay and showed up to a restaurant where I had gotten a table for four, and it was me, that person, and my two cats, that'd be one difficult dinner.

We thanked Paul for his help, and he reminded us to put in a good word with Betsy. I told him I couldn't forget if I tried. Then we made our way toward that cave again, this time with a different destination in mind. This whole mess started at the McCarthys'. If I was going to get to the bottom of it, I needed to focus my search there. I knew Frank or Yanni (or Mark Fontaine, for that matter) would never let me in the front door, but the tunnels offered a new solution. At least one of them had to know something about the growing body count.

I knew the way to the Hunts', and if they and the McCarthys both lived on the southern half of the island, then all we had to do in theory was get back to those two doorways in the tunnels—the ones with the M and H on them—then go in the M door instead of the H. This was assuming M was for McCarthy.

Easier said than done, of course.

No one will tell you this, but secret tunnels suck. You think it'll be some fun adventure, but fifteen minutes in, you're swatting off prehistoric bugs and somehow your elbows are bleeding. Not only that, but you can't stop thinking about how you've exposed yourself to asbestos, and not only have you ruined your health, you've also ruined the health of a beautiful librarian with no personality faults who happens to be your new best friend (non-cat).

We managed to make it back to the cave where we'd first entered the tunnels, but once we plunged into the darkness, we struggled to navigate.

Our intention was to head south, but often as we walked, the tunnels would turn abruptly, and there would no longer be an option to continue south. Several times we thought we were onto something and making progress when we'd end up at a closed door we'd never seen before with no way to enter it. It was almost as if these tunnels were purposely designed to mislead newcomers, especially if they didn't enter them from a house.

The fifth time we arrived at a closed door, Joan pulled out her phone to use as a flashlight. As much as we wanted to keep a low profile, time was running out. Right away, the light from her screen showed something on the door we hadn't seen before. Joan shined her phone's flashlight on the door. At eye level, right around where there would be a peephole, the door had a small etching of an animal. After studying it closely, we both decided it was, of all things, a mongoose.

"*Herpestidae*," Joan whispered.

"You get one more Latin name, then you're cut off," I whispered back.

I had an idea. Surely we weren't the only ones who'd been completely turned around in these tunnels. There had to be a system for those in the know. I asked to borrow Joan's phone and walked back several paces, holding the light along the wall. Sure enough, the etching of the mongoose was there, too. We recognized the one door Sybil had taken us through, which also had a mongoose etched at eye level. So the mongoose likely marked the Hunts' property. The door was locked, but it meant we were at least on the south side of the island. Now we just had to look for the other families' symbols.

When we were presented with a new tunnel to go down, we would first run our hand along the wall and find an etching. Joan would hold up her phone light (the battery was now down to 30 percent), and we were able to identify whether it was still the Hunts' property or another family's. What we hadn't realized before was that multiple tunnels led to the same property. The Hunts' alone had at least four tunnels that we counted. But through this system, and Joan's awareness of cardinal directions, we were able to locate either the Petersons' or the Jorkavics' domain (marked by a bear) and the Tylers' (marked by a water buffalo).

"*Bubalus bubalis,*" Joan muttered.

"That's your last one. I hope it was worth it."

"In fact, it was," Joan said, raising her chin a little higher.

With the Hunts', the Petersons' or the Jorkavics', and the Tylers' properties demarcated, we felt we had a better sense of direction. Our educated guess was that the bear meant we were north, the water buffalo meant we were central, and the mongoose meant we were south.

"We're closer than ever," I said.

"I feel it, too," Joan said.

The first tunnel we came to with a new animal etched into the wall was a rooster. Joan's phone battery was down to 21 percent, so after seeing the initial carving, we tried to identify the remaining symbols through touch. Our fingers came to recognize the comb and the exaggerated tail feathers on the entrances of the next three tunnels we found. But the question remained, was this the McCarthys' place or possibly the Jorkavics' or the Petersons'? Bradford Tyler's warning rang in my head: *beware the rooster and bat.* I mentioned this to Joan to gauge her take.

"Permission to reference Latin? If it's for the case?"

I let out a long sigh. "Yeah, go for it."

"The surname Jorkavic is typically Croatian, Slovak, or Slovenian, and the name itself has roots in the George family. Do you know what *George* means?"

"A curious monkey?" I asked.

"George means farmer. And what's iconic to a farm? A rooster," she said. Even in the darkness, I could make out a twinkle in her eye. She was loving this.

"So you're saying that rooster means it's the Jorkavics' property?" I asked.

"Exactly," Joan said. "Which means the Petersons' place is marked by the bear, and whatever animal is left demarcates the McCarthys!"

Damn I was glad to have that bookworm around. Without Joan, I would've been wandering those nasty tunnels until I was fifty.

We encountered five rooster-marked tunnels before we finally arrived at a new animal. I told Joan she could reserve her phone battery. I could tell what this thing was with my eyes closed. There were wings with claws at the ends and a little round head. I couldn't help but notice two tiny fangs coming out of the creature's mouth. The etching made my ass hurt all over again. There was no question—the McCarthys' family symbol was, of course, a bat. We needed to follow the bat etchings. Was Bradford Tyler telling me to beware of the Jorkavics and the McCarthys? And this from the grown man who pet toads in the middle of the road. What could he know?

One bat tunnel led to another, which led to a locked door. On a whim, I reached for the keys I'd pocketed that morning and tried them one by one. Joan's phone battery had dwindled down to 10 percent, but we both agreed using the last of her battery to light our way was worth it.

Finally I found the key that worked. The door opened onto a set of stairs. I left it unlocked in case we needed a speedy escape. Joan shined her phone light on the staircase, and I counted three stories. Past that, it was pitch-black, but I anticipated more stairs. Oh, my poor, sweet ankle.

"When's the last time you used a StairMaster?" I asked.

"It was 1992," Joan replied. "Czechoslovakia as a country still existed."

I took a deep breath. "Let's get this over with. Could you shine the light around the base of the stairs?"

As Joan moved the beam of white light along the ground,

something caught the light. I ran over to it. There, lying on the ground, was my phone! Sure, the screen was cracked, and it might've been broken beyond repair, but this meant something crucial. This was the secret stairway I'd been on before. This would lead us straight into the McCarthys' house.

We began our slow ascent with me in front and Joan in the rear. She turned off her phone's flashlight to conserve the remaining battery, and our eyes adjusted to the surrounding dimness. Slivers of light had come through where the walls must've met the old wooden flooring. I informed Joan about the wretched state of that narrow staircase The wood was soft, often rotten, and I may have even broken a few steps a couple of days ago. She understood and proceeded with caution.

"Slow and steady," I said. "The most important thing is that no one hears us."

As the stairs went on and on, our breathing became heavier. If I was correct in my estimations, we'd started at the basement level, and if we walked up three stories, we'd arrive at the secret book-case door.

After two flights, I paused midstep when I heard what sounded like a squeak. Joan stopped right behind me, caught her breath, then whispered, "What's wrong?"

Then I saw beady eyes and a flash of a tail.

"Rat," I said. "Rat on stairs."

Without skipping a beat, Joan squeezed past me.

"I got this." She moved toward the creature, and in an instant, the air smelled like peppermint and the animal had scampered away.

I stammered, "What did you—how did you—?"

"Peppermint oil. You don't work in a New York City library for decades without keeping a vial in your pocket at all times. With-out this stuff, I would've been picked apart for meat years ago. He'll warn his friends. They won't be bothering us again."

"Joan, be honest. Are you a superhero?"

"Close enough," she said, now taking the lead.

I'd lost count how many stairs it'd been, but it felt like we'd been climbing for half an hour when I spotted the outline of two doors. One of these had to be the false bookcase on the third floor. Joan and I both held our ears to the wall, and when we heard no movement on the other side of either door, it was time to make a choice.

"Right or left door?" I asked Joan.

"Left," she said.

"Why?"

"Because of that," she said, pointing to a dark smudge across the doorknob. She held her phone light up, and I gasped. It looked like dried blood.

I turned the ancient doorknob, avoiding the blood as much as I could, and pushed the door open. It must've weighed a hundred pounds and its hinges whined.

The light from inside the room was blinding compared to the shadow world of the staircase we emerged from. Joan and I must've looked like creatures from some kind of lagoon—squinting, draped in cobwebs, creeping in from a dark abyss. You know, how every bachelor dreams of his bride.

Once my eyes adjusted to the brightness of the empty room, I took a moment to look around. It smelled like roses in here. My confusion quickly turned to alarm as I realized I had no idea where we were. Our threshold was not a fake bookcase, but what appeared to be a door the same color as the cream walls.

It was a small room with a daybed, a nonworking fireplace (too clean to be functional), and a desk and chair facing a window. A handmade flag of a bear, a rooster, a bat, a mongoose, and a water buffalo was framed and hung above the fireplace's mantel.

"Wasn't that on the ship, too?" I asked. "And on the wallpaper in the hallway under the Hunts' place?"

Joan nodded. "And the etchings in the tunnels." I could tell she was spooked. I was, too, but the rose smell was getting to me more. It was so familiar.

On top of the desk sat several blond bob wigs on head stands. I walked over to examine them closer.

"That looks like your hair," Joan said.

"Or Lenore Fisher's," I said, then I froze. There on top of the desk was the same off-white stationery with the scalloped edges I'd seen slip under my attic door. The cards that had told me to watch out for Mark Fontaine and to leave the McCarthys' house, and that had contained the instructions for Sybil. At least one of them had smelled like roses, just like this room.

I looked out the window and realized we were facing the back of the house. I recognized the McCarthys' garden and patio furniture. From this distance, we looked to be about three stories up—Caitlin's floor. If we'd chosen the other door, I realized we'd have come through the false bookcase. But the bloody doorknob had led to this room.

That's when I saw Frank emerge from the back door with a watering can. He briefly looked up in our direction. Either he was tending to the garden or he was onto us. I ducked and hissed for Joan to duck, too. This brought me face-to-face with the desk's drawers.

Curiosity has always gotten the better of me. When confronted with a drawer, how many of us can honestly say we'd prefer to leave it closed, never knowing what's inside? Even Schrödinger would've opened that cat box eventually. He'd need to either feed the poor thing or have a cat funeral. (It's worth noting that my cats, Meatball and Meatloaf, will never die. That's the promise they made to me with their eyes. I said, *Blink twice if you'll die one day,* and they stared at me for ten minutes straight. And sure, I *was* holding tuna.)

From my crouched position, I slid open the top desk drawer. Inside, there were hundreds of small plastic baggies, all containing dozens of chalky blue tablets. I removed a bag and held it low so Joan could see from where she was kneeling.

"Are those what I think they are?" Joan whispered.

"Whoever's desk this is, they enjoy scopolamine."

Joan crawled closer to me as I opened another drawer. "The last time I did drugs, I was twenty-four in Washington Square Park," she stage-whispered. "A guy—we called him Drunk Harry—offered me and my friends some shrooms, and we had the most wonderful afternoon . . ."

Then I saw it. "Joan, I already love this story, but we may have to continue it another time." I pulled a bloody letter opener out of the drawer and showed it to her. "We may have just found Josh's murder weapon."

Joan staggered over to the daybed and sat down. It was possible all this was taking a toll. She was used to shelving books, and at worst, chastising people for watching porn on the library computers. How could I put her through all this? She had such a nice, peaceful life before I came into the picture.

Suddenly Joan jumped up with a start.

"What's wrong?" I whispered.

"I think I sat on something," she said, now searching the daybed. Then she found it. "Come here! Quick!"

I crawled over to see what she was looking at. On the daybed, nestled in the blankets, was a red leather strap-on. The dildo attached was white and appeared to be made of marble. I didn't plan on touching it, and it looked enough like marble, so I was going with that. On the back, where the leather was stitched together, there was a sewn-on label. Using the blanket as an intermediary, I lifted the device closer so I could read it. The label said: *The Rooster.*

"So this thing is called The Rooster, the Jorkavic family symbol is a rooster, and there's a rooster on that flag. So this is the family strap-on?" I said.

Joan furrowed her brow, looking closer at the flag above the mantel. "Have you ever studied heraldry?"

"If you tell me what heraldry is, I might know if I've studied it," I said.

"Heraldry is the system for which symbols are used in coats of arms," Joan said.

"Oh right. *That* heraldry. Yeah, no, I have not studied that, Joan. But I'm assuming you have?"

"Well, your assumption would be correct! I've always been fascinated with coats of arms ever since I was in grade school." In her reverie, Joan retreated to the daybed, surprising herself once again by sitting on the strap-on. "Oh dear!"

I kicked it off the bed and it landed with a thud. Hopefully Frank was still outside watering those plants. Joan patted the daybed and I sat down next to her. Behind us, there were a dozen identical cream-colored throw pillows. We both sat with our feet dangling off the edge.

"Where was I? Oh yes! In heraldry, each symbol has a specific and universally understood meaning, so when you put it on your crest, it's clear what you're trying to convey about your family or group. For example"—Joan pointed to the flag—"the rooster there symbolizes virility or braveness, depending on the context. The bat represents watchfulness, the bear means strength, the water buffalo signifies wealth, and the mongoose? Well, everyone knows what the mongoose does."

I gave her a blank stare until she told me what the mongoose did.

"They kill snakes," she said.

"So we're talking about a flag that represents wealthy, strong, watchful, virile people who kill snakes?"

"Think about it. This flag was on the boat, the only way to and from the island for most people. These animals are etched into the tunnels. I don't think these people are huge supporters of the ASPCA. And like Bradford Tyler said, 'Beware the bat and the rooster.' I hate to be the one to cry cult, but, Marie . . ."

"You might be onto something. The drug-fueled parties, the isolation from the city . . . Are we dealing with a sex cult?" I asked, queasiness churning in my stomach.

"We might be. And what do all sex cults need?" Joan asked.

"Condoms? No, lubricant?" I was getting too granular.

"All sex cults need a leader," Joan said.

But who was the leader? Edmund and Sierra Hunt, who were buying up all the properties? Or someone who would stop at nothing to prevent the Hunts from usurping any more land and power? I walked over to the window to see if I could still spy Frank watering the garden, but he'd disappeared. Turning around, I noticed some papers peeking out of a desk drawer I hadn't seen before. I opened the drawer and peered inside, careful not to disturb the way the papers had crumpled there. They seemed to be some kind of deed of sale. Scanning the text, I spotted the signatures of Mark Fontaine and Sierra and Edmund Hunt. Were the McCarthys planning on selling their property to the Hunts, as well?

That's when it occurred to me: only Mark had signed the deed, not Caitlin. But the house was in Caitlin's family name. The Petersons had already sold their place to the Hunts, and from what Carla said to me at Josh's memorial, she was considering selling, too. It looked like the McCarthys had also gotten an offer. But now Caitlin was missing. Had they killed Caitlin because she wouldn't sign? Were the Hunts murdering anyone who stood in the way of their acquiring all the island's property?

There was something about this room. Maybe that it had a bloody doorknob? Or that one door was locked and the other led in from a secret staircase? Or maybe it was the several blond wigs identical to mine sitting on the desk, or the bloody letter opener, or the marble strap-on, or the scalloped stationery, or the fact that it smelled so much like roses it was like we were sitting in a bush.

"Joan?"

"Yes, Marie?"

"I think we're in the killer's room."

Joan took a moment to look around calmly. "Yes, I think you're right."

26

But whose room was it, was the question. This was the third floor, which was Caitlin's floor, but the flag and the wigs didn't seem like Caitlin's. She liked things clean and white. There was also the very real possibility that Caitlin was dead, which we had to factor in. This room had to belong to someone with access. Frank or Yanni were both options, but Mark Fontaine seemed worthy of consideration, too. He was the one who told me the third floor was Caitlin's, which could have been a lie to put me off the trail.

My brain really started spinning when I realized it could be anyone who came in through the tunnels, like we had. But who would actually do that? The Tylers' butler was suspicious. And after today, I certainly wouldn't rule out Sybil. Whoever it was, their drug stash connected them to the Hunts.

Paul had told us the sex party would be at the Hunts' place that night. The way I saw it, we could either wait in this room for the killer to come back (when they would probably kill both of us), or go to the Hunts' sex party and look for someone wearing a blond bob wig or offering people little blue pills or stabbing someone with a letter opener. The thing they don't tell you about being a private detective is if you *see* the crime happening, it saves you a lot of work.

"Hey, Joan, how do you feel about going to a sex party?"

She stood up from the daybed and posed seductively against the frame. "I thought you'd never ask."

Suddenly I thought of Betsy Clench, a woman whose only desire was to be a part of this elite sexual debauchery, who would be absolutely heartbroken if we went to a sex party without her.

With the island's limited service, we used the last sliver of battery on Joan's phone to turn on her own hot spot and call Betsy through the wifi. Thankfully, she picked up. Betsy was in lower Manhattan, drinking at that same bar in the South Street Seaport.

"Betsy," I said. "It's Joan and Luella. Will you come to a sex party with us tonight?"

"*What!* Are you serious? Fuck off! Are you fucking with me? You want me to go . . ." She was already sobbing at this point. "I'm going to a sex party! Manifestation really works! I can't believe it! Fuck, there's so much to do. I gotta get waxed. I gotta get tested. I gotta get new underpants. It's really happening! *Charlie, I'm going to a sex party!*"

"Who's Charlie?" I asked.

"He's just a random guy sitting next to me!" We heard Betsy initiate a crisp high five with the random guy named Charlie.

Joan estimated we had two minutes until her phone died completely, so for the remainder of the conversation we talked fast. Betsy was to sneak the ferry back to Murder Island as soon as possible. We gave her directions to find the tunnels with the bat etchings and climb the stairs to this room. Luckily I'd left that tunnel door unlocked. We would wait for her here, and in the meantime, hopefully the murderer would not return.

It'd be at least a couple of hours before Betsy found her way to us. By the time she got here, we'd only have a little time to get ourselves ready. Betsy was in charge of bringing outfits. Not knowing if tonight's party had a theme, I told her to go for *Eyes Wide Shut* couture. I had a feeling she'd run with it, and no matter the theme, we wouldn't be too far off the mark.

In the meantime, we examined every detail of the room we were in. I looked for hairs inside the wigs and found nothing, which was suspicious. Joan did a thorough inspection of the desk for anything I might've missed. Both of us looked at the marble strap-on from a moderate distance.

I started to think the bloody letter opener and deed were displayed on purpose, as if to redirect us, but I couldn't understand why. The killer would have to know we'd get in here, and that we'd taken the tunnels, and that we were onto them. That cat-and-mouse feeling was back. I couldn't shake the sense I was being played with.

Then we both heard footsteps approaching. Quickly, Joan ran and hid in the doorway we'd entered, while I stupidly got under the covers of the daybed and tried to still my breathing so it wouldn't look like the twelve throw pillows had come to life. I should've gone with the doorway. If given the choice, always go with the option that allows you to stand. Makes it a lot easier to run away if necessary.

I heard the door unlock, and I broke out in a cold sweat. The murderer was here. Had they heard us rummaging around? Could we have been quieter? Was this the end? (Astute readers will understand this was not the end, as there's more of the book left.) A small part of me hoped it was Betsy Clench who had secured some keys, but the timing was all off. It had to be the killer.

Then I heard someone say, "Luella?" It was a man. The blankets were suddenly itchy on my damp skin. This was a form of torture used by the military, I was sure of it, but I tried to wait it out. Maybe he'd leave.

But he didn't leave. "Luella, are you in here?" I thought I recognized the voice but stayed as still as I could, breathing slowly through my mouth to keep quiet. I could feel individual fibers of the blanket burning against my bare legs. Next case, I'd be sure to wear leggings the whole time. This was horrible.

The next thing I knew, the blanket was being yanked off me, and while there was the immediate relief of fresh air, I was confronted with the face of the likely killer.

Yanni Toumis held the blanket with his right hand and the bloody letter opener in his left. "What the hell are you doing in here?"

Just then, Joan popped out of the doorway holding her dead cellphone like a weapon.

"Get any closer and you're a goner," Joan said.

"Same," Yanni said. "Who the fuck are you?"

"I'm your worst nightmare," Joan said. What were the chances I was friends with the one librarian who talked like Sylvester Stallone?

"Yanni, is this your room?" I asked.

"Shut up!" Yanni said as he covered my mouth with his hand. "Frank's just down the hall and Mark should be home any minute now. You shouldn't be here, so keep your voices down."

I pulled the rest of the blankets off and sat up. "How did you know we were in here?"

"For people trying to be discreet, you two make a whole lot of noise. Now you," Yanni said to Joan. "Sit on the bed with her." Joan did as she was told. "I tried to make it clear. It's not safe for you here," Yanni said.

"Are you going to kill us?" I asked.

For a minute, Yanni looked from Joan to me as the space between his eyebrows creased. Finally he broke the silence with a gut-busting cackle.

"You think I'm the killer? Why would I be the killer?" He threw his head back and laughed harder.

If you ever suspect someone of being evil, and then they laugh like that, it'll confirm all your suspicions.

Yanni wiped tears from his eyes and collected himself as his evil laugh died down. "Ah, I needed that. Thank you."

"Is this not your room?" Joan asked.

"No! And I'm not the killer. Why would you think that?" he asked, emphasizing his words with a shake of the bloody letter opener. "Oh, this?"

Both of our eyes followed the weapon as he slowly set it back down on the desk.

"I'm the one who's been protecting you this whole time. I'm the one trying to get you out of here, which apparently has backfired, since you're back, and now you've brought a friend!"

"Why are you protecting me? I don't understand," I said.

"The killings began when you came to Murder Island. I think this all has something to do with you."

27

asked Yanni to expand upon this theory of his. Putting two deaths on the newcomer is convenient and all, but there had to be more to it than that.

According to Yanni, Frank was working with Mark Fontaine on something private. In the last few weeks, he'd seen them huddled in corners, murmuring to each other. Whenever Yanni would enter a room, they'd pretend to go about their respective business. Yanni had been close to Frank at one point, even thought of him like a father figure, but over the last couple of years something was off.

Yanni had asked Frank what was going on between him and Mark, but Frank only brushed him off. He got the sense they were plotting something together. Especially when the meetings became more frequent leading up to Josh Jorkavic's murder.

Joan nodded and seemed to be following along better than I was.

"So wait, whose room is this?" I asked.

"I'm not sure. I've seen both Mark and Frank enter it. When I heard that thud up here, I stole Frank's keys and ran up, hoping to catch someone doing something."

Joan clicked her tongue, nodding toward the strap-on flopped on the floor. "The Rooster." I knew that thing would get us in trouble.

Yanni picked it up by one of its leather straps. The marble phallus swung gently midair. Really mesmerizing imagery, a hypnotist's delight. "Looks like someone could have a lot of fun with this thing," he said.

"Maybe one of us could wear it to the party tonight, see who takes an interest. That might lead us to the killer?" I said.

"Oh, I wouldn't go to that party if I were you. I know these types. That killer is striking again tonight, and if I had to guess, Luella, you're next. Whoever it is, they won't want to be caught. I'm sure by now the killer knows you never left the island."

I swallowed the lump in my throat. "So if we want to catch the killer in action, the party is the place to do it?" I asked.

"You're not listening to me!" Yanni shouted. I immediately thought of what the Tylers' butler had said to me, about listening more and speaking less. Their messages were eerily similar. Were Yanni and the Tylers' butler working together? All his talk about Frank and Mark huddling in corners, maybe that was intended to put us off the scent.

Yanni slammed the strap-on on the desk with a clunk. A moment later, we heard more footsteps approaching.

"Someone's coming!" Yanni said in an urgent whisper. The color drained from his face as his eyes darted back and forth between Joan and me.

"Maybe it's Frank! If so, remember you have his keys," I hissed. "He can't get in without his keys!"

Just then the footsteps stopped in front of the door. We all heard the nearby floorboards creak under the person's weight.

"If he finds us in here, we're all dead," Yanni whispered.

Hold the door, I mouthed. Yanni ran over to the door and leaned against it with all his weight concentrated in his shoulder blade. Someone on the other side banged repeatedly. The wooden door wavered in its frame, and soon Joan and I were both throwing our weight against it, too.

"Who's in there?" a man yelled from the other side of the door. The voice was raspy and angry. It had to be Frank's. But that meant as long as we were in here with Yanni, Frank didn't have his key, which bought us some time. I only hoped we weren't aligning with the murderer.

"It's not safe here," Yanni whispered. "You need to go. Now!"

"But Betsy Clench is coming to meet us!" I said.

"Meet her somewhere else! You don't realize how much trouble I've gotten you out of this week. But there's only so much I can do if Frank finds you two here."

I looked to Joan and she nodded, already heading toward the door from which we entered.

Frank's banging got louder. *"Let me in!"* he screamed.

"If you see Betsy, tell her to wait for us!" I whispered, then quickly followed Joan out of the room. My knees were shaking as we descended the rickety, dark staircase, and more than once I missed a step entirely. I'd left my walking stick in the killer's room, and this time my other ankle took the hit.

I didn't want to admit it to Joan, but I was officially terrified. This case felt more dangerous than anything I'd ever worked on. We were on a private island with no law enforcement, and whoever the killer was, they were likely rich and powerful, or at least deeply connected to the rich and powerful. If we lived through this, I planned to do a lot of things differently next time around. Mainly, not get involved.

We hurried down the stairs, Joan in the lead, me tripping after her. Whether it was adrenaline or pure fear, something was giving us momentum. Finally it occurred to me to ask Joan where we were going.

She stopped in her tracks. "I don't know. I was just running."

In the darkness of the stairwell, Joan reached out her hand until she touched my shoulder. Then she gave it a squeeze, and I felt all the tension and panic start to melt away.

"What should we do?" she asked. And for the first time in hours, I found I could actually think clearly.

"I'm not sure what time it is, but Betsy must be arriving soon. We should stay within the house to intercept her."

"Right," Joan said.

"I'm sorry this is nothing like the library," I said. Joan was silent for a moment, then let out a barking laugh, which didn't stop. I hadn't even meant it as a joke, and Joan was doubling over, wheezing. I tried shushing her but it was no use.

Joan eventually got control of herself, taking a few deep breaths.

"This gig is not for sissies. The tunnels and staircases, the running for your life, the stealing of the murder weapon."

"Wait, what do you mean 'the stealing of the murder weapon'?"

In the dimness of the stairs, I spotted in Joan's hand the dull glimmer of the bloody letter opener.

"You took it! Joan, you're amazing!"

"I do what I can. Now before Betsy gets here, take me to the scene of the crime. Walk me through what happened to Josh Jorkavic. I feel like we're closer than ever before."

Maybe it was all bullshit, but Joan was giving me hope. We hightailed it to what I calculated was the basement. The stale incense smell was encouraging. Sure enough, when we opened the stairwell door, we'd made it to the red antechamber I'd seen the night of the McCarthys' sex party.

The room was chilly, and Joan marveled at the grotesque decor. She ran her fingers along the unlit candelabra resting on the credenza.

"It's right out of Poe," she murmured.

"That's comforting," I said.

In the semi-darkness, I led Joan to the main basement area and into the hallway that led to the cement room.

"At some point in the night, Josh was taken into this room where his neck was slit open. He bled out over this drain."

"And he was likely drugged," Joan said.

"Right, otherwise there would have been bruises or other signs of struggle."

"But then the next morning you found his body in the antechamber where we came in? So he would have had to bleed out during the party, then get moved to that room afterward," Joan said, her brow furrowing.

"The night before, I'm almost certain I saw Lenore Fisher walk in blindfolded, but I'm not sure what time that was."

"If they knew the right arteries to cut, it could take three minutes for Josh to bleed out. Then moving his body to another room would take another fifteen minutes. Longer if the murderer was working alone."

"What are you getting at, Joan?"

"There were three hallways coming off the main room in there. One that led to this room and one that led to the antechamber, so where does the third hallway lead?" Joan asked.

"The sex swing room," I said.

"Hold on a sec. What do you think Lenore Fisher meant when she talked about the little prank?" Joan asked.

We both started running toward the third hallway as fast as we could, my ankles be damned. Inside the third room, there was the bed and sex swing I'd seen earlier. What I hadn't seen before was a closet. I looked to Joan then took a deep breath and opened it.

Inside was an enormous console, with various buttons lit up and labeled. We looked closer at the labels. There was a button labeled *Party Noise,* and another labeled *Floor Creak.*

"What if there wasn't a party the night Josh Jorkavic died? What if they only tried to convince you there was?"

"Why would they do that?" I asked.

"Why would they do any of this?" Joan said.

"But the sounds that night, Joan . . ." I said, but my head was spinning. Something wasn't adding up. I reached out and pushed the button marked *Party Noise.* All around us, the moans began again. The moans I'd heard that night I snuck down to the Mc-Carthys' party. I thought about what Sybil had said about the Hunts' house being wired for blackmail, and this recording didn't seem so far-fetched.

"Wait! Turn that off!" Joan said with worry in her voice. I hit the button again, but the moans only got louder. "Turn it off now!" Joan shouted.

Again, I hit the button. This time the room fell silent.

"It must be on a two-setting system," I mumbled. But it was too late. Now I heard what had made Joan so nervous. Footsteps approaching on the basement stairs.

What do we do, Joan mouthed to me. I shook my head. I didn't know. The footsteps were now in the hallway just outside this room; I could hear them clearly. The person wore heavy shoes and walked at an even pace. I saw tears rolling down Joan's face, and I wrapped my arms around her. I felt her whole body tremble with fear, and I held tighter.

The door swung open, and Yanni stepped in. I found myself breathing for the first time in a minute.

"Holy fuck," Joan yelled, wiping her nose. "Please stop doing that, sir!"

"Next time don't hit the moan button. God, you two are terrible at sneaking around. Get upstairs, your friend is here." We followed Yanni back up the narrow staircase to the killer's room.

My ankles wobbled and my calves spasmed, and it occurred to me I'd never done so many stairs in my life. The gams were rightfully upset. After Murder Island, I promised myself no more exercise.

We entered the killer's room once again to find Betsy Clench lounging on the daybed. She was wearing one of the murderer's blond wigs under her sailor's hat and was pulling it off exquisitely.

"Gals," Betsy said, tipping her sailor's hat to us.

"That's it!" I said. Finally, I had a plan.

28

I couldn't help but notice Betsy in the blond bob wig looked an awful lot like both Luella van Horn and our new friend Lenore Fisher. I knew they wouldn't let Betsy into the party if they knew she was the ferry's first mate. But if they thought she was a VIP wearing a wig for anonymity like Ms. Fisher, they might. That would free me up to go there as someone no one on Murder Island had ever met: Marie Jones. But this plan put both me and Betsy at risk. There was a chance I was a target, which meant Betsy would be the new target. Part of me feared this was another setup, but I knew if I was going to catch the killer by tomorrow, this would be the only way.

Before all that, I'd have to come clean about my double identity to Betsy and, unfortunately, Yanni, which felt risky. What if they went public? What if they abandoned me right then and there because I wasn't the suave, sexy private eye they thought I was? Before I could dwell on it anymore, I removed my wig and let them decide for themselves. If they were going to abandon me, I'd rather know sooner than later.

They were having an ongoing conversation about what Betsy's fake name should be. The debate was between Betty and Sarong, with Joan pushing for Betty and Yanni strongly in favor of Sarong. Betsy seemed excited by both options. I sat there in my wig cap, but their conversation kept going. I cleared my throat, which caused them to briefly pause.

"You need a lozenge?" Betsy asked.

"My wig is off," I replied.

"Looks like it," Yanni said.

"I'm not really Luella van Horn—" I said, but Betsy cut me off.

"Ludacris, it doesn't matter. So you wear a wig, so what?"

"Wait, you knew I wore a wig?" I asked.

Betsy looked to Joan and Yanni before looking back at me. "Well, sometimes your hair slips off your head."

"And it's always perfectly coiffed," Yanni said.

"And it looks like a wig," Betsy said. "A nice wig. But definitely a wig."

"Ah," I said. I felt something inside me deflate. I wasn't fooling anyone.

"But that doesn't matter," Betsy said. "Who cares if you wear a wig and have those big fake veneers. I'm going to a sex party tonight because of you. You've made my dreams come true, Labubu!"

Joan chimed in, too. "Wear the wig, don't wear the wig, you're still an incredible private eye."

Joan and Betsy looked to Yanni to add something to this pep talk. He cleared his throat and finally said, "I've been wanting to get back at these people for ages. If you weren't here, it'd never happen."

I removed the wig cap and shook out my frizzy brown hair. "Let's do this."

Yanni had heard tonight was the infamous Underwear Party, which made me feel a little sick. He snuck out to grab some of Caitlin's old lingerie. Betsy was beyond stoked. Joan said nothing, but the twinkle in her eye gave something away. I had to accept it: my friends were sluts.

Betsy had brought with her three theatrical half masks, their insides stamped with PROPERTY OF NYU TISCH COSTUME DEPARTMENT. Turned out that guy Charlie she was sitting next to at the bar was a graduate student there, and like everyone who crossed paths with Betsy Clench, wanted to help. Yanni came back with an armful of Caitlin's lingerie in various shades of white and cream.

"You look like a pervert," Betsy said.

"Don't make me do that ever again. If anyone caught me, I'd be fired on the spot," he said, heaping Caitlin's underwear onto the daybed. We sifted through the pile for something that could possibly fit each of us. Caitlin was a tiny woman, and it was clear we'd be pushing the limits of what these garments were capable of. Respectfully, Yanni offered to turn away while we disrobed.

Even if the lingerie was small, it was better than what we were all currently wearing. Between the three of us, it was like we were competing in a World's Ugliest Underwear Contest. The elastic around Betsy's right leg was loose, Joan's was from 1987, and mine sagged like a wet diaper.

Eventually we found something that would work for each of us. Betsy wore an ivory negligee that went down almost to her hip; Joan wore her own bra (brown, full coverage, reinforced two-inch-thick back straps) and a cream-colored slip; and I got a silk camisole and a garter belt situation I'd rather not get into here. All I'll say is it was a shit ton of hooks. Getting it on basically earned me a degree in civil engineering.

We all wore the masks for anonymity. The finishing touch was putting my wig on Betsy. I tucked her short hair into the wig cap and placed the blond wig over that, combing the bangs just so to cover any wig lines. I smiled to myself. She looked just like Luella van Horn. *Who did that make me?* I wondered.

Yanni agreed to take us to the party so we wouldn't get lost, and just as we were about to leave, Betsy spotted the strap-on.

"And who are you?" she murmured, picking up the apparatus and attaching the leather straps around her hips. The marble penis poked through the negligée. "Okay, now I'm ready!"

"You sure you're okay doing this?" I asked Betsy. "What if they try to kill you thinking you're me?"

"Then I'll try to kill them, and I'll give you the credit."

I shook my head. There was no reasoning with this woman.

Knowing Mark would already be at the party by now, Yanni searched for Frank. When he couldn't find him, Yanni declared the coast cleared and we snuck out the front door, piling into an old golf cart Yanni claimed the McCarthys didn't remember buying. He drove us to the Hunts' compound. Even if we were practically naked and going to track down a murderer, it was nice not having to travel via darkened tunnel. My ankles agreed.

We pulled up to the Hunts' front door. Before Yanni even stopped the golf cart, Betsy had already hopped out and was jogging in place. The strap-on bounced near the hem of her negligee.

"Wait a minute," I said. "Let's go over the plan one more time. We go in there, we divide up and look for someone who's acting suspicious. Maybe they're giving out those blue pills or trying to get someone away from the party, or they react strangely to that strap-on."

"The Rooster," Joan clarified, looking at Betsy.

"Right. And once we find them, we call out for the others. Do not apprehend them alone. They will be dangerous," I said.

Joan reached around in her left bra cup. "That's why I brought this!" She held out the bloody letter opener.

"Joan, it's a little unconventional to protect yourself with the potential murder weapon," I said. She responded with a salute.

Yanni wished us luck, and Joan, Betsy, and I walked arm in arm toward the entrance. Even if they did spoil the evidence, I had to admit it was fun being part of a little team.

"Damn, this thing is heavy," Betsy whispered, adjusting her marble attachment. She thrust back and forth a few times. "This is going to take some endurance."

As we approached, Sybil opened the door but didn't seem to recognize us. She only nodded and welcomed us solemnly. The NYU masks were doing their job.

Inside, the party was already in full swing. Underwear had been the theme, but at this point most people were already naked. Luckily we weren't the only ones with the mask idea. Several people kept their faces covered. I spotted Mark Fontaine talking to an older man in a mask near the baby grand piano. Mark squinted at me, and I quickly turned away.

I scanned the expansive living room, where people had spread out in the early stages of lovemaking. There were more people at this party than usual. I only recognized half of them. Edmund and Sierra Hunt were busy "Eiffel Towering" (Betsy taught me the phrase) an older gentleman. I spotted Carla Jorkavic talking to

Lenore Fisher, whose resemblance to Betsy Clench in my wig was uncanny. The only people who seemed to be missing from the core group were Caitlin McCarthy, obviously, and Bradford Tyler. I wondered where he was.

Betsy's strap-on was quickly the life of the party. She was beckoned to a dark corner to demonstrate the power of the marble phallus. Joan was so nervous, she ordered an Old Fashioned and chugged half of it. I got a club soda. I needed to stay alert.

We both kept an eye out for suspicious activity. Mark Fontaine got up abruptly and sauntered over to Lindsay Peterson, whispered something in her ear, and palmed her something that Lindsay slipped into the pocket of her satin robe. Joan and I looked to each other. Was Mark targeting his next victim?

We followed him down a dark hallway, large votives lighting the walls from below. I couldn't see five feet ahead of me, but I felt Joan nearby, and then I smelled roses again. I thought immediately of the secret third-floor room and the note cards. I heard the ice in Joan's drink tinkle against the glass.

"Was that you?" she asked me. "Did you just touch my glass?"

"No," I said. I was too disoriented to understand what was happening, but I should've known.

"Hello?" I said, addressing the darkness. "Is someone there?" No one answered, and soon I could no longer smell roses.

The hallway eventually led us toward a kitchen. Two people could be heard talking inside, and we lingered in the dim hallway to listen.

"You're not Luella van Horn . . ." a man's voice said. I knew that voice. It was Mark Fontaine.

29

What I know now is that Joan Clyborn is a wild card, but I did not know it then. If I had, I would've told her not to do exactly what she did.

Before I could stop her, Joan jumped into the door frame with the bloody letter opener raised high.

"Let her go," Joan said. I moved closer to the door to see who was with Mark Fontaine. He was holding Betsy Clench by the throat. He'd backed her into a corner right as Joan stepped in to save the day with the letter opener.

The kitchen was immense, and Mark held Betsy at least thirty feet from us.

"Mark, step away from her," I said.

Mark looked up, surprised, then regained his focus on Betsy. He kept one hand on Betsy's throat while he used his other hand to nervously rub his neck. "None of this makes sense . . . Something is wrong!"

"What do you mean?" I asked.

"Luella's supposed to be back in the city, and . . ." He turned to face Betsy. "No, this isn't right at all. Who are you?" Mark held Betsy's neck tighter, and her face began to turn purple.

Joan charged at Mark with the letter opener pointed directly at his heart. "*Let her go!*" she screamed. They both toppled to the ground, eventually bringing Betsy with them. Mark yelled in pain, clutching his chest.

I ran over to assess the damage. Would the third death on this island be Joan's fault? Then I noticed there was no blood.

"Damn, that thing is dull," Mark said, pointing at Joan's letter opener. He rubbed his chest some more. "If you've bruised me, I'll sue you for everything you've got."

If the letter opener couldn't even break skin with momentum, what did that mean for it being the murder weapon that killed Josh Jorkavic? Was it possible this was just a severe-looking letter opener? If so, why was it bloody?

Now that I was closer to Mark Fontaine, he squinted at me again. The man really needed his glasses back. "*You* are Luella," he said, pointing a stubby finger at me. "So who's she?" he asked, gesturing to Betsy. "And where's my wife?"

Out of the corner of my eye, I could see Joan dusting herself off. But Betsy was gone.

"Where's Betsy?" I asked Joan. "Where did she go?" Joan shook her head, her eyes revealing a deep fear. "We need to find her!" I shouted, then we both turned to go.

Then came the sound of metal scraping against wood. "Now wait a minute. I asked you a question," Mark said, brandishing a butcher knife from a nearby block. "You're not going anywhere until you tell me where my wife is. I know you know."

Both Joan and I put our hands up and backed against the kitchen wall. This was the second time I'd been cornered by Mark Fontaine in a stranger's kitchen on Murder Island. My mind raced. What did I know? Two people had possibly been murdered, and Endeavors was somehow involved. Caitlin McCarthy had been cheating on her husband with Josh Jorkavic. The Hunts were planning to buy up the island's properties. And Murder Island was basically one giant sex cult that stayed clandestine because the people involved were so rich and powerful that if anyone let anything slip, it would come back to haunt them. It was structured so that keeping quiet was in everyone's best interests. That's why people like Walter Stanford didn't last long around here. Then there was the bloody letter opener too dull to be a weapon, and all those blond wigs in that room on the third floor. Who was behind it all? Was it the man standing in front of us holding a knife?

"We need to find Betsy. I'm afraid she's in danger," Joan whispered to me. I nodded. I mean I was on the same page. We just needed to get past Mark's knife, which would require some ingenuity.

"I've come back to get another rabies shot in my ass," I said with as much conviction as I could muster. "Dr. Tyler said I'd need one at exactly midnight tonight to stay on schedule, otherwise I'll start foaming at the mouth."

"You have rabies now?" he asked.

"I was attacked by a bat while staying on your property. And I will be filing for worker's compensation in small claims court, where I'm sure nothing else illegal will come up for you or your family if my lawyers start digging around. If your property is important to you, I would drop the knife now, before that lawsuit expands to include assault with a deadly weapon."

There are two problems with threatening to sue the über rich. One: they have access to better lawyers, and two: they have so much money they don't give a fuck. This is a major lesson I learned that day when my threat did nothing to stop Mark Fontaine.

A large marble island marked the center of the kitchen. Mark and his knife were currently on one side while Joan and I were on the other. Suddenly Mark lunged toward us, and we ran the other way around, narrowly missing the tip of his blade. Mark was faster, and I could feel the heat from his body as Joan and I ran into the walk-in pantry and slammed the door behind us. I could see the doorknob wiggling and needed to think fast. We could only hold him off for so long. He wanted us dead, and he was the type who got what he wanted.

"What do we do?" Joan asked.

That's when I got an idea. One of my dumber ones.

"When I say *help,* let Mark in."

"*What!* Why?" Joan said.

There was no time to explain. I left Joan to hold the pantry door while I found baking soda and poured half the box into my mouth. It was so salty I started crying, which only furthered my cause.

"Help!" I gabbled, giving Joan the signal.

Mark yanked open the pantry door to find Joan dumbstruck and me foaming at the mouth. It certainly conveyed *rabies in full swing.* Mark's face took on a panicked expression as he backed out of the pantry.

"Don't let him get away," I tried to say, but the foam kept coming and coming, and I retched up the baking soda I'd accidentally swallowed. Joan whipped out her letter opener and chased Mark out of the kitchen. Meanwhile, I just had to throw up a little bit more before I could join in on the fun. When I finally caught up with Joan, she was standing outside the Hunts' front door, panting. Mark was gone—she'd lost him.

We tried to formulate a plan. Mark was still our main suspect, and his running away didn't lend him any more credibility. So the agenda was catch Mark, find Betsy, and get the hell home. It seemed doable when we put it like that.

"Marie, I don't feel right."

"What do you mean?" I asked.

"In the hallway, someone put something in my drink. I think it was that blue pill."

Just then, I clocked someone with a blond bob walking toward a white Range Rover in the driveway.

"Look," I whispered to Joan. "Maybe it's Betsy." She nodded.

We quickly followed the blond woman. "Betsy?" I shout-whispered. "Betsy, is that you?"

The woman turned around. It took me a minute in the moonlight to distinguish her delicate features, her wide-set eyes, now furious. It took another minute to realize she wasn't dead.

"Caitlin?" I asked.

Caitlin McCarthy was wearing a blond wig and a white leather jumpsuit that looked like it cost the same as one hundred acres of land in Michigan.

"Are you two wearing my underwear?" Caitlin asked.

I didn't want to answer that. "How are you alive?" I asked instead.

"We thought you were dead," Joan said.

"I was almost dead, which is basically the same thing. There's no time for questions. As long as Mark is out there, we've got to go! I tried to warn you!"

"What about Betsy?" I asked.

"I'm sure she's with Mark! Come on, get in! We can't let them get away!"

We quickly got into Caitlin's car. I was in front and Joan sat in the back. Before we were buckled in, Caitlin pressed hard on the gas pedal. I was thrown back and scrambled for my seatbelt.

Caitlin drove down the one-lane road at eighty miles an hour. If we had a head-on collision with someone going the opposite way, we were toast. I grabbed onto my seatbelt buckle as if that would help. The road curved, and Caitlin took it fast, so everyone in the car, including her, was swept to the opposite side.

"What do you think Mark plans to do with Betsy?" I asked through clenched veneers.

"I'm not sure. You know he killed Josh Jorkavic? And you've been digging around too much. He plans to kill you, too, Luella. He's got those zombie drugs, and he's built up a tolerance, but he got Josh to overdose, and he almost did the same thing to me. We need to get to the city where there is actual law enforcement before it's too late."

"I thought we were trying to find Mark and Betsy? Why would we go into the city?" I asked.

"Well, if we catch Mark . . . we'll need back up!" she said, her foot not letting up on the gas.

We had just zoomed past the Tylers' castle when the Range Rover buckled. Something was in the road, and as Caitlin drove over it, we all felt it. It was something big, like a deer.

"What was that?" I asked, turning to look out the rear window. First thing I saw was Joan passed out in the backseat. Then I saw what we'd hit.

"Stop the car!" I yelled. Caitlin swerved to the right side of the road but stayed in the driver's seat.

"What the fuck!" Caitlin screamed. She slammed on the horn, which blared in the quiet night. I jumped out of the car.

Bradford Tyler was lying still in the middle of the pavement. A tire track stained his creased khaki shorts. I called out his name as I ran toward him.

His eyes were closed and his limbs sprawled out, making him resemble a starfish. I knelt on the ground beside him and felt for a pulse. There was a faint one.

"Bradford!" I called again. "Bradford, it's Luella. Can you hear me? Can you open your eyes for me?"

I sprinted to the Tylers' front door and began banging on it. "Help!" I screamed. "Somebody help!"

Within a minute, the Tylers' butler had burst out the door, running toward the street with me right behind. He dropped to his knees and tenderly took Bradford's round face in his large hands.

"Sir! Sir, can you hear me?" he asked, gently shaking him.

Bradford's eyes fluttered open, and he looked at the two of us. His voice was soft and throaty as he spoke. "It's over, it's all over. Thank god."

"Sir, stay with me now!" The butler rose to his feet and scooped up Bradford like a baby, like I'd seen him do before. "I'm going to get his wife. He needs medical attention now!"

"Wait!" I said. "My friend! She needs help, too!"

The butler followed me over to Caitlin's car, where Joan was lying in the backseat.

"Get her up," he said sternly. I opened the car door, and with strength I didn't know I had, I pulled Joan out and stood her next to me, propping her up with my shoulder under her arm. The butler held a phone light into her eyes.

"She's been drugged with scopolamine. It will wear off eventually. She'll be fine, but later, she won't remember anything that's happened. Be careful with her now, as she'll be very impressionable on that nonsense."

"Joan?" I asked. "Joan, can you hear me?"

"I can!" she said softly, rubbing her eyes.

"Can you stand on your own?" I asked. She nodded, and I eased out from under her. "Thank you," I said to the butler.

With that, he ran back to the house with Bradford in his arms. Behind us, we heard Caitlin's wheels screeching against the pavement. The front of her car had a human-sized dent in it, and she may have killed Bradford, and still she was driving off.

"Where's she going without us?" Joan asked.

And where'd she get that wig? I wondered. Caitlin was alive, blond, and didn't give a damn about possibly killing Bradford Tyler. Was she possibly out of her mind with fear? Joan had been drugged, and Mark Fontaine was on the lam because he likely killed Josh Jorkavic and planned to kill Betsy. With all this excitement, I really would've preferred to be wearing something besides Caitlin's tiny lingerie.

30

The butler stopped midway up the sidewalk and turned to us with Bradford's limp body in his arms.

"You need to follow her," he said, fishing something out of his pocket. "Take Bradford's car. Do not let Caitlin get away with this!" He tossed Joan the car keys, which she caught, because she's more coordinated than any drugged librarian should've been. I yanked them out of her hands before she could get herself into the driver's seat.

"Will he be okay?" I asked him.

"I don't know," the butler said. "I hope so."

"Will she?" I said, looking at Joan.

He nodded. "Of course. The high only lasts an hour, and as long as she's with you, she's safe. But I wonder who gave it to her, because whoever it is, they must've wanted her pliable."

"Very cool," Joan said, flashing the butler a peace sign. I grabbed her hand and put her in the passenger seat.

Murder Island obviously had no streetlights, and by the time I figured out how to start the Tylers' car (that key fob thing was for the birds), Caitlin was long gone. So were Mark and Betsy, for that matter. Still, there were only so many places on the island one could go. I decided to head toward the dock, since Caitlin had mentioned she wanted to get to the city. There was always the chance at least one person on this island was telling me the truth.

I was going sixty down a dark road when Joan scared the shit out of me by shouting, "How'd we end up here?"

"We're chasing Caitlin."

"Why?" she asked.

"Because she almost killed Bradford Tyler and she's our only living witness."

"Oh," Joan said, then was silent for a moment. "What about the other guy?"

"Mark Fontaine?" I asked. "What about him?"

"Are you sure he's the killer?" she said, now somehow holding a packet of peanut M&M's.

"Where'd you get those?" I asked, temporarily distracted by the existence of food. It'd been awhile since we ate. She surprised me by popping three into my mouth. "Thank you," I said, chewing. They were the most delicious things I'd ever tasted. The combination of sugar and that little bit of protein was just what I needed to fire up my brain again.

"Joan, you don't think Mark is the killer?"

"No," she said calmly as she popped another couple of M&M's into my mouth.

I chewed gratefully. "Why not?"

In my peripheral vision, I saw Joan turn to face me. "You're so beautiful," she said.

"Thank you, Joan. Mark Fontaine had means and motive to kill Josh, and Caitlin just told us he tried to kill her, too. He also might have Betsy right now. Why don't you think Mark is our guy?"

She didn't answer, and instead chose that moment to nuzzle my shoulder. "We need to find Betsy."

"I know," I said, patting her head.

We got to the dock fifteen minutes later, and I parked on a side street. The moon was high in the sky and the roads were empty, painting the downtown area an eerie silvery white.

We had just gotten out of the car when Joan grabbed my elbow. "Look!" she said, pointing at the sky. "Aliens!"

I looked up and saw a helicopter descending on the shore. So that's how Caitlin was getting to the city. I grabbed Joan's hand as we ran toward it, but the helicopter was farther away than I thought. By the time it landed, we were still nearly three blocks away and wheezing. Joan hunched over gasping for breath, her hands on her knees, while I accepted the fact that both my ankles would probably fall off.

I saw two figures running toward the helicopter, one dragging the other one, but I couldn't tell who they were in the darkness. We had to get closer, and we didn't have much time. The helicopter was already midair by the time we got close enough to see two blond wigs. For some reason, Betsy Clench was on that helicopter with Caitlin.

"Betsy!" I screamed. "Betsy, we're here!"

But the sound of the helicopter's blades drowned me out as it lifted higher and began flying west, toward the water.

"How did Caitlin and Betsy end up together?" Joan asked. I was wondering the same thing. Did Mark Fontaine manage to capture them both? Something wasn't making sense.

Joan had brought the bag of peanut M&M's with her and was continuing to eat them by the handful. "I don't think Betsy's safe at all." Joan began sobbing.

"Joan, it'll be okay! We won't let anything happen to Betsy!"

She was silent for a moment, then looked at me with a blank stare. "Do we have any more of those chocolate morsels?"

31

"They're going to Manhattan, right? So we need to get to Manhattan," I said to Joan, who kept nodding at me even though it was clear she was retaining none of what I was saying. "But how do we do that?"

She nodded solemnly.

"No, Joan, I'm *asking* you, how do we get to Manhattan?"

"We go the way we came," she said, slowly pointing to Betsy's boat.

I considered it for a moment. "You know, that's not a bad idea."

We walked over to where Betsy had moored the ferry. After a few false starts, I finally got the rope knots untied. Joan stood back and sniffled.

"We'll get you more peanut M&M's once we get to the city, Joan. Please stop crying."

"This isn't going to end well," Joan said between sobs.

"Joan, this is not the time for prophecies."

"Have I ever told you you have the most beautiful teeth? They look like index cards . . ." Joan began mumbling to herself while I yanked her up onto the ferry's deck. Drugged Joan required more patience than I was equipped with. I dragged her onto the bridge, which was where the command deck was stationed. And if you think I knew all these words before I went on a boat, think again. I'm out here googling stuff like "boat floor" and "hot place on boat where I had to steer inside" like the rest of you.

The command deck was equipped with two phones, a bunch

of dials, maybe fifty buttons, and what looked like a joystick. I turned to Joan.

"Do you know how to operate this thing?" I asked.

She nodded confidently, then began licking the window. I rubbed my temples and let out a long sigh. *The perks of having a partner,* I thought.

Surveying all the possible buttons and knobs, I bit my lower lip. "Okay, this should be like driving a car. Except the road is water. And the car is a boat. Right, Joan?"

Joan kept licking the window, which I took as an affirmative. The key had been left in the ignition (thank you, Betsy!). I turned it and the damn thing came to life. Step one, done!

The ferry deck rumbled under my feet. Now I just had to push the right button or buttons that would make it go. Then I heard a rap at the door and saw the knob jiggle.

"Who's in there?" a man's voice yelled. I knew that voice. Mark Fontaine. How was he possibly on this boat with us? And what did that mean for Caitlin and Betsy's situation on the helicopter?

Before I could process what to do next, Joan yelled, "It is I, Captain James Beauregard, sir!"

What are you doing, I mouthed to her. She shrugged and smiled at me.

"Captain Beauregard, I'm warning you, I have a weapon. Do you hear it?" Mark banged something against the metal door, making a loud clank. "I will spare your life, if and *only if* you do as I say," he said. "Take me to Manhattan now!"

"Aye, aye, sir! Captain James Beauregard is on it!" Joan yelled. I ran my finger repeatedly over my throat to stop her from saying any more. She finally took the hint.

"I'll be right outside this door. There will be no funny business!" he shouted, clanging his weapon against the door once more.

If there wasn't pressure before, now our lives were on the line. *Buttons, buttons, buttons,* I thought. *Might as well push them all.* It took several combinations, but somehow (and I'll never know exactly how), I got the boat moving. Then there was the issue of directions.

"Joan?" I said, causing her to temporarily pause her close-up palm examination. "You don't happen to remember how to get to lower Manhattan, do you? Or maybe your phone could come alive again?"

"The current is moving southeast to northwest. If we follow the current, turning sixty degrees after we pass Rat Island, we should see the Statue of Liberty. It's a clear night and the tide is low, so I don't foresee us having any trouble."

I was so relieved to hear this. It almost sounded simple! Then I remembered Joan was high. "Joan, did you just make all that up?"

"No," she said emphatically.

"You promise? Because if you're making all that up, and we don't make it to Manhattan, Mark Fontaine will kill us."

"He won't kill us, and we'll get to Manhattan," she said. "Then I'll get more M&M's." She closed her eyes and licked her lips.

I'll be honest, I blacked out for most of that boat ride. Every few minutes, Mark would bang on the door, threatening Captain Beauregard's life. The waters were so turbulent it had made Joan seasick. She was hurling loudly in the corner of the bridge when Mark asked what was going on.

"It's never taken this long before!" he yelled.

"It's the winds, sir. They're blowing east," Joan said between retching. I had to admit, Captain James Beauregard was pretty convincing, all things considered.

By the time we saw Lady Liberty, I was ready to believe in god. Or Joan. Or a combination of the two. All that vomiting had sobered Joan a bit, which was helpful because I hadn't thought of a plan for how to get us off the boat. Maybe Mark wouldn't kill James Beauregard (he'd want a ride home after all), but I couldn't imagine him deciding to let Joan and me live once he realized who we were.

Somehow I parked the ferry with the help of several old men who were spending their evening hanging around the docks. Six of them shouted at me at the same time, all with different instructions, but eventually they got me moored at Pier 24.

"Captain, I'm leaving now. You stay right where you are!" Mark hollered.

Joan was busy resting her head on her knees in the corner when I demanded she get with the program. *Speak,* I mouthed.

"Not to worry, sir," Joan shouted. "I seem to have come down with a case of ol' seaman's worms!"

"What in the hell is old seaman's worms?" I whispered, but Joan only shook her head and held up her hands. She was coming down from the drugs, and she was out of ideas.

"Well . . . if you want to stay alive"—he rapped his weapon once more against the bridge door—"don't follow me!"

My eyes grew wide as they met Joan's. The only thing we had going for us was that Mark would be looking over his shoulder for a man named Captain James Beauregard, and he couldn't see shit without his glasses. The last people he expected to see were Joan Clyborne and Marie Jones. That could work to our advantage.

I waited until I stopped hearing his footsteps on the deck, then I pulled Joan to her feet. "Let's go!" I said. She groaned in response. "If we can prove Mark is the killer and find Betsy and Caitlin, I'll buy you a chocolate milkshake."

"Okay," she grumbled. "Did you know the first milkshake ever served was at a Walgreens in Chicago in 1922?"

I breathed a sigh of relief. Joan was back.

32

As we got off the boat in front of all my old-man helpers, I realized we were both still wearing a tiny woman's expensive underwear.

"Prepare yourself for hoots and hollers," I said under my breath just as the first catcalls began.

"I'm in love!" a man with a scraggly beard shouted.

"I have a wife but I'd leave her!" said another one with only one visible tooth.

"I've died and gone to heaven! Two angels walk before me!" This from a man wearing suspenders but no shirt.

"I'd take Viagra for you two!" the shortest one yelled.

We hobbled as fast as we could toward FDR Drive. Eventually the men's voices were drowned out by sounds of passing traffic. I scanned under the streetlights for any sign of Mark Fontaine. At last, I spotted him limping west at the crosswalk, and we hurried to get closer. The ideal distance for trailing someone in New York is half a city block.

"I'm sorry, why are we following him?" Joan asked. Of course, the drugs made it so she remembered nothing.

"Mark might have plans to kill Caitlin. Caitlin's with Betsy, so Mark may lead us to both of them. Save Betsy, figure out what to do with Caitlin, and apprehend Mark without getting ourselves killed."

"Got it," Joan said. "Why am I in someone else's underwear?"

"That's a conversation for another time, Joan! We're losing him!"

Mark was moving faster now. He headed south on Lexington and through Madison Square Park where he did a loop, then started running north on Madison Avenue. He looked over his shoulder, and we quickly ducked behind two tree trunks.

"Where do you think he's going?" Joan asked.

"Not sure. I get the sense he's trying to lose us. He must know someone's following him."

"Speaking of . . . do you know that man?" Joan asked, pointing to someone fifty feet behind us. I turned, and my body broke out in a cold sweat as I saw his outline illuminated by the neon sign of a halal cart. I'd know that figure anywhere.

"C'mon. We gotta go," I said, quickly hobbling uptown. I didn't care if we found Mark Fontaine, but we needed to get the hell away from Taylor Bell. I was starting to think that man had put a goddamn AirTag on me.

Joan followed me, turning once more to catch a glimpse of the man who gave me such a fright. "He's gaining on us," she said. I figured.

"Quick! Let's go up Sixth Avenue. Fewer tourists means faster locals." We ran west to Fifth, then north until Thirty-Third Street, then west again until we hit Sixth Avenue, where we tucked into a bodega to catch our breath. The owner glanced up then pretended to ignore us. We were back in the city, all right.

"We're practically at my library," Joan said between gasps. I looked out the glass door for signs of Taylor Bell approaching, but I couldn't find him. It was possible we'd lost him.

Joan bought two blue Gatorades with a damp, rumpled ten-dollar bill she'd fished out of her full-coverage bra. There'd been a letter opener in there plus cash—that thing was like a Mary Poppins bag. Joan offered me a Gatorade, but I declined. I still couldn't drink the stuff since the *Sex Island* case, where I'd been slowly poisoned by antifreeze Gatorade cocktails. She chugged them both, then screamed, "*I feel alive again!*" She pounded her chest and the bodega owner buried his face in his newspaper.

That's when I saw that day's headline: STATEN ISLAND FIERY BREAK-IN, ACQUITTED MURDERER TO BLAME. I felt like I was dreaming. "Can I see that paper?" I asked.

"It'll be a dollar twenty-five," the bodega owner said.

"To *see* the paper?"

He tutted. "I don't know where you've been."

Joan fished the damp change back out of her bra and plopped it onto the counter. The man tossed me the paper like he didn't want it anyway.

I read the cover story hungrily. I needed to know *where* in Staten Island, *which* acquitted murderer. The more I read, the more the walls seemed to close in around me. The bright overhead lights flared and it was like I could smell everything in there at once: the rat poison, the cold cuts, the off-brand candy, the dust. My vision blurred. I felt something soft rub against my bare arm. A long-haired white cat came into focus. It had a pink nose and black paws and a swooping belly. That was the last thing I saw before I fainted.

I woke to a woman shouting, "Marie!" I turned my head in the direction of the voice. Joan was bent over me with a cold wet washcloth.

"Taylor Bell set my ex-husband's house on fire. He's the man who's been following us, and I think he's trying to kill me," I said, trying to sit up. People sound less crazy when they sit up. That's something I took from social work.

The bodega door jingled, and the four of us (including the cat) looked up. Taylor Bell stood in the doorway. In my nightmares, I'd played out this scenario countless ways. But each time, I'd wake up before he could do anything to me. Right at the last second, I'd find myself lying in my own bed, sheets kicked to the floor, drenched in sweat. But this time, it was real. Taylor Bell was standing before me in the flesh. I tried staggering to my feet.

"Marie Jones, we need to talk."

33

steadied my breath. "What are you doing here, Taylor?"

"Someone's trying to frame me," he said.

"I've heard that one from you before," I said.

"I mean it," he said. I looked at his large, callused hands. The bitten nails, the hairy knuckles. I thought about what those hands had done, what they were capable of doing again. He continued. "I didn't break into your house."

"It's not even my house, it's my ex-husband's."

"I know," he said. His white T-shirt clung to his chest and his dark brown hair matted against his forehead. He must've been running for a while.

"You shouldn't know where my ex-husband lives," I said. "You shouldn't be in my life, you should be in jail."

"Do I call the cops?" the bodega owner asked.

I nodded my head, but Taylor yelled, "Don't! Marie, you need to hear me out. You know me better than anyone. I was your client!"

The bodega owner looked to Joan and wordlessly handed her a rusty crowbar, which she accepted and held at the ready. Taylor clocked this but continued to speak directly to me.

"I'm not some manipulative monster. I know you think I am, but I didn't kill my wife, and I'm not trying to kill you."

"Then why'd you break into my ex-husband's house?" I asked.

"You're not going to believe me, but I was framed. I wasn't there! I mean, I was there, I'll admit that. I was trying to find you, but I didn't break in. And I didn't set that fire. But I'm certain whoever did is trying to get to you through me. You're in danger, Marie. I want to help you."

Of all the what-the-fuck moments in my life, this was making it into the top five.

"Why were you trying to find me?" I asked. Joan lifted the crowbar ever so slightly.

"For years, you've been convinced I'm a cold-blooded killer. We were close once. I needed to set the record straight."

"I've fallen for this act before. I'm not doing it again," I said, nodding to Joan, who promptly moved in front of me with the crowbar ready to strike. "If you'll excuse us, we have a case to solve." I walked backward to the bodega's entrance and Joan followed. The bells jingled once again, and I maintained eye contact with Taylor as Joan and I stepped out. "Don't follow us."

Before the door could shut, Joan tossed the crowbar back to the bodega owner, who saluted her. Once we got around the corner, it all hit me.

"Mark Fontaine is long gone," I said, feeling the sense of failure creep in. "I'll be honest, Joan, I don't know what to do now."

"Let's go to the library," Joan said. "We'll be safe there to plan our next steps." She hailed a passing yellow cab and we hopped in. It was late, and there wasn't much traffic. The night air was cool, so I rolled down my window, letting the breeze ruffle my frizzy hair. Couldn't do that in a wig.

"So that's Taylor Bell. I remember reading about his murdered wife. I must've read about you, too. He was your client?"

"Long story," I said, looking at the moon from my open window.

"You know, even if we don't solve this case, we got really close to it. That's why they're running from us," Joan said.

"How do you know?"

"I'm a librarian. I know everything."

We were three blocks from the library when I saw strange red lights in the night sky accompanied by the sound of wind beating against metal. "Is that . . ." I began.

Joan looked up. "A helicopter. What are the chances . . ."

"Sir, follow that helicopter!" I yelled to the cabbie.

"Lord," he mumbled. "I swear, y'all are the last crazy people I'm dealing with tonight. After this, I'm going *home*."

The helicopter seemed to be heading toward Times Square, which meant we had to head to Times Square, which made the cabbie grumble even more. But if Caitlin and Betsy were in there, it'd all be worth it. This would mean Mark was heading to Times Square, too. I realized I was still shaking from my encounter with Taylor Bell, but I had to focus. Times Square, Josh Jorkavic, the zombie drugs, the weird animal symbols, Caitlin McCarthy, Mark Fontaine, the extremely limited real estate that was Murder Island. When you put it all together, what did it mean?

We were nearly at Forty-Second Street when Joan tapped me on the elbow.

"Marie, why do you think Caitlin was wearing a blond wig?"

"Maybe to disguise herself from Mark?"

"But doesn't Mark Fontaine being the killer make a little too much sense? I keep thinking about how Caitlin's wig looked an awful lot like yours."

I instinctively ran my hand along my hairline. My mind raced through everything I'd seen, everything that had happened. Caitlin in the helicopter with Betsy, the blond bob wig, the locked room, the secret stairs, the sex parties, the affair, the bat, Bradford Tyler. Caitlin had hit him with her car then driven off. But the crazier thing was, he felt relieved.

"Joan. What do you think Bradford meant when he said it was all over?"

"He must've recognized Caitlin's car. He must've known Caitlin was the one who hit him."

"I think you're right, Joan. Mark might not be our killer after all. But that makes this case a whole lot more complicated."

34

The helicopter descended on a skyscraper helipad on Forty-Fourth Street and Eighth Avenue. The cab dropped us off a block away, at the corner of Forty-Fourth and Broadway. From fifty stories down, I could still make out two blondes stepping out into the floodlights, one grabbing the other. But then who was piloting the helicopter?

"C'mon," I said, clutching Joan's hand. "I see them!" We were moving west toward the building when I got the feeling someone was behind us. I turned to see a Times Square Iron Man only three feet away.

"Not interested," I said as curtly as possible, pushing myself to hobble faster through the throngs of Times Square tourists, even at this late hour.

"Why is Iron Man following us?" Joan asked, moving swiftly through a family with three young children on leashes. I turned my head to check. She was right. Iron Man was chasing us like we were that purple guy played by Josh Brolin.

"Do you think it's Taylor Bell?" Joan asked. I could sense the panic in her voice. It was cruel to involve her in all this. I knew there was an alley coming up, and I yelled for us to duck in there. The alley had three dumpsters and a stage door for a new musical called *MenoSTART*.

We both doubled over, trying to catch our breath. My ankles throbbed, and I found myself crying from the pain. But there was no Iron Man in sight. We'd lost him. I was so relieved.

"Ooh, I've wanted to see that," Joan murmured, reading the stage door sign.

Just then, he appeared under the orange streetlight. I could see the scuff marks on his bulky costume, the runs in his tights.

"*What do you want?*" I yelled.

He stepped closer.

"*Get away from us!*" Joan screamed.

Iron Man reached for his helmet. The Rolodex of who it could be whipped through my mind—Taylor Bell, Mark Fontaine, Yanni Toumis, Frank Fisher? It could even be a homicidal stranger for all this night was bringing. Then the helmet was off, and I couldn't believe my eyes.

Popping out from the bulky costume, Leslie's head looked like a piece of Pez candy. Leslie, as in my ex-husband. As in the man who refused to let me live in the house we once owned together that was now burned down. As in the last person in the world I expected to see.

"Leslie, you're Iron Man?" I screamed. My voice was hoarse.

"Marie, I've been running after you for blocks now. Do you know how heavy this costume is? Why didn't you slow down?"

"I don't know, Leslie, maybe because you looked like fucking Iron Man!"

"Right," he said, nodding. "I do embody the character fairly well."

"Leslie, is this what you meant by getting into acting?"

"It's just a gig. Paying my dues, you know. Everyone's gotta do it," he said, stretching his neck from side to side.

"Who is this?" Joan whispered to me.

"Who are *you*?" Leslie asked, trying but failing to fold his bulky plastic-sleeved arms.

"Um. Leslie, this is my friend Joan. Joan, this is my once-practical ex-husband, Leslie."

"I'm an actor," Leslie said, shaking Joan's hand with his enormous Iron Man glove.

"I'm a librarian," Joan said. Leslie nodded approvingly. What an asshole.

"I've been so worried, Marie. After our house caught fire, I tried to call but I couldn't reach you. I thought you might be in danger. Then I saw you step out of that cab! It was a sign. You needed my help."

"I needed your help before!" I shouted.

"I told you! I'm staying with my friend Davis, and there's no room for you!"

"I still don't know who the fuck Davis is!" I said.

"That's the problem, isn't it?" Leslie spat.

Joan cleared her throat. "I don't mean to break up this reunion, but I'm afraid we may have lost sight of Caitlin and Betsy. They got out of that helicopter minutes ago. They could be anywhere by now."

"Actually, I know exactly where we can find them," I said.

I'd only been to that Endeavors office once, to pick up a check. It was in Times Square, on the fourteenth floor, which was really the thirteenth floor, which is why I always remembered it. If Caitlin was going to Times Square (of all places), this had to be where she was heading.

The three of us made quite the group. Two women wearing only lingerie plus Iron Man running through Times Square. A dozen people asked us for pictures, but Leslie said that was low for a typical night and he could give us some pointers if we wanted. I told him we'd pass.

The old building was a rare sight among the flimsy new skyscrapers that made up the current city skyline. Like the Chrysler Building, the Endeavors office building still maintained its art deco appearance, inside and out. Or at least that's how I remembered it. The front doors were locked.

Leslie banged on the glass with his Iron Man glove. An exhausted-looking security guard slowly approached the door, only to shout, "I've already let in three of yous on the roof. *The building is closed!*" then walk back to his station somewhere out of sight. So he already let in three people—Caitlin, Betsy, and who? Mark? Or the helicopter's pilot?

Certainly our method actor would not be deterred. "What would Iron Man do?" I asked Leslie.

He banged on the glass once more. The security guard lumbered back, rubbing his eyes. That's when I saw the top of the man's red undershirt. There was the unmistakable crest of a blue-and-white shield. I knew this one. This was Captain America's.

"*We are closed,*" he said with a growl.

"Put your helmet on," I murmured to Leslie, and he did.

"Captain America, Iron Man needs to have a word," I said. This was insane.

"What'd you say to me?" the security guard asked.

"Iron Man needs to save . . . Batman." I was flailing.

"Spider-Man," Joan whispered. God, she really did know everything.

"Iron Man needs to save Spider-Man. Only you can help them, Captain America. Avengers unite."

"Avengers assemble," Joan and Leslie whispered together.

"Right. Avengers assemble," I said.

He unlocked the door and popped his head out. *This was a start.* "What in the hell are you talking about? Is this because of my shirt?"

"Well . . . yes," I said.

"My kid gave me this shirt. He loves Captain America. But I don't give a shit about comic books because I'm a grown man."

"Well . . ." I said. "Does your son have a birthday coming up?"

"Sure. Two months from now. Why?"

"What would your son think about a surprise visit from Iron Man?"

"For free?" the security guard asked.

"If you let us into the building, then sure," I said. Even through the helmet, I could sense Leslie's eyes boring into me. Whatever. He was the one who decided to be an actor. A gig's a gig!

I thanked the security guard, who introduced himself as Darrell. He lived all the way up in Yonkers, and he hoped Iron Man would be able to learn his son's favorite TikTok dance in two months' time. I assured him Iron Man could do anything, which ultimately included grumbling at me the whole elevator ride up to the fourteenth floor. I hoped it was worth it. There was the possibility that Endeavors had moved offices, or that Betsy, Caitlin, and Mark were somewhere else, or that we were on the wrong trail altogether. All I could do at this point was hope my intuition was correct.

the fourteenth floor. I hoped it was worth it. There was the possibility that Endeavors had moved offices, or that Betsy, Caitlin, and Mark were somewhere else, or that we were on the wrong trail altogether. All I could do at this point was hope my intuition was correct.

35

An ancient gilt elevator let us out on the fourteenth floor. Leslie's costume squeaked as he walked out, and I quickly shushed him.

"Tony Stark never got shushed by his ex-wife," he said under his breath.

"With that outfit? I bet he did," I said.

At the elevator bank, there were three corridors, which meant three ways to go. There was no directory, of course. When you have the big bucks, who needs directories? Marbled glass doors etched with names I couldn't read lined each darkened hallway. I couldn't see farther than ten feet down any of the corridors. As I recalled, the Endeavors office was at the very end of a long hall, but I was hazy on exactly which hall that was.

You know in horror movies when they all decide to split up and you think *Why would you idiots split up? At least one of you is going to die!* But it seems to make sense to the characters, and so you just have to watch knowing something bad is about to happen? Well.

We decided to split up. To be honest, it was my idea. I couldn't risk us choosing the wrong hall and the killer getting away. This cat-and-mouse game had gone on long enough. There would be no more mousetraps. It was time to trap the cat.

Joan took the left hall, Leslie took the right, and I took the middle. The plan was to meet back at the elevator bank in five minutes, whether we'd found the Endeavors office or not. If anyone found it, we agreed we'd all three go in together.

Walking down the center hallway, I tried listening for sounds of human life but could only hear the blood rushing past my ears. Why was I so nervous? I'd confronted so many criminals in the past. Was anything really so different about tonight? Then I thought of Joan and Betsy and even stupid Leslie. How they got so tangled up in this—it was careless of me. These people had passions and friends and family who loved them. They didn't need to be doing this. I'd put them all at risk, and I had a feeling it would only get worse from here.

When I heard hushed whispers coming from the end of the hall, I knew I'd chosen the correct path. Maybe I sent Joan and Leslie down the wrong ones on purpose. Maybe deep in my subconscious, I wanted to protect them. I knew at least three minutes had passed. Soon they would each be heading back to the elevator bank. That's when they'd realize they'd been spared. They could go home, eat a meal, hang out at the library together. Anything from a safe distance. This was my battle to fight.

I found myself standing in front of the same door I'd faced years ago. ENDEAVORS had been etched into the glass along with a bat in midflight. This family and their fucking bats. I could see human-sized shadows moving behind the marbled glass, and I reached out for the doorknob and turned it slowly.

Inside, the office was dark but for the most part as I remembered. There was the front desk, the floor-to-ceiling windows with a view of upper Manhattan, and across the room, the heavy leather and mahogany furniture. I knew I'd seen shadows, but now the office was still. Too still.

I felt the blade at my throat before I could make a sound. I couldn't see who was behind me, but I could tell from the blade's pressure they didn't want me scared, they wanted me dead. I tried pushing them off with my flailing arms, but the person was smaller than I anticipated and more agile. At that moment, Joan and Leslie were probably meeting back up, wondering if I'd lost track of time.

I'd gone about this all wrong and it would probably cost me my life.

36

"Move," the voice behind me said.

With the blade at my neck, I was guided into an interior office. I gave up trying to turn around to see who was about to kill me. Instead I focused on staying alive. This office had velvet drapes over the large picture windows, an antique rug, and a low leather couch pushed against one wall. Across from the couch, there was a carved wooden desk the size of my twin bed. Tied to the desk chair with her mouth duct-taped shut was none other than Betsy Clench.

"Betsy, are you okay?" I choked out. With the duct tape, she could only respond in whimpers. I mean, I wasn't doing so hot myself.

"Shut up!" my attacker yelled. I knew that voice, the small hands. Caitlin.

"I know who killed Josh," I said.

She pressed the blade against my windpipe. Air was getting harder to come by. Suddenly she threw me to the ground. I landed on my face and gratefully gulped in air. There was a crunching sound, and it took me a minute to realize my big, beautiful veneers had broken.

I tasted blood, and my cheek burned from where I'd skidded across the rug. When I reached up to touch my face, my hand came away bloody. I wiped it on the side of my camisole, making a reddish-brown handprint on the ivory silk.

"What did you just do?" Caitlin said in a low growl.

"I'm bleeding," I said.

"That's my camisole. You just wiped your blood on my camisole," she said, pointing at me with her blade, which I realized was a letter opener.

"Cool it, Caitlin," a raspy voice said from the shadows. Something about being back in this office made everything click. This was who I'd heard on the phone all those years back. This was F.

"So you're in on this, too, Frank?" I asked. He slowly stepped into the light. There were bags under his eyes, and it looked like he hadn't shaved in a while.

Frank glanced at me. "You look different," he said.

"Yeah, well, my face is bleeding," I said, my broken veneers whistling on the S's.

"Must be her hair," he said to Caitlin. "You sure that's Luella van Horn? Not some impostor?"

"Yes, it's actually her," Caitlin said, shaking her head.

"I said I'm sorry about the mix-up, it was dark and I had to work fast," Frank said.

"You thought Betsy was me? That's why you kidnapped her? What do you want from me?" I asked.

"Shut up," Caitlin snapped, then turned back to Frank. "Look. Luella's here now. You did a good job, Papa Bear." She walked over to Frank and kissed him softly on the mouth. "Now let's get this over with."

Frank shakily pulled a brass dagger-shaped letter opener from his tuxedo jacket pocket and moved toward me menacingly. Somehow there were now three letter openers in play. I knew Joan still had hers, plus Caitlin's, and now Frank's. "Look familiar?" he asked.

"How long have you two been . . . working together, so to speak?" I asked.

"We're in love. And we've been in love for a long time. Ever since Caitlin turned eighteen," Frank said.

"That's very convenient," I said, then turned to Caitlin. "Didn't Frank basically raise you? Isn't that a little weird?"

"Frank and my father were always close. Even now that Daddy's in jail, they still write letters and talk on the phone. This was our way to tell him about us—we figured it'd go down easier with you on a platter."

"That's why you wanted to kidnap me. To tell your father, Dave McCarthy, about your fucked-up relationship with your house manager?" I asked.

"That's what this was all for?" a man's voice asked. We all turned to see Mark Fontaine standing in the backlit doorway, the butcher knife from the Hunts' kitchen clutched in his hand. "What's going on, Caitlin?"

"Mark, it's over. You need to sign the divorce papers. Let this marriage die," Caitlin said.

"Mark, Caitlin's having an affair with Frank. And here's your proof. Technically, I've done my job, so I'll be going now," I said, struggling to my feet, but Caitlin kicked me back down to the ground. This time I landed on my ass, right where I'd gotten my rabies shot. I groaned in agony.

"Shut up!" Caitlin yelled. "You're staying right here. You worked for Mark, now you'll work for me. I'll pay you double to figure out how Mark killed Josh Jorkavic."

Cat and mouse, I thought, and took a deep breath.

"Against the sex cult bylaws, you started having a public affair with Josh in order to rile up Mark," I said. "You wanted Mark out of the picture, so you basically set the stage for him to murder Josh Jorkavic, and Frank arranged for me to be on the island so Mark would get caught. Meanwhile, you and Frank were the ones actually having a serious longtime affair. But your plan failed."

"What is she talking about?" Mark asked Caitlin, who wouldn't even look at him.

I continued. "Mark got the scopolamine from the Hunts and slipped it into Josh's cocktail to make him overdose. It was known to happen, and it could be written off as an accidental death. That night, Josh got more wasted than usual, but he wasn't dying. He'd built up a tolerance."

"Fuck," Mark muttered.

"Someone had to finish the job, so they lured Josh into the cement room where they slit his throat with"—I looked at the letter openers in Caitlin's and Frank's hands and the knife in Mark's—

"one of these blades," I said. "Josh's blood was drained and his body was repositioned, making it look like some cultish sacrifice."

"How do you know Mark wasn't the one to slit his throat? He wanted Josh Jorkavic dead!" Caitlin growled.

"I gave him the pills, I admit it. But I didn't slit his throat, I swear! At least I don't think I did." As he spoke, Mark began to weep. "I can't remember. I was on so many pills, too."

"See, he doesn't even know what he did!" Caitlin yelled.

"But you do, Caitlin," I said. "When I discovered you were all connected to Endeavors, I knew I was roped into this nightmare for putting Dave McCarthy in jail. Mark didn't want a divorce, and you knew you'd have to get creative. You led me to believe you were having an affair with Josh Jorkavic. I was supposed to leave the breadcrumbs for Mark to kill Josh. You counted on me to figure Mark was the culprit, so he could be put away and the divorce would be finalized. Then you'd be free to basically be with your uncle. But the question remains, who finally killed Josh Jorkavic?"

Mark threw up his arms. "See, this is what happens when you're in a sex cult, Caitlin! The lines blur! She's right, you're practically fucking your uncle! And it's sick!" Mark shouted through tears. "I only wanted to save our marriage! I love you!"

"Sometimes people are better off divorced," someone said from the doorway. And that someone was my ex-husband, Iron Man née Leslie. I tried mental gymnastics to interpret what Leslie said in a positive light, but as you can imagine, I was having trouble.

Joan strode up next to Leslie, holding her letter opener. If you're counting, all three letter openers were now accounted for, plus the butcher knife.

"Make another move, and you're mine," Joan said, menacingly pointing her letter opener toward Mark, Caitlin, and Frank. A muffled celebratory "Joanie!" came from Betsy's duct-taped mouth.

"Why are there so many goddamn letter openers?" Frank asked.

"We're rich," Caitlin said. "We can have as many letter openers as we want."

I quickly glanced at Joan in time to see her rolling her eyes in disgust, then I got myself to a standing position, leaning most of my weight on the ornate desk.

"What'd we miss? Who's going to jail?" Leslie asked.

"No one is going to jail," Mark growled. "There's no proof of anyone doing *anything* wrong. Caitlin, we will not be getting divorced. And Frank? I want you gone, and I will personally make sure you never work again."

"But there is proof," I said. "The person holding the murder weapon is the killer. And Joan, who might that be?"

Joan took a deep breath and smiled. "First, the knife can be ruled out. We saw Mark retrieve it from the Hunts' kitchen. What slit Josh's throat was one of these letter openers. But what you must know is that brass letter openers came to prominence in the late nineteenth century."

"Oh my god," Caitlin mumbled.

Joan ignored her and continued. "Envelopes at that time were closed with wax seals, which were easy to pry open with a dull but heavy blade. As envelope technology advanced in the early twentieth century, wax seals were replaced with a horse glue adhesive that, when wetted, sealed the paper more completely, requiring a slimmer, sharper blade in order to effectively open a letter. Later in the century, brass office supplies fell out of favor and were quickly replaced by silver, which is a much softer metal that easily tarnishes."

"Go, Joan, go!" I cheered.

"Our murderer is the person holding the brass letter opener from the early twentieth century. The only letter opener strong and sharp enough to slit a human throat," Joan said, looking at Caitlin.

"He wasn't dead!" Caitlin shouted. "The plan was foolproof, nearly perfect, but of course, Mark fucked it up like he fucks everything up. It's because of those stupid drugs!"

"You were the one who got me hooked on those things in the first place! You told me they were safe!" Mark yelled.

Caitlin prowled the room, ignoring Mark's outburst. "He could barely function when Frank stole his glasses, and that was step one."

"You stole my glasses? Why?" Mark asked Frank.

"You couldn't see five feet in front of you without them. That was necessary for our plan to work," Frank said, then turned to me. "There was no party the night you found Josh's body. It was a setup. The sounds, the smells, it was all theater. Mark was told they were having an intimate get-together that night. A few friends: Mark and Caitlin, Josh Jorkavic, Lenore Fisher, that's all. We outfitted Lenore with a blond wig to match yours. We knew you'd eventually make your way down to the basement. You were never one to stop investigating, even when it wasn't smart. When you got down there, we wanted drugged Mark not to be alarmed. He was abusing those scopolamine pills and he couldn't see anything. He wouldn't know you from Lenore. We wanted him thinking he'd get away with it and you knowing something was off. Lenore only thought it was a prank. Don't blame her in this."

Lenore Fisher, I thought. Why would Frank protect Lenore Fisher?

"She mentioned she'd never been on the island as a guest. She's your daughter," Joan said.

Frank nodded solemnly. "I couldn't be there for her when she was growing up. I was always here. But she agreed to help me out one last time if I never bothered her again." A sadness overcame Frank. His shoulders slumped and his eyes began to water. But Caitlin paid him no mind.

"It was perfect. Mark would kill Josh, you would nab Mark, and Frank and I could finally come clean to Daddy with a special present for him. A dead Luella van Horn. But things weren't going according to plan. Josh was bouncing back. Someone had to finish the job!"

Before anyone could blink, Caitlin ran across the room, the letter opener gripped tight in her right hand. She lunged at me, and although I tried to dodge her, Caitlin cut my arm. I screamed as the pain registered and the blood began to pour out of me. She'd gotten my brachial artery. Leslie and Joan ran toward Caitlin, but they were held back by the two men who loved her, Frank on Joan and Mark on Leslie. I screamed, swatting at Caitlin, but Caitlin was stronger and the letter opener was sharp. My blood was getting everywhere. Caitlin lifted the letter opener again, just above my heart. This was it. I would die in this room.

That's when I heard a thud. Suddenly Caitlin sank to the ground. Behind her, Betsy Clench's chest heaved as she gripped the shaft of The Rooster, now wet with Caitlin's blood. Betsy then swung the marble phallus against Mark's face and Frank's back. Both of them collapsed soundlessly as she ripped the duct tape off her mouth. "They really thought they'd tie up a first mate with these basic-ass knots? I got out of those things twenty minutes ago."

"Betsy, what the hell? Why didn't you help us?" I asked.

"Honestly, the whole thing was pretty hot. I was supposed to fuck a bunch of people tonight, but instead I got kidnapped. Frank thought I was you, so he grabbed me at the party. Something about those wigs, man, really screams Loolie van Horndog. Seems like you were the one who was supposed to be tied to a chair. And now you're gonna fault me for getting my jollies despite the odds? I thought we were friends."

"Come here," I said, bringing Betsy in for a one-armed hug (the one not hemorrhaging). "I'm so glad you're safe."

Joan embraced both of us. Then I felt Iron Man's stupid plastic arms wrap around us, too. So this is what people called friendship. I had to admit—it was worth the hype.

37

We called Captain America at the security desk and told him what went down. Soon the place was swarming with first responders. All three of our unconscious perps were arrested. Caitlin for murder, Frank for aiding and abetting, and Mark for assault. The EMT wrapped my bloody arm in a tourniquet and strongly suggested I go to the hospital, but I declined. I had an appointment to keep.

Betsy hooked the marble strap-on back onto her harness and the four of us walked out of that building with the swagger of superheroes: Iron Man, Library Woman, Strap-On Sailor, and The Toothless Wonder. We walked into the nearest diner and ordered four chocolate milkshakes to process everything we'd just been through.

"So Mark drugged Josh, but it was Caitlin who slit his throat?" Joan asked.

"And Frank who helped arrange the whole thing. He'd used me years ago to put her father in jail and get him out of the picture, then they both used me to frame the husband, get rid of him, too."

"So that room on the third floor, that was Caitlin's room?" Joan asked.

"I think that was where Frank and Caitlin . . . uh . . . spent their time together. All those blond wigs were worn to misdirect Mark. They knew he couldn't see without his glasses," I said.

"So what do you think Sybil threw in the river?" Joan asked.

"The note, the tarp, all of it must've been to convince us Mark had killed Caitlin as well as Josh. Caitlin and Frank tricked Sybil, too."

"Wonder who it was in that tarp, though," Joan said.

"Maybe Josh Jorkavic," Betsy said, slurping up the last of her milkshake. "His body never made it onto the boat. I checked once we got to Manhattan. We had no cargo." She glanced over at the milkshake remaining in my glass. "You gonna finish that?"

Leslie shook his head. "This case sounds like hell, Marie. You really prefer this to doing social work and being married to me?"

"Just drink your milkshake, Iron Man," I said.

38

Money can be great, but as far as New York City goes, it sure goes quickly. I signed a new lease with my landlord and was able to stay in my apartment. I also spent a chunk of hard-earned cash on new veneers. I asked my dentist, Dr. Frank, if we could work out a deal for a discount if I spread his name around town. And let's just say Dr. Frank is the best! You gotta go see Dr. Frank! Have I mentioned my dentist, Dr. Frank? He's amazing.

I'm almost hesitant to tell you how it all turned out this time. It's not a big shocker that the rich and powerful can maneuver their way around the US legal system, but that doesn't make it any less upsetting.

Caitlin McCarthy was charged with manslaughter and sentenced to five years in a minimum-security prison with a possibility for parole. I mean, if that isn't a slap on the wrist, I'm your Aunt Sally. She orchestrated a complicated, manipulative plot, killing a man in cold blood to force her husband into a divorce. I'm sure she'll get out in less than three years. I can't imagine what she'll cook up during her time in the clink. I made a note to keep an eye on her. To this day, Mark Fontaine has not granted her a divorce, and they are still oh so unhappily married.

Mark Fontaine was charged with second-degree murder, which is murder without too much preplanning for laypeople. Overdosing Josh Jorkavic was a crime of passion, his lawyers said. Plus that didn't even kill him. Caitlin was the real murderer, they claimed. He was sentenced to two years in prison and fourteen months of community service. When I told Betsy Clench about his sentence, she had a great line. "I've got a community service project for that guy: go to Antarctica and shovel snow!" It's like the woman is a slutty time traveler from 1925. I love her.

Betsy is still working as the first mate on the Murder Island ferry. I can now say I have a friend in New York City who operates a boat. And isn't unlimited boat access the ultimate goal of living in New York City?

Oh, Betsy and Paul, aka Caviar Guy, tried hooking up a few times, but she got bored. Apparently he was too vanilla for her. A couple of months ago, she met a new guy at a sex party underneath a Gristedes, and they've been hitting it off. She says they share a lot of the same kinks. I haven't met him yet, but hopefully soon.

Frank got sentenced to ten to fifteen years in a minimum-security prison. Same one as Dave McCarthy, funnily enough. Frank was charged with aiding and abetting the murder of Josh Jorkavic. Why did he get ten to fifteen years and the two who actually killed him get much less time? Well, why do you think?

As far as the Murder Island folks go, all that fucking and sucking slowed down significantly once the Hunts acquired the McCarthys' property as well as Carla Jorkavic's. As the majority owners of the island, they put the houses on a short-term rental site, where any riffraff with enough money could come stay on Murder Island. They took down the flags and stopped having parties. They realized the whole sex cult vibe was a little off-putting to vacationers. I do wonder if the tunnels are still operational.

The Tylers retained their fortress in the center of the island and still live there today. Bradford Tyler's leg was amputated after the car accident, but he still spends his days wandering the roads around his castle, looking for creatures big and small. I wrote him a letter asking how much he knew and what he meant by all that "beware the bat and rooster." He wrote back to say his butler had tipped him off that something was going down between the Jorkavics and the McCarthys and it involved me. When I asked to speak with the butler, Bradford said the man had suddenly left his position. They have Yanni Toumis as their butler now.

Leslie and I are working on our friendship. We try to meet once a week at a diner for milkshakes. We sit there as long as possible without trying to kill each other. And once the thought of killing the other person pops into one of our heads, we stand up, leave cash on the table, and gently excuse ourselves. These meetings tend to last fifteen to twenty minutes. But they used to be ten, so that's progress.

Joan Clyborne and I have remained good friends. Whenever I get a new case (which has been often, thanks to the news coverage of this one), I go straight to the library and we get to work. Every Sherlock needs a Watson, otherwise he's just some asshole with a drug problem. Joan makes my work smarter, and I guess I make her life more exciting. She knows about Marie Jones and Luella van Horn, and she thinks it makes me "multi-faceted." I made her put that in writing, then I framed it and put it up on my bathroom wall above the litter box. When people love you no matter what, it's good to have reminders everywhere, especially in places where you and your cats take dumps.

Until this case, I really thought I was going through life alone. Every decision I'd made in the last few years only served to further isolate me—the divorce, the move, the job, the secret identity. Looking back, I wonder if I siloed myself on purpose with this Luella van Horn/Marie Jones split, like I didn't need the support or even deserve it. But I found out it's not so bad having friends who know your secrets. Betsy Clench says "double identity means double the love." And you gotta listen to Betsy Clench. She operates a boat!

I woke up this morning to someone banging on my door and both my cats crying. When I opened the door, Sophie stood there with a stack of my mail. Luckily, this time she was wearing a shirt. Then without saying a word, she shoved the pile at me and walked away. The cats desperately tried to follow her out but I closed the door just in time. Honestly, what do they see in her?

Amid the pile of bills I could now finally pay off, I was surprised to find a letter addressed to Luella. I used the tarnished silver letter opener Joan had stolen from the McCarthys and carefully pulled out the letter, which I've copied below:

Dear Luella,
For decades now, Murder Island has been impenetrable. I should know. I wrote the only book on the matter. And I paid the price. After what they did to my publishing career, I ran out of money and became destitute. The only work I could get was as a valet. The Tylers hired me as an act of sympathy. Over the years, I proved my loyalty to their family and was promoted to head butler, which was my most recent post.

You and your friends, you changed everything for me. I realized Murder Island no longer holds the power over me it once did. It's a wonderful day when a young private detective comes in and shakes everything up. I'll never be able to thank you for all that you've done. I've decided to leave Murder Island for good, and in my old age, rekindle my true love: writing. One day, my dear, you may find yourself in my next book, *Sex on Murder Island,* and I hope you will be flattered.

Most sincerely,
Walter Stanford

EPILOGUE

The sun was setting behind us as Joan and I walked toward the marina on East Twenty-Fourth Street. I wore my Luella wig and had new sturdy veneers. (Enter promo code VENEER30 for 30 percent off your next Dr. Frank visit!) Joan's long gray hair was French braided and her glasses hung on a new beaded chain around her neck. By now, the days were getting shorter and the weather was chillier.

We were heading to meet Betsy Clench and her new boyfriend for one-dollar oysters at a nearby café. Though they'd been dating for a couple of months, Betsy claimed he was shy, so this would be our first time meeting him.

I spotted Betsy first in her white sailor hat. Her boyfriend kissed her neck, and all we could see was a swath of his dark wavy hair. Betsy giggled, swatting at him. I cleared my throat and Betsy smiled.

"You're right on time!" she said. "Babe, meet my friends, Luella and Joan."

The man stopped kissing Betsy's neck and slowly turned to face us.

"This is my sexy boyfriend, Taylor," Betsy said. "Taylor, these are my sexy friends."

Joan's jaw dropped, and I told myself to keep breathing.

"Oh, we go way back," Taylor Bell said with a smile. We sure did.

ACKNOWLEDGMENTS

Thank you to Jesse Shuman, Cassie Gitkin, Faren Bachelis, Dan Denning, Chelsea Woodward, and the Bantam team for your guidance and wisdom.

Thank you to Abby Saul at the Lark Group for everything you do.

Thank you to Dylan Marron, Todd Clayton, Ashley Brooke Roberts, and Mike DiCenzo for offering your time and insight on early drafts that might not have made much sense. Thanks to the Murder of Crows writing group, Ankita Saxena, Silvija Ozols, and Gina Hagler, for reading pages and saying nice things that kept me going.

Thank you to the Firestone family, the DiCenzo family, the Talve-Goodman family, Jason Klorfein, Vern Co, Kent Ochse, Hannah Vaughn, Alyse Landry, Felix Deemer, Donovan Wong, Bari Finkel, Gabrielle Lewis, Kristina Rivero at Books Are Magic, Shane Mullen at Left Bank Books, Heidi Bender at Split Rocks Books, Alex Adan, Manolo Moreno, and the Greenwich House Comedy Workshop. You guys are nice, and I love that.

Thank you to everyone who read *Murder on Sex Island* and keeps rooting for Luella van Horn, even though she is kinda bad at her job.

And no thank you to my dog who tried to thwart me at every step. That animal doesn't understand why I would write a book when I could be playing fetch with him. Our power balance is not right.

ABOUT THE AUTHOR

Jo Firestone is a comedian and writer best known for her work on *After Midnight with Taylor Tomlinson, ZIWE,* and *Joe Pera Talks with You.* She is the author of *Murder on Sex Island* and the co-author of two card games: *Punderdome: A Card Game for Pun Lovers* and *Fruits.* She lives in New York.

jofirestone.com